Other Arabesque books by

Janice Sims

in the Bryant family trilogy

Waiting for You
Constant Craving

One fine Day

Janice Sims

ARABESQUE®

ONE FINE DAY

An Arabesque novel

ISBN-13: 978-0-373-83014-5
ISBN-10:   0-373-83014-9

www.kimanipress.com

Printed in U.S.A.

To all the Amazons out there who keep holding it down for their loved ones and for the rest of the world! You're magnificent women, and you inspire me every day.

Let her own breasts intoxicate you at all times.
With her love may you be in an ecstasy constantly.
—*Proverbs* 5:19

I am woman. You are man
A universe of differences conspire to
prevent our coupling, but we foil its plan

God knew what He was doing when
from Adam's rib He created Eve
A fast learner, Adam soon discovered that
in Eve he had someone with whom to cleave

His better half
His life
His support system
His wife

—*The Book of Counted Joys*

Chapter 1

Jason Bryant whipped the Ford Explorer into the parking lot of Aminatu's Daughters and parked right behind Sara Minton's cherry-red Mustang convertible, thereby blocking her exit. If there was one thing he knew about Sara, it was that she was a hard woman to pin down. This way, she wasn't going anywhere until he'd issued his invitation.

He climbed out of the SUV's cab, his long muscular legs flexing beneath a pair of Wrangler jeans. The heels of brown leather cowboy boots announced his arrival as he walked across the hardwood floor of the bookstore.

He noticed right away that there was another strange woman behind the counter in the coffeehouse section of the bookstore. Strange, in that she was new to him.

The rate of employee turnover at Aminatu's Daughters astounded him. He'd counted more than ten new employees within the past year. All of them had been women and all of them had been brown-skinned. They worked a few weeks, and then moved on.

He made a point of speaking to each and every one of them in order to prove his theory that none of them could claim English as their native tongue. The woman today was in her early twenties, had dusky brown skin, dark brown eyes and a very short afro.

Jason walked up to the counter. "Hi, how are you? I'm looking for Sara. She's here, isn't she?"

"We have wonderful mocha lattes," the woman said cheerfully. She turned to gesture to the coffee machine behind her.

"Thank you, no," said Jason. He smiled gently. He couldn't be sure, but he would wager that she was South African. She had the same lilting cadence to her voice as Nelson Mandela: a musical tone that was beautiful to the ear.

Upon hearing that he did not want a mocha latte, her expression became so sad that he changed his mind. "Oh, okay, I'll take a small one."

She smiled broadly. "Miss Sara is working in her office," she said once the sale was under her belt.

Jason laughed softly. It was obvious she intended to earn her keep around there.

"Thank you. I'll be back for my coffee." He turned and walked across the bookstore section and into the hallway. The first door he came to was the storage room. The second was the employee lounge. Next, he came to Sara's office. The door was closed.

He knocked and waited.

"Come in!" he heard Sara's distinctive husky voice call.

When he walked in Sara was sitting behind her

desk, and Gary Pruitt was sitting on the corner of it looking right at home. He was wearing an expensive suit, as usual. Jason didn't think he'd ever seen the man in anything except a suit. But then Gary was the most successful attorney in town. He had to look professional. Jason, who used to work as an attorney himself, could recall how looking professional was a part of the job.

These days, as a gentleman farmer, his chosen title for his job as a vintner, he wore jeans or khakis and sturdy denim shirts. The last time he'd worn a suit it had been to his brother Franklyn's wedding, which had taken place over a year ago.

"Am I interrupting anything?" Jason asked lightly as he entered the room.

"No, no," Sara said quickly. She rose and Jason leaned over and gave her a peck on the cheek. Her smooth brown skin had a light flowery scent and, as always, Jason's heartbeat accelerated as a result of being near her.

Jason straightened and Sara gestured to the chair in front of her desk before she sat back down. "Have a seat. Gary was just telling me that he and Kat are having a dinner party next Saturday night and wanted to know if you and I could come."

Jason brightened. He knew he had no reason to be jealous of Gary. All indications were that he was happily married. He was a newlywed, in fact. But why did he have to spend so much time with Sara?

"If you can, *I* can," he told Sara. Oftentimes, her schedule was packed tighter than his. Unless there was some kind of an emergency at the winery like a wine press breaking down, he worked only from sunup to sunset. On the other hand it wasn't unusual for Sara to be called away at a moment's notice.

He never knew the life of a bookstore owner was so exciting. He had noticed, too, that practically every time she went out of town, either a new employee arrived or an old one departed. There had to be some connection there.

"Barring emergencies, I'm free," Sara said.

"See you at eight," Gary said, rising. "There'll be six of us and we're having seafood."

"I'll bring a few bottles of our best Chardonnay," Jason offered.

"I'm looking forward to it," Gary said with sincerity. The Bryant Chardonnay was among the most delicious in the wine world.

He and Jason shook hands, and Gary left.

Sara got up to go sit on Jason's lap. Wrapping her arms around his neck, she bent her head and kissed him on the cheek. Then lower, at the corner of his full, sensual mouth.

Jason regarded her suspiciously through slits. "Are you ever going to get down to business? Because I could be doing something fascinating like watching grapes grow."

"When I'm good and ready," Sara said, smiling. She enjoyed taking her time, kissing his face and neck before getting to his mouth. Anticipation was titillating to her.

She could feel Jason's state of arousal on her bottom. Patience wasn't his strong suit. But she'd known that about him before she'd taken him into her bed. She had known that sometime soon after they'd become intimate he would want a commitment from her.

Jason had made changes in the past year and a half. And those changes had not come easily for him.

Formerly a sought-after divorce attorney in Bakersfield, he'd moved back home to the quaint town of Glen Ellen to take over his family's winery. He'd made sacrifices to do it. Among them, a freewheeling life of revolving-door relationships in which the only thing that interested him about a woman was how attractive she was and how good she was in bed.

Surprisingly, he didn't miss the women. Perhaps if he'd made an effort to develop a genuine relationship with any of them, he would. But he'd avoided anything serious. You couldn't miss what you'd never had.

Now, though, he knew what he wanted. He wanted a good woman in his life. He wanted children with her and he wanted to leave behind a legacy, like his parents had done. Something lasting.

Sara knew all of that about him because he'd told her. Oh, the late-night talks they would have after making love! They would talk about anything and everything.

First loves. The first time they'd ever *made* love.

Their favorite books, movies, foods. The people who had helped shape them into the people they were today. They even talked about those painful high-school episodes in which Sara had been ridiculed and Jason had stood by and said nothing to prevent it.

She didn't blame him. However, he blamed himself.

She knew how hard it had been for him to fit in at Santa Rosa High. And the bus ride between Santa Rosa High and Glen Ellen, during which she and he had been the only black students, had sometimes been pure hell.

He sat up front with the rest of the football players, laughing and cracking jokes.

She sat in the back, hunkered down, her nose in a

textbook, hoping all the while that no one would say anything to her. *Please, God, just make me invisible!*

It didn't help that she was overweight, wore glasses, and had skipped a grade. The kids regarded her as a freak of nature. But she had hoped, the entire two years that she rode the bus with Jason Bryant, that he would say something nice to her. He never did. He simply looked at her with sympathy in his eyes. She hated him for that. He could deride her like the rest of them, but she didn't want his pity. She was glad when he'd graduated. The next two years, she was the only black student on the bus between Santa Rosa High and Glen Ellen, and that suited her fine. She grew tough. They made her grow a thick skin. They made her turn inward and realize what a strong, competent person she could become if she wanted to. It was trial by fire, and she had passed.

Now, as she embraced the man who had once been the boy she'd hated, she found that she only wanted to love him. Her present life, however, made that impossible.

She needed to make some changes of her own.

Finally, she kissed him full on the mouth.

His response was immediate and passionate. He pulled her closer and she lost herself in the feel of his mouth as he patiently and thoroughly made love to her with his tongue. She moaned softly. Desire engulfed her, and he feasted on her mouth as though it was the most pleasurable act in the world. Now, at this moment, nothing else mattered to him except her complete and utter enjoyment of his mouth on hers, her breath mingling with his and her body ripening under his sensual assault.

He had a one-track mind when it came to giving her pleasure, and she thought that a good characteristic for a lover to have.

They came up for air, and gazed lovingly into each other's eyes. His were the color of brandy, hers were a more mellow shade of brown, almost like caramel.

His hands caressed the back of her head, her braids between his fingers. Hers pressed against his chest. "Will you go riding with me tonight?" he asked softly.

Her full lips turned up in a smile. "Love to. There's a full moon."

"Good, we can watch it come out. Can you be there by seven?"

"I'll be there."

"Afterward, I'll cook for you."

"Mmm," she moaned. "Too many sensual pleasures, and I just might give in to you and become the mistress of the Hacienda, after all."

She immediately knew she'd made a miscalculation. She'd joked about his asking her to marry him much too soon after the fact. It was still a sore point between them. One that wasn't going to go away without some serious negotiations.

His eyes grew distant in an instant. He attempted a smile in order to cover up the hurt she had unconsciously inflicted but it wasn't much of a smile. Instead of responding to her comment, he said, "Look, you're busy. I should go."

She reluctantly stood up. After which he also rose.

She could have stood aside and let him go, but it wasn't her way to let things slide. Smoothing her skirt, she said, "Jason, I didn't mean to sound flip. I realize how much it took for you to ask me to marry you. And I'm truly honored that you want to."

His gaze relentlessly held hers. "But not enough to accept."

"One day I'm going to make you understand why I had to turn you down for now."

"One fine day," he said quietly. He smiled ruefully. "Remember that song? It was about unrequited love, too."

"That's not what's going on between us," she denied.

"You say you love me but you won't marry me." It was a statement, not an accusation. He was past the blaming stage or feeling as if something was wrong with him because she had turned him down. He sensed that she loved him. Sometimes he could feel the love she had for him so powerfully, it left him breathless.

That's why he had been completely stupefied when she'd said no to his proposal.

"I adore you, Jason, you know that."

"I know that you desire me," he allowed. "I know that sometimes what you feel for me is so overpowering that it scares you. What I don't know is, *Why* does it scare you? Why aren't you free to let yourself go?"

Once again, her answer was, "Soon, soon. I'm working on it."

He bent and kissed her forehead. "All right. You work on it. In the meantime, I'll accept whatever you have to offer. I'm easy."

He smiled gently.

Tears sat in her eyes.

"Don't cry, mystery girl," he said. "I'm a lawyer, I know all about confidentiality. You'll tell all when you're able to. I'll be waiting with bated breath."

He kissed her cheek, tasting her tears.

She watched him go, and wiped her tearstained cheeks with the pad of her thumb.

Some people made their lives needlessly complicated. She wasn't one of those people. What she did in secret was for a good cause, and her being careful to keep it secret was of the utmost importance. Innocent lives depended on her discretion.

She had to make a choice. Her secret life, or Jason.

The way her heart felt torn at this moment, she knew that she wanted the latter.

She had never known anyone to leave the organization. There were only two reasons the organization allowed anyone to leave it. One was death.

She sat down in front of the computer and entered her password. Earlier, she'd logged on to the organization's Web site. There were two messages waiting for her. One was from their leader, the highest-ranking woman in the United States government.

Congratulations on your last assignment. Your present charge is very important to the people of South Africa. We are certain that those who seek her would never think that she's been spirited away to a tiny hamlet in Sonoma Valley, but we encourage you to be extremely careful. We're working very hard to expedite her safe passage to her final destination. With respect...

Then the leader had signed her personal signature.

Sara smiled as she exited the message. If anyone ever suspected that the woman closer to the president than his own wife was head of a secret organization of women who aided foreign nationals, her career would be over. Yet another reason for her to be discreet.

She quickly read the other message. It was from another sister in the organization, a physicist who lived in Tucson, Arizona. She'd met her a few months ago at their annual convention in New York City where they'd become fast friends.

Hi, Sara, the message read.

If you haven't already heard, Dr. M'boto insisted on returning to her homeland and was killed as she stepped off the plane. I'm heartsick about it. She believed that the only way to prevent nuclear proliferation in her country was to sacrifice herself, the one scientist in the grip of the government who could make it happen for them. When they killed her, their hopes died as well.

Sara, of course, had heard about Dr. Victoria M'boto's assassination. And she knew Dr. Katharine Matthews-Grant had done everything in her power to convince Dr. M'boto to remain in Tucson and under the protection of the organization. Sara dreaded the day when she lost one of her charges. She wrote a very sympathetic note to Kate, telling her how sorry she was that Dr. M'boto had seen no other way out of her dilemma.

After she'd replied to Kate's message she sat at the desk, thinking about her recruitment and initiation into the organization nearly six years ago.

But then her mind went to Billy, her husband of only two years, who had been killed in a car crash while returning from a business trip to Philadelphia. He specialized in entertainment law and represented some of the country's highest-paid athletes.

At the time Sara was assistant creative director at a large advertising agency. She rarely left work before 7:00 p.m. and that evening when she got home she went straight into the tub for a relaxing soak. It was a Thursday, and she wasn't expecting Billy back until

Friday evening. She planned to cook dinner for him as a welcome-home surprise.

She was the one who got a surprise when, after she came out of the bath and slipped into a plush robe, someone rang the doorbell.

Cautious by nature, she peered through the peephole before calling, "Yes? Who is it?"

"Mrs. Minton?" came a deep male voice.

"Yeah!"

"Mrs. Sara Minton, wife of William Minton?"

Nobody called Billy William. He used to say that that was his father's name.

Still cautious, she answered, with the emphasis on the junior, "William, *Jr.*"

"Yes, William, Jr., Mrs. Minton. I'm Detective Aaron Green of NYPD. We've been informed by the Pennsylvania Highway Patrol that your husband was involved in a serious car accident."

Sara quickly opened the door and swung it wide. "What?" Her voice was barely above a whisper.

The two police officers stood there, not moving an inch, perhaps waiting until she invited them in. But she had no intention of inviting them in. To invite them in would be acknowledging that they were there on deadly serious business.

"Was he hurt? Is he in the hospital in Philadelphia? He went there on a business trip." The questions were spilling out of her, fast and furious. She didn't wait for them to reply. "What hospital? Do you have the name of the doctor I need to speak with?"

"Mrs. Minton," Detective Green ventured softly. He was a slim man with dark hair and soulful brown eyes that were fairly dripping with sympathy. She didn't like the look in his eyes.

She looked at his partner instead. She was a brown-eyed blonde who was about the same height as her partner: five-ten. She looked straight into Sara's eyes with a kind, intense expression that seemed to be pleading with Sara not to lose it. *Be strong, sister,* it said.

That was when Sara knew they weren't there to tell her Billy had been injured. They were there to tell her that he was dead. There was no hope in either of their expressions.

She stepped back from the door. Still barefoot, she looked down at her feet and somehow they seemed to be very far away. Afterward, she would realize that she was having a mental episode in which her mind was seeing things in a distorted way.

Panic had seized her brain.

She stumbled backward, her hands clutching the wall for support. Detective Green caught her before she fell. The woman police officer, whose name Sara would later learn was Carla Farrell, acted in concert with her partner. She shut the door, and together they helped Sara to the couch, where they made her sit down. Carla then went into the kitchen, grabbed some paper towels, folded them over several times, and held them under the tap. By the time she returned to the living room, Detective Green had convinced Sara to lie down with her feet raised above her heart. Carla Farrell placed the cool towels on Sara's forehead, and sat on the floor next to her.

"Just lie there for a few minutes until you come to yourself again, honey," she said.

Sara concentrated on breathing. For a moment, she had

felt as if she was going to lose consciousness. The woozi-ness had passed but she still felt weak and nauseous.

"Is he dead?" she asked, her voice cracking.

"I'm sorry," Detective Green said. With downcast eyes, he continued, his tone filled with compassion. "They told us that the driver of the car that hit him fell asleep at the wheel. Witnesses said that by the time they got to your husband, he was already gone."

"And the driver of the car that hit him?"

"He died from his injuries a few minutes after they got him to the hospital."

"Oh." She didn't know what else to say.

They would not leave her side until her friend Frannie Anise rushed over to stay the night. Frannie, a free spirit from Northern California, the thing they found out they had in common within two minutes of meeting each other upon Sara's arrival in New York City, worked at the United Nations as a tour guide.

Frannie was with her round-the-clock until her parents arrived from Glen Ellen.

Sara seemed to float through the day of the funeral. Her head felt light as if she was on something even though she had declined the tranquilizers her doctor had offered to prescribe for her.

Her parents stayed for two weeks, doting on her. When they prepared to leave, they begged her to go home with them for a while. Sara, however, felt that if she didn't soon get back into her regular routine, she would lose her mind.

That was a mistake.

Without Billy, her life had lost its flavor.

Sara thought that she had permanently built up her self-esteem when she had been a bullied teenager. She had become a diehard optimist who didn't allow anyone to bring her down. Life's challenges didn't faze her in the least.

But two months after Billy's death, she was sitting at the breakfast table on Sunday morning, the day she and Billy always spent together, and for the first time in her life she had suicidal thoughts. She looked at the knife in her hand, a bread knife, and wondered just how deeply she would have to cut her wrist in order to bleed out swiftly enough so that no one would be able to save her. She'd read somewhere that people who attempted suicide by slitting their wrists rarely cut deeply enough to reach that vital artery deep down past all the insignificant veins. Slitting your wrist was often messy, but it wasn't a good way to off yourself.

She found herself wishing she'd allowed her doctor to prescribe those tranquilizers. Pills were probably much more efficient. As she sat there turning the knife over and over, the blade flashing, she caught her reflection in it and saw how desperate she looked, dark circles under her eyes, dry, cracked lips. Utterly hopeless.

She placed the point of the knife against her wrist, deciding that she was simply going to test herself, see if she had the guts to do it. Pressing down a little harder, she felt a little pain but she hadn't even broken the skin. She pressed harder and this time the tip broke her skin and blood immediately began to pour slowly from the tiny hole.

She actually smiled happily.

She pressed down a bit harder, a hopeful expression on her face.

Then, someone loudly knocked on her door.

She ignored it and went back to the task at hand.

They knocked even harder, then Frannie's voice yelled, "Sara! I know you're in there. Open the door! Open this damn door or I'll break it down!"

Sara laughed at her threat. Frannie Anise was five-three and must have weighed a hundred and five pounds, tops!

She got up and went to the door. "Go away, Frannie, I'm busy!"

"Busy moping around that apartment. Open up. I'm getting you out for some fresh air."

"It's August. There *is* no fresh air in the city in August. Just heat, and a lot of cranky New Yorkers complaining about it."

"It's hot as hell in this hallway. The least you can do, after I've come all this way, is to invite me in for a cold drink."

"I'm not dressed for company."

"Who cares? If you really want to be alone, I'll drink and run."

Sara was silent for several minutes.

"I'm really hurt that you won't even open the door," Frannie said. "I thought I was your best friend."

"You are my best friend, but I need to be alone. A best friend would understand that."

"I haven't seen you in nearly a month. You won't answer my phone calls or my e-mails. What am I supposed to think? Unless I can look into your face, I'm not going to leave here. You know me. You know I mean it."

"Yeah, you're as pigheaded as they come."

"I'll get you for that pig remark. And I'm Jewish. We're not known for giving up."

"You're only half Jewish!"

"Yeah, but the other half is African-American. You *know* we don't give up!"

Sara peered down at her bleeding wrist.

She opened the door and fell into Frannie's arms.

Chapter 2

Frannie made Sara shower and dress, after which they got in a cab and went across town to an apartment building on Amsterdam Avenue. On the cab ride, Frannie didn't say a word about the thick bandage covering Sara's wrist, for which Sara was grateful.

She'd told Frannie that she'd cut herself while trying to split a breakfast bagel.

The building was quite old but well maintained. It had a redbrick facade and a dark green awning over the entrance. Sara guessed that Frannie must have been a frequent visitor because the elderly gentleman at the desk in the lobby waved them past without first inquiring after their reason for being there.

As they waited for the elevator, Frannie said, "I've been wanting to introduce you to this group of women for a long time but, the fact is, you haven't needed them until now."

"What do you mean?" Sara asked.

"You'll see," said Frannie with a mysterious smile. "One more thing, try not to stare at them. Some of them are very well known. I'm counting on your discretion."

"Ooh," intoned Sara. "What is this, a secret society or something?"

"Don't be ridiculous. It's simply a group of women who want to change the world by helping other women. We're hoping that you'll consider joining us."

"What if I don't want to join?"

"After you hear what we're about, you will," Frannie said with confidence.

"I'm not big on joining clubs," Sara said as a warning. "I was wooed by four sororities when I was in college and managed to avoid signing up with any of them."

"This is nothing like a sorority," Frannie told her.

"It's a charitable organization?"

"Of a sort," Frannie said.

A couple of minutes later, Frannie was knocking on the door of the penthouse.

"Wow," said Sara. "Are you sure all the funds you collect go to unfortunate women? Or does the person who lives here get kickbacks?"

Frannie laughed. "All of your questions will be answered soon."

"You're not a secret organization of call girls, are you?"

"If I weren't so glad to hear you cracking jokes, I'd bop you upside the head for that," Frannie said, laughing.

Sara was about to respond to Frannie's threat of violence when the door was opened by the Honorable Secretary of State, Eunice Strathmore. Sara had to mentally command herself to close her mouth because it was suddenly hanging open in surprise.

"Francesca!" the secretary of state cried, obviously delighted to see Frannie.

The two women warmly embraced.

A gentleman in full butler regalia closed the door and stood aside as if awaiting further instructions.

"Ladies, we're lunching in the next room. The food is buffet style, but Avery is mixing the drinks. What will you have?" said the secretary of state.

"A mimosa," Frannie said at once.

"Iced tea, please," Sara said, trying to keep her tone relaxed.

"My pleasure," said Avery, a tall African-American in his late sixties. His silver hair was thick and wavy, neatly trimmed, and combed back from a handsome coppery-brown face.

The secretary of state watched him go. She was in her midfifties, though she looked not a day over forty-five. Trim, attractive, she wore her short dark brown hair in a tapered cut that always looked freshly styled. A minimum of makeup graced the face that was known the world over.

Around five-five, she was rumored to jog every day and work out with weights three times a week, all to relieve stress. Sara guessed it was working for her, because her face was free of worry lines, and the twinkle in her eye appeared genuine.

Turning to Sara, she grasped her by both hands and peered up at her. "Welcome, Sara. Frannie has told me all about you. May I express my sympathy on the loss of your husband, Billy? My heart goes out to you. I, too, was a young widow."

Sara remembered that the secretary's husband had been in the military and had been killed in action more than twenty years ago. They had two children, a girl and a boy, both adults now, of course. She had chosen not to marry again.

"Thank you, Madam Secretary," said Sara.

"Call me Eunice, dear. We're all just women here."

Eunice warmly placed Sara's hand through her arm and led her into the next room where perhaps twenty women were sitting on couches and chairs enjoying luncheon on china plates and drinking from crystal champagne glasses. Conversation and laughter was heard throughout the room.

All conversation ceased, however, when Eunice re-entered the room with Frannie and Sara in tow. Frannie was greeted with more warm hugs, after which she introduced Sara to everybody.

Sara knew she would not recall all of the names of the women who formed a multicultural group. They were of African, Asian, Hispanic and Caucasian extractions. Their membership was obviously not limited to African-Americans.

She recognized several famous faces. A couple of actresses; a CEO of a major company; a multimedia magnate who could have bought and sold all of New York City, she was so fabulously wealthy. Sara was slightly in awe of them but recalled Frannie's admonition not to stare and tried her best to keep her eyes in her head.

She and Frannie were encouraged to partake of the buffet. Sara was glad for the opportunity to speak with Frannie in private. So, as they filled their plates at the buffet table, she whispered to her friend, "Oh, my God, that was Eunice Strathmore. I read she was in New York! But she's supposed to be attending a summit."

"She can't be in meetings every minute. Whenever she's in town, we get together to discuss business. Occasionally, one of us brings someone to be considered for membership. Today, that's you."

"But, why didn't you ever tell me you knew the secretary of state and," she looked around them, "Phylicia Edwards, my favorite actress, for God's sake?"

Frannie bit into a large shrimp and closed her eyes in ecstasy. "Like I said earlier, all of your questions will soon be answered."

As they turned away from the buffet tables, Phylicia Edwards called out, "Sara, Frannie, join me, there's room on my couch."

Holding their plates and placing their glasses atop coasters on the coffee table in front of them, they got comfortable.

Sara observed that Phylicia was every bit as beautiful as she looked in the movies. In her late thirties, she was petite and had delicate bone structure. Her golden-brown skin was unmarred by age or injury and her dark, liquid brown eyes seemed as guileless as a young child's.

Sara knew her estimation in that instance was faulty. Phylicia was not innocent by any means. She had fought her way to the top in Hollywood. She was not one to mince words about directors and producers whom she'd left whimpering like babes in her wake. Nobody messed with Phylicia Edwards and got away with it.

She was a warrior.

"How old are you, darlin'?" Phylicia asked Sara.

She was eating fast, obviously enjoying her food. But

she didn't talk with food in her mouth. She swallowed first, then spoke.

"I'm twenty-four," Sara told her.

Phylicia's eyes stretched. "I would have guessed twenty-one. You look fresh out of college."

"I graduated from college at twenty. I saw no reason to stay any longer than three years if I could get my bachelor's degree in three years' time. I went to graduate school at NYU once I came here. That's where I met my husband."

"I never went to college," Phylicia told her. She speared a piece of melon, chewed it thoroughly, swallowed, and said, "By the time I was twelve I was an expert at avoiding the hands of my lecherous stepfather. Two years later, I left home because he became more aggressive. I went to L.A. to live with my older sister who knew all about the bastard. She hadn't been as lucky. But she refused to allow that episode in her life to define her. She went to school and became a teacher. I got to go to high school in L.A. and when I was sixteen I went to test for a role on a sitcom, got it…"

"Hocus Pocus," Sara said excitedly. "I used to love it when I was a kid."

"Be careful, you're dating me," Phylicia joked.

Hocus Pocus had been a sitcom about a family of African-American witches. Kind of like *Bewitched,* but with more flavor.

"It didn't last very long," Phylicia went on. "But at least I got my foot in the door and the rest, as they say, is history, or herstory. Now, tell me, Sara, do you want to be in advertising for the rest of your life?"

"What did you all do, read my file?" Sara joked.

"Something like that," Phylicia confirmed. "We all got the memo on Sara Minton."

"I don't really know," Sara said wistfully. She had yet to put a morsel of food in her mouth and didn't know how in the world Phylicia managed a conversation while consuming everything on her plate.

Phylicia saw Sara's eyes on her plate and laughed. "After loads of Hollywood lunches I've learned to eat fast and talk out of the corner of my mouth. Especially in the lean years when somebody else was paying. You also learn how to pack your purse with food without being found out. Girl, I could eat for days on what I pilfered at a party. Sorry, you were telling me what you want to do with your life."

"I don't really know," Sara said again. "Before Billy died I thought I was reasonably happy working at the ad agency. But now, I'm not so sure. When I was a kid, I dreamed of owning a bookstore probably because I loved books so much, but I haven't entertained that notion in a long time."

"You know," Phylicia said. "Our childhood dreams often tell us things about our personalities that we sometimes forget when we become adults. I'm not saying a grown man should go be a cowboy because he wanted to be one when he was a kid. But I do believe everybody should do something adventurous every now and then."

Emboldened, Sara asked, "What have you done that was adventurous?"

"Last month, when I was filming in Ethiopia, I helped the wife of a government official escape out of his clutches. We went into his compound dressed like visiting nuns and when we left she and her two children were likewise attired. They were safely in Sudan before he realized they were missing." Her tone was conspiratorial the whole while.

She's talking about a movie role, Sara thought skeptically. However Phylicia, as she would soon learn, was telling the absolute truth.

A few minutes after everyone had finished eating, Eunice got up and went to stand in front of the huge fireplace. All of the ladies gave her their undivided attention.

"I'm so happy to see you, my sisters," Eunice began, a warm smile on her face. "This year we celebrate over one hundred and forty-one years of existence, ever since an ex-slave woman who was a member of the Underground Railroad started a secret organization of women, black and white, who would aid women and children by helping them escape dangerous situations. Her name was Celestine and in 1860 when she started her secret society she referred to the members as Aminatu's Daughters after the Nigerian princess, Aminatu, who gained wealth and fame by being a fierce warrior and who built walls around the city of Zaria in order to protect her people from invaders. We are still fierce warriors and we are still protecting the people!"

There was uproarious applause. The ladies got to their feet and gave their leader a standing ovation.

Eunice smiled benevolently and gestured for them to sit down. "Francesca has brought her best friend, Sara, to meet us. Sara is recently widowed, and some of us know what an emotional time that is, how we're suddenly unsure of our direction in life." She looked directly into Sara's eyes, her own hypnotic. "The one thing that saved me, Sara, when I lost Zachary, was getting out of myself. I volunteered in the neighborhood, at my children's school. It was at that time that I got involved with politics and I also went back to school and got my doctorate. I became an expert in foreign affairs. With my first assignment overseas I got to witness firsthand the subjugation of women in the country I visited. I won't name the country. There are so many like it, where women are considered second-class citizens or, worse, as chattel. Women in the United States don't know how good they have it compared to a lot of other women all over the world. So, after some research, I discovered Celestine and her story. And I realized that with the help of good friends, I could finish what Celestine had started. So, we pooled our resources, both financial and intellectual, and we started to do something about our sisters in countries where they had no rights. And since 1999, we have aided over five thousand women and children by educating them, where needed, and relocating them. Not always to the States, either. We have branches in over twenty countries."

Her curiosity up, Sara asked, "But how do they contact you? How do you know who needs your help?"

"I'm the secretary of state," Eunice said without bragging. "Special reports come across my desk all the time. Plus, we have people in governments all over the world who report cases of abuse. For example, I suppose you read about the Ethiopian woman who was going to be stoned to death for adultery while the man she had sex with, and whose child she gave birth to, got off scot-free?"

Sara nodded in the affirmative. The case had been in the news for weeks. Many countries expressed their outrage at the severity of the punishment, but apparently none of them had the authority to step in and remove the poor woman. Three days before her sentence was to be carried out, she disappeared from her prison cell. No one knew how she had escaped. Officials claimed the prison guards were guilty of taking a bribe to let her go. Prison guards swore they were innocent of such dirty dealings.

At any rate, she was not apprehended. The Ethiopian government had no proof of a conspiracy, so they let it go. They had bigger problems to worry about. They did, however, promise to keep an eye out for the young mother and if they ever caught her, she would then be put to death for her crime.

"She's living in France now," Eunice said. "She's getting training to become a nurse and she and her child, whose father is still in Ethiopia and enjoying his freedom, are happy and healthy."

For the first time since Billy's death, Sara began to feel as if her life might still have a purpose. That day, sitting among so many accomplished women, she felt as if her spirit had gotten a much-needed boost.

She started asking questions, and the ladies were delighted to answer them.

"Do you have to be a Republican to get involved?" was her first question. She knew the secretary of state's political affiliation, and she assumed that many of the women who were undoubtedly well-to-do shared their leader's political views.

"I'll answer that one," Phylicia said. "Honey, we don't care how you vote. Or if you vote at all. Politics don't enter into it. I can't stand Eunice's boss."

Some of the ladies laughed.

"Well, it's true," Phylicia said. "And Eunice knows

it. I've told her often enough. My point is, we only care that you're passionate about what we're doing, and that is saving innocent women and children."

"Where do I sign up?" Sara asked.

The ladies laughed good-naturedly

"You don't sign up," Eunice told her. "You're branded." And she went to Sara, turned around, lifted the right corner of her blouse and showed her the tiny, black crossed spears that had been tattooed just above her right buttock. "The spears of Aminatu."

Sara's tattoo was on her chest, on the top of her left breast.

Jason thought it had been done on a dare when she was in college.

Sara didn't join Aminatu's Daughters the day the secretary of state flashed her. She was advised to wait at least thirty days before deciding. It wasn't a decision to be made lightly.

She didn't change her mind, though, and a month and a half from the day Frannie introduced her to the organization she was tattooed in a ceremony in the same penthouse apartment on Amsterdam Avenue. Shortly afterward she was given an assignment.

Today, six years later, she had assisted in the liberation of more than a hundred women and children. And even though her actions could be considered outside of the law, she had no regrets.

"Hey, Jake, how's it going, my man?"

Jason was in the produce aisle at the supermarket when he heard Erik Sutherland's voice behind him. His eyes narrowed slightly as he considered the yellow squash in his hand. Jake was what he'd been called by his football pals. Erik had been leader of the pack back then.

In a sense, he still was. He was the richest man in town, and he was running for mayor.

"Hello, Erik," Jason said as he turned to regard the hefty six-foot-four redhead.

"You cook?" Erik asked. "You don't have a woman to do that for you?"

"No," Jason said, trying to keep the annoyance out of his tone. "Unlike some men who are barely beyond the knuckle-dragging caveman stage, I know how to cook."

Erik was thirty-six and had the beginnings of jowls and a beer gut. Jason supposed he didn't get much exercise these days. He was too busy ridding the streets of Glen Ellen of illegal aliens. Not that Glen Ellen had a huge illegal alien problem. It had none, as far as Jason could see. But Erik was from the alarmist school of politics. There were only so many jobs for permanent residents to begin with. Imagine the panic among citizens if they thought illegal aliens were after their source of livelihood?

Erik picked up a peach and bit into it. "I heard you were dating Sara Johnson. She sure turned into a beauty, didn't she? Talk about your late bloomer. Remember how awkward she used to be?" He still called Sara by her maiden name.

"No, I can't say that I do," Jason said. "If she seemed awkward to you it was probably because she was trying so hard to get out of your path. You never passed up the opportunity to make pig noises at her or call her out of her name."

Erik licked peach juice from his lips. "Yeah, I was a

real prick. I admit it. Now, God is getting me back because my own daughter is a little chubby and she's getting picked on at school." He finished off the peach and had the nerve to place the pit among the other peaches in the display. "To make it worse, she's a bookworm and spends more time at that bookstore of Sara's than she does at home. I can't blame her. Since her mom divorced me and gave me custody I haven't been much of a father."

Jason found himself feeling sorry for him. He supposed even for blockheads like Erik life had a way of forcing them to readjust their way of thinking.

Okay, he gave Erik the benefit of the doubt where his daughter was concerned. But what was up with ridding Glen Ellen of illegal aliens?

"I have to ask," he said. "Where exactly are all the illegal aliens you're hoping to run out of town on a rail?"

Erik laughed softly. "Now, there, my friend, is a conundrum. But the fact is I don't have to produce the illegal aliens. Simply the threat of them will make folks vote for me."

"So you're trying to get elected on a platform of fear," Jason deduced.

"Hey, just because we don't have the problem now doesn't mean we won't have it in the near future. The government's plan to crack down on illegal aliens hasn't exactly been foolproof. Once Southern California is full of 'em, they'll be coming north."

"You really are an idiot," Jason said, shaking his head.

Erik laughed louder. "You need to borrow a sense of humor, my friend."

"And you need to grow a conscience," Jason countered.

"Oh, that's right," Erik said, remembering a salient point about the Bryant family. "You have Haitians working for you. Tell me, are they American citizens?"

"You know damn well they are!"

"Calm down, I only asked a question." His blue eyes narrowed. "When did you get to be such a tight-ass? You used to be one of the guys."

"This isn't high school, and this town is not one of your cliques. You can't rule everyone simply because you're the biggest guy or the richest guy around anymore. Grow up, Erik."

Jason had been filling his handheld basket while he'd been talking to Erik. Finished shopping now, he turned to leave. "Have a nice day."

Erik picked up another peach and bit into it. "Yeah, you too, old buddy. And be sure to tell that pretty Sara Johnson I said hello."

Chapter 3

If Sara had had any shame at all where Jason was concerned she might have second-guessed herself to the extent that she would have stayed home that night. But she wasn't going to pass up the chance to see him again, even if it meant a continuation of the strained conversation they'd had earlier that day.

After work, she went home and showered, changed into a pair of loose-fit jeans and a long-sleeve shirt, put on her boots, brushed her braids, grabbed her jacket and sped over to the Hacienda in the Mustang.

The Mexican-inspired architecture of the Hacienda gave the 3000-square-foot house romantic appeal. Every time Sara drove up to it, she expected Zorro to come riding up on Tornado, his black steed, and sweep her up behind him.

No wonder she melted whenever Jason pulled her up

behind him on his equally handsome black steed, Indigo. Jason had named the three-year-old Indigo because the stallion was so black it had a purple-blue sheen to its coat.

Sara knocked on the door with not a little temerity. Reckless confidence might be the death of her, but a faint-hearted maiden wasn't liable to win her true love, was she?

Jason pulled the huge door open and looked down his nose at her. He was wearing jeans and nothing else but he still managed to look haughty, as if she were the one who had to pass muster to enter his sanctum.

Sara smiled at him. "Am I welcome?" She took a step backward. "Because I can leave if you don't want me here."

His hand shot out and firmly grasped her by the arm.

Sara turned and went into his arms. They made a half turn as they embraced, and he shut the door. He bent his head, she raised up on her toes, and they kissed passionately.

"I told you I was easy," he murmured when they parted. He smiled enigmatically.

Sara couldn't detect any leftover hurt feelings in that confident gaze of his. Sometimes his mercurial nature confused her. He definitely kept her on her toes.

She wondered, for example, how much longer he would put up with her lack of communication? She asked only that his patience lasted long enough for her to get Elizabeth, her new charge, placed in a suitable situation. After that, she was going to resign from the organization.

Hopefully that shouldn't take more than a few weeks. Eunice had assured her they were working hard to get Elizabeth placed.

She smiled brightly up at him. Their lower halves were pressed firmly together and she, being highly susceptible to his nearness, was becoming more and more aroused.

"Are we going for that ride you promised me?" she reminded him.

"Yes!" His teeth flashed in a gorgeous smile. He loved their rides together in the moonlight. "I'll get dressed."

He gave her a quick buss on the lips and was gone.

Sara went to the kitchen to see what that divine smell was that had been enticing her since she'd stepped foot in the house.

The house was made of very thick stone and was cool in summer and drafty in the winter months. There was Mexican tile, a different shade in each room, throughout the house. Handmade rugs offered some relief from its stark beauty. The furnishings were good solid wood and leather pieces, the colors in earth tones with splashes of bold color here and there. Simone Bryant had truly designed a beautiful family home over the years. Sara could imagine living there and putting her own stamp on it.

The kitchen, Simone's pride and joy, obviously, was equipped with everything a chef could want—durable and reliable cookware, lots of counter space, a double oven, and a restaurant-size Sub-Zero refrigerator.

Sara walked over to the stove and lifted the lid on the Dutch oven. The aroma of stewed chicken made her mouth water. There was something very appealing about a man who could cook. She supposed some of his mother's culinary talent had rubbed off on him. Come to think of it, his brother was a chef, too.

She went and got a fork from the cutlery drawer and

dipped into the stewed chicken, spearing a nice chunk. She closed the lid and blew on the steaming treat.

Jason came into the kitchen just as she was putting it in her mouth.

"Caught you!" he said, laughing. "A little hungry, are you?" He had put on a long-sleeve shirt, a denim jacket and his brown leather boots.

Chewing, Sara said, "It smelled so good, I couldn't resist."

Being the gentleman he was, Jason offered to forgo the ride and feed her instead.

"No, no," she cried. "I'm looking forward to our ride."

A few minutes later, Sara was sitting astride Indigo behind Jason with her arms wrapped around him. They were riding through the vineyards, which were bathed in moonlight.

Indigo's gait was slow enough so that they could talk comfortably.

"These grapes are going to become what kind of wine, again?" she asked. She was woefully ignorant about the wine business but was willing to learn.

"Zinfandel," Jason told her.

"That's a red wine, right?"

"Right, red or rosé, which is a light red."

"How old were you when you had your first glass of wine?"

"Five or six," Jason told her. "Every Christmas we were permitted one glass, up until we were eighteen, at which time we were considered old enough to determine how many glasses we wanted and when we wanted to drink them. Of course, when we were kids the Christmas glass of wine was perhaps only large enough to hold half an ounce. And the moderation with which our parents treated wine made all of us into near teetotalers. None of us will have more than a glass of wine with dinner to this day."

The side of Sara's face was pressed to his back and his voice vibrated in her ear. She liked the sound of it. "Are you glad you came back home?"

She'd never asked him that question. She was afraid he would say he wasn't happy here. She closed her eyes and hoped for a positive reply.

"I'm happier than I ever thought I could be," he said without hesitation. "I told you how I mentally fought against going into the family business?"

"Yes, you said you didn't want to be like your father, so you excelled in school and became a lawyer, a profession so removed from being a gentleman farmer, as you like to think of your father, that no one in the family would ever presume to ask you to take over."

She laughed when she was finished.

"What's so funny?" Jason wanted to know.

"Then, your sister came along and talked you into it."

Jason didn't want to tell Sara that she had also been a determining factor in his decision to come back home. He was already smitten with her at the time and wanted to get to know her better.

"I was unhappy being a divorce lawyer, too. I was tired of seeing so many marriages go up in smoke."

"You don't miss being a lawyer at all?" Sara asked, incredulous.

"Nah, I had my fill. Now that I look back I realize I was just running from the inevitable. I belong here. This place is in my blood, no matter how hard I try to deny it."

Sara hugged him tighter and with a broad smile on her face, sighed happily.

"Does that make you happy?" Jason asked.

"Yes, it does. I'm glad you love it here. So do I. I wouldn't want to live anywhere else."

"After living in New York City?"

"I love New York. I always will. But Glen Ellen is home. After Mom died and Dad moved to Florida to live with Uncle Ed, I didn't even think of selling the family home and moving away."

"I'm grateful you didn't."

"There are not that many black folks left."

"There weren't that many to begin with," Jason said. "According to the African-American historian on this area, my mom, the Bryants were the first blacks to live here. And it was lots of years before anyone else black moved here."

"My mom and dad came in the late seventies when Mom inherited a lot of money and bought property here. She was the one who loved farming, not Dad. When she died he couldn't go on without her. Yeah, this is definitely a lonely place for black folks," said Sara. "I bet there aren't twenty African-Americans living in this area. The high school kids have to go to Santa Rosa to attend school, and last I heard Claude and Rosaura's two kids were the only black students at the elementary school."

"But Santa Rosa's not that far away, and it has a sizable African-American community. We're not that isolated from our culture," Jason said reasonably.

"Hasn't that always been the place to go when you wanted soul food, or had to get your hair cut, or your hair styled? Or actually wanted to date a sister or a brother? I didn't date anybody from here when I was in high school."

"I know. The first guy who kissed you came from

Santa Rosa. I remember Kyle Bailey, that little pip-squeak, he was two grades behind me."

"That little pipsqueak shot up several inches over the summer of his junior year and led the basketball team to the state finals his senior year. For a hot minute I was the most popular girl in school because he was my boyfriend. Then, he dropped me for Susie Kent, and my moment of fame fizzled so quickly it made my head spin."

She laughed at the memory now, but back then, like most sixteen-year-old girls would have been, she was devastated. She'd wound up going to the senior prom with her father. Her mom had insisted that she would regret it if she did not go. She'd been right.

Her father, a big, handsome brown-skinned man made the girls swoon with envy. Some of them had even asked him to dance with them, but he told them his dance card was filled. He and Sara danced every dance together.

That still was her favorite memory of her father.

"Where is he now?" Jason asked of Kyle Bailey. "I'll go kick his butt right now."

Laughing, Sara said. "Forget it. Last I heard, he was happily married with a houseful of kids. More power to him."

"Did he marry Susie Kent?"

"No, she married a pro basketball player, got divorced two years later, married another jock, divorced him and decided to give marriage a rest for a while. I saw her at our tenth-year class reunion. She said she owned a boutique in San Francisco. Her divorce settlements had left her pretty wealthy, so she didn't need to work but liked to stay busy."

Jason chuckled. "You believed that?"

"The point is, she did," Sara told him. "I had no way

of knowing if she was telling the truth or not, but I hoped that she was happy. She had this kind of desperate look in her eyes that made me wish for something good to happen to her. That was two years after Billy died, so I wasn't in the best mental health myself."

In the beginning of their relationship, Jason had tensed up whenever she mentioned Billy Minton, but now, after learning how good he had been to Sara he no longer felt uneasy listening to her talk about him. He was sure that if he had met Billy he would have liked him. He was glad that Sara had had a good marriage.

He'd known too many women who felt that they had been damaged by their marriages. He had represented some of them.

Thinking about Billy sometimes put Sara in a melancholy mood, though. In fact, he felt her slump against him now, a sure sign that a blue mood was building. He quickly changed the subject. "Guess who sends you his regards?"

She sat up straighter, her curiosity engaged. "Idris Elba?"

Now, that irked him. Elba was Sara's favorite actor of the moment. No, not just her favorite actor. He was convinced that the British actor lived in her sexual fantasies.

He chuckled. "No, and if he called I wouldn't give you the message. So quit hoping. No, your secret admirer is your former tormentor, Erik Sutherland. I saw him in the supermarket this afternoon."

"What do you mean by secret admirer? I haven't even seen him since I moved back."

"He said you'd really blossomed. He called you pretty."

"That makes my skin crawl. Where could he have seen me and I wasn't aware of being *seen* by him?"

"That's another mystery," Jason said. "Anyway, he

seems to regret his past behavior towards you and said that God was punishing him for it by allowing his own daughter, who happens to be a little overweight, to be picked on by kids at school."

"I know Melissa," Sara said sympathetically. "She's a sweet girl. She's grown attached to Frannie who thinks she's a work of art in progress."

"There's another mystery," Jason said. "Your friend, Frannie Anise. Doesn't it strike you as unusual that when you left New York she quit her job and followed you to California? That's not something most girl-friends would do, not even best friends."

"Northern California is home for her, too. I told you, she grew up in San Francisco. Her parents still live there. It wasn't such a stretch for her to move back here."

"Are you sure she's not in love with you?" Jason asked seriously.

"Frannie's not gay."

"I've never seen her with a guy."

"You've got a suspicious mind."

"It's one of my many faults," Jason admitted. "I wonder about those trips you take. I wonder about those women who work in the bookstore for short periods of time and then disappear as if they never existed. I'm wondering when the new woman, who I think is from South Africa, will disappear. I have questions that need answers, and you have all the answers and won't give them to me. Excuse me if I'm suspicious."

"I understand how you feel."

"But you have no answers."

"I'm afraid not."

"That's what I thought." He made a noise with his

tongue, a signal for Indigo to break into a canter. The big stallion seemed to have been waiting to stretch his strong legs and for the next twenty minutes he got a good workout while his riders clung to each other in silence.

Later, as they slowly rode into the yard, Jason said, "I'll take care of Indigo. You can go on inside, I know you must be tired."

"No, I'm not tired at all. I'd like to help."

In the barn, after Jason had removed Indigo's bit, stirrups and saddle, Sara gently wiped the sweat off him with a soft cloth used specifically for that purpose. Afterward, they took turns brushing him down.

Finished, Sara patted his strong neck. "Good night, handsome."

They left him in his clean stall where he had fresh oats and water.

Silently, they walked to the house from the barn. The full moon illuminated their path. Even if there had been no moon tonight, there were security lights at the top corners of the back of the barn and at strategic points around the house.

Jason was in a pensive mood. Everything about Sara, lately, was a mystery. She seemed to delight in helping him rub down Indigo moments ago. Last year, she'd gone into the vineyards and helped with the harvest, working as hard as anyone else.

It was obvious that she knew what becoming a vintner's wife would entail. It also appeared as if she would welcome that kind of life. Therefore it continued to puzzle him as to why she'd turned down his proposal. He was irritated with himself to still be dwelling on it, but he couldn't help himself.

He would have to change his way of thinking. He was basically a future-focused person. The present concerned him only for its momentary pleasures. He looked at life as in constant flux, and unless you planned for the future, you would be caught unawares.

He didn't like surprises. He knew that it was impossible to predict the future. But those who prepared for it were better equipped to cope with unpleasant surprises. In his future-focused mind he saw himself and Sara together. He had been seeing himself and Sara together ever since that night he had kissed her in the wine cellar during Erica and Joshua's wedding reception here at the winery.

Once in the house, they went to separate bathrooms and freshened up before dinner.

They dined in the kitchen, talking and laughing about their day.

It was mid-October, the start of the rainy season, and Sara told him that several of the ladies who had come into the store that day had mentioned someone had told them that El Niño would cause severe climate upheavals this year. "We could have floods and maybe even a tsunami, they said."

"You're not listening to the rumor mill, are you?" Jason asked with a skeptical laugh. "Every year, somebody predicts the end of the world, and all we get here is a little rain from November to December. The same thing will happen this year. Nothing's changed in this area in a long time. We're blessed with a wonderful weather system."

"Yeah, but what if they're right this year? What would flooding do to the vines?"

"There would be destruction of Biblical proportions," Jason joked.

"Okay, drop it," Sara said, laughing softly. "I can see you think my patrons are a bunch of lunatics."

"Just tell me this, was one of the doomsayers Mrs. McClarin?"

Sara nodded in the affirmative as she forked more of the delicious stewed chicken into her mouth. She narrowed her eyes at him. What could he have against dear sweet Mrs. McClarin? Mrs. Mac, as the kids had referred to her, had been her fourth-grade English teacher. She had retired twenty years ago but her mind was as sharp as ever.

"It was Mrs. McClarin who said she saw Big Foot eating out of the garbage can in her backyard last year. Pete Baumgartner told me about it."

Pete was the local sheriff's deputy.

"Yeah, well, Pete Baumgartner got a D in her fourth-grade English class and he's had it in for her ever since. Maybe she *did* see Big Foot eating out of her trash can."

Jason threw his head back in laughter.

Sara loved seeing him like this, with his guard down and supremely relaxed.

Those whiskey-colored eyes of his were so enticing at these moments. But it was his mouth that had been her undoing from the beginning of their relationship. She couldn't look at it with its sensual lines without wanting to know how it would feel to be kissed by him. Once her lips had touched his she couldn't resist wanting to kiss him again and again. Just the thought of kissing him aroused her.

His laughter under control, he met her eyes across the table. Placing his knife and fork in his plate, he wiped his mouth with the cloth napkin, dropped it onto the plate, and got to his feet. "Are you finished?" he asked softly.

Sara tipped her head back slightly in order not to break eye contact. "Yes."

The pulse in her neck thumped excitedly. She'd already put her utensils and napkin in her plate. Now, she sat there almost primly, looking up at him.

They had not made love in more than two weeks. Ever since the night he'd proposed. Unfortunately, all of their present problems stemmed from that night. If he wanted her again maybe he had decided to forgive her for turning him down.

Jason went to her and held out his hand to her. Sara placed it in his and he slowly drew her to her feet and pulled her into his arms. She tipped her head back, anticipating his kiss.

She closed her eyes as his face descended toward hers but quickly opened them again when she felt his lips on her forehead instead of on her mouth.

Jason smiled warmly at her as he straightened up. "It's getting late, and we both have to get up early. I'll walk you to your car."

Sara schooled her features. She would not let him see how much his rejection had wounded her. If emotional detachment were his objective she would show him how it was done.

"You're so right," she said, her tone eminently reasonable. "I'll just get my jacket." She hadn't bothered to bring her shoulder bag inside. It was locked in the car. Her car keys were in the pocket of her jacket.

He was still holding her by the arms. She turned her back to him, breaking his hold. Walking to the coat tree near the back door, she grabbed her jacket and put it on.

They walked side by side through the house to the front door where Jason opened the door for her and followed her outside. Sara peered up at the sky once they had descended the steps that led to the stone circular driveway.

"Thanks for a lovely evening," she said when they were standing in front of the Mustang. The tension between them was palpable. Sara fought the urge to throw herself into his arms and beg him to forgive her.

Jason didn't dare touch her again because he was on fire with the desire to make love to her. He was only a man. But he had his pride. He wouldn't make love to a woman who didn't love him enough to marry him. He'd said he was easy, but he wasn't stupid. This was a war of wills and he was going to be the victor. No. He didn't want her to come crawling back to him, begging him to forgive her. But even if he had to take cold showers every night and run ten miles each day, he would not take her to bed until this matter was settled between them.

And the only way that was going to happen was if she said yes to his proposal.

That was his final decision.

However, as he gazed into her upturned face, her almond-shaped eyes golden in the bright moonlight, and her mouth looking especially inviting, he knew he was going to suffer mightily for his convictions.

Sara had been watching him while he wrestled with his thoughts. She could guess what was going on behind those hooded eyes of his, and she didn't doubt for a moment that she would emerge victorious in this test of wills.

But just so he knew what he was fighting for, she tiptoed, grabbed him and kissed him soundly. Jason, caught off guard, thought of breaking it off but her mouth felt so good on his he immediately capitulated.

He held her firmly against him. Her arms went

around his neck. His hands molded her shapely body to his, moving downward until they rested on her firm buttocks. Their bodies pressed closer together as they hungrily sought the temporary satisfaction a kiss afforded. As soon as Sara felt his manhood growing hard against her belly, she withdrew her tongue from his mouth and disengaged herself from his embrace. "I'd better go. Don't want to keep you from your *bed*."

She jerked her arm out of his grasp, and reached for the door's handle.

Jason calmly stepped aside and let her get behind the wheel of the Mustang.

"I know that it seems like I'm sending mixed signals, Sara," he said, "but I'm having a hard time knowing exactly how to handle this situation. Do we go on as if nothing has happened between us and continue making love? Or would it be better to call a moratorium on sex until we know where we're going? I don't know the best course so I'm winging it."

"Let's just agree on the last choice, all right?" Sara said as she started the car. "It might do us both good to be celibate for a while. But don't play with me, Jason. I didn't turn down your proposal because I wanted to hurt you. I had a very good reason for doing it. I can't tell you that reason right now. No amount of psychological blackmail on your part is going to get your answers any quicker. Believe it or not I'm trying to do the honorable thing here."

Jason was shaking his head in the negative. "You're killing me with all this secretive crap. If you trusted me, you would be able to tell me anything. If you don't trust me, then you don't love me. It's as simple as that."

"Nothing's as simple as that!" Sara cried. "The fact is,

Jason Bryant, you're a spoiled brat who doesn't really know how the world works. You think you're sophisticated because you were a hotshot attorney and therefore you've seen it all. But, believe me, you need years of maturing before you'll be truly enlightened. Good night!"

With that, she put the car in Drive, hit the accelerator, and sped out of his driveway.

Chapter 4

"Sara, darn it, slow down. What is the matter with you this morning? You know I don't have the legs of a gazelle, like you do. Mine are more like a Dachshund's!" Frannie protested as they set off on their jog the next morning.

Sara ran in place a few seconds while Frannie caught up with her. She smiled at the comical sight Frannie made with her abundance of black frizzy hair done up on top of her head. She resembled one of those toy trolls people liked to keep on their desks.

"Nothing's the matter with me," she said. "What makes you think something's wrong?"

"You're running as if the hounds of hell are after you," Frannie told her. Beside Sara now, she peered up into her face. "And you have that 'don't mess with me' glint in your eye. You're mad at somebody. How many guesses do I get? Oh, wait a minute, I don't need to guess. It's Jason, isn't it?"

Sara picked up her pace again.

Frannie ran harder to keep up. "Okay, okay, I get the message. You don't want to talk about it. Even though it would help to talk about it. My mother says a friendly ear is worth more than a year on a psychiatrist's couch."

"Your mother's a psychiatrist!"

"Yeah, but she's an *ethical* psychiatrist. If she thinks a patient is better served by simply talking to a good friend, she'll tell them to save their money."

"That's ethical, all right," Sara agreed, laughing. She slowed down. "Okay. Yesterday he came into my office all sweetness and light, talking about how he's easy and he's willing to wait for me. He invited me to dinner, with the promise of more afterward."

"More of what?" Frannie asked, her delicate brows arched in curiosity.

"Do you want to hear this, or not?"

"Just wondered what made you think he was suggesting sex later on? After all, you two haven't been together in that way since he proposed, right?"

"I really do tell you too much about my personal life."

"You know I live vicariously through you. So don't stop the supply now that I'm hopelessly *hooked.*"

Sara laughed. "I could tell there was the promise of more because of his body language. We were affectionate at the office, very affectionate, almost to the point of having sex on the desk."

"It has been awhile, huh?"

"Exactly. We hadn't kissed like that since before the proposal. Of course I would think that he'd decided to give me the benefit of the doubt and resume our physical relationship!"

"I see your point."

"Thank you!" Sara took a deep breath and continued. "But later that night, after dinner, he got up and made a move on me so similar to his old self just before he used to jump my bones, that I got all hot and bothered. He went to kiss me. I closed my eyes, and what do you suppose happened then? He kissed me on the forehead as if I was his baby daughter whom he was kissing good-night! Then, he said it was getting late and he would walk me to my car."

"After making like Valentino?"

"Yeah, girl, had me about to pant like a dog."

"The scum!"

"That's what I'm talking about!"

"Oh, he's definitely still mad at you," was Frannie's considered opinion.

"I know."

"You're doing all you can," Frannie said sympathetically. "You wouldn't have accepted your last assignment if you had known he was going to propose. But Elizabeth was already under our protection before he popped the question."

"Bad timing."

Frannie nodded her agreement, her frizzy hair bobbing up and down. "You're making a huge sacrifice for that *schlimazel*."

"What does that mean in English again?" Frannie was always tossing out a Yiddish word or two that Sara had to have translated.

"It means someone who's prone to mistakes or plagued with bad luck."

"It *was* all just bad luck when he proposed. I was so ready to say yes, I could taste it. But I couldn't because Elizabeth needs us."

"Oh, girl, I do feel for you," said Frannie. "But, now, lend me your ear because I actually have a problem that I could use your help with."

"Fire away."

"Melissa is hinting around about setting me up with her father. The poor kid wants a mother so badly, she's considering me for the job!"

A pickup truck that they recognized as belonging to Joe Rizzo, a local olive grower, slowed down next to them. "You ladies in those jogging shorts does an old man's heart good!" Joe yelled.

"Get on to work, you pervert!" Frannie yelled back at him, grinning. Joe meant no harm. He often bought her a beer at the tavern on a Saturday night. Fifty-nine, and a widower the past five years, he was so busy fending off most of the single women of a certain age that he didn't have the energy for serious flirting. At least that's what he'd told Frannie.

Joe laughed heartily. "Enjoy your day, ladies."

"You too!" Sara called.

"Anyway," Frannie said, continuing the conversation Joe had interrupted. "Yesterday when she dropped by the store after school she asked me if I'd come to her sixteenth birthday party tomorrow night. Fool that I am, I immediately accepted. I like her, and I was flattered that she'd asked me. Then, I remembered that her father is the same creep who used to make your life miserable when you were her age and now I regret that I accepted so fast."

"I'm all for sisterly solidarity," Sara told her. "But

you don't have to feel offended by him on my behalf. Jason told me that Erik said he regretted being an ass back then. If you want to go to Melissa's party, then go. But what makes you think she's going to try to fix you up with him?"

"She told me to wear something sexy, as if she would know anything about sexy. She wears clothes so big they're practically falling off her body."

"That's the style these days. Plus, since she's a little heavy she thinks it camouflages her body."

"I'd love to give her a makeover," Frannie said. "Do you think she'd be offended if I took her shopping for her birthday?"

"Make it a girls' day out and I don't see why. Invite me and Elizabeth along and she won't feel as if you're targeting her."

"Good idea. We can hop over to Santa Rosa before the mall closes tonight. Are you sure you're free tonight? I'm pretty sure Melissa is. But I wonder if her dad would object?"

"Yeah, I don't have a love life anymore, remember?" Sara said with a laugh. "And why should Erik object?"

"His daughter going shopping with three black women?"

"I wish he *would* object," Sara said. "I have a few choice words for him that have had nearly twenty years to simmer at the back of my mind!"

Frannie laughed. "Now, watch yourself. You may be talking about my future boyfriend if his daughter has anything to do with it."

"I'll pray for you, girl."

"Don't pray too hard. I've seen him around. He's got a nice tush. You know I go for big guys."

"He's six-four, Frannie, more than a foot taller than you. Isn't that *too* big?"

"Oh, please, I once dated a guy who was six-seven. He could almost put me in his pocket. But it was nice while it lasted."

"What was nice about it?"

"Do I have to tell you about the main advantage of dating a tall guy?"

Sara actually blushed. "No, don't say it."

Of course, Frannie had to say it now. "It sort of leaned to the left and, girl, I had to go around the corner to get on it."

"You ought to quit!" Sara cried, laughing. Knowing Frannie's history with men she was happy that Frannie could still joke about sex.

"Well, lately, all I've got is a few good memories," Frannie said wistfully.

Later, back at the house, the three housemates, Sara, Frannie and Elizabeth, had breakfast together. Elizabeth had slept in while Sara and Frannie had their morning jog. When they returned, they heard her in her bedroom's shower. Sara and Frannie went to their rooms and showered and dressed, too. By the time Elizabeth came downstairs Sara had prepared their breakfast of scrambled eggs, ham and toast.

Frannie was pouring coffee in mugs at their place settings when Elizabeth came into the kitchen and gave them a timid, "Good morning."

Elizabeth was twenty-two, had light brown skin and dark brown eyes. She wore her natural black hair in a short afro. Although Elizabeth was a genuinely shy and modest young lady, she was under the organization's protection because she had led a walkout of nearly five hundred gold miners in Johannesburg. Since apartheid had been abolished working conditions had improved for blacks; however, there were still some throwbacks to a colonial system that in many aspects resembled slavery.

The government passed laws to protect workers, but the gold-mining companies failed to comply. A group of miners, led by Elizabeth's father, Edward, wrote down and presented to their bosses their grievances which included the need for better pay, health insurance, an on-site infirmary and more frequent water breaks.

Two days later, Edward Mbeki was gunned down while walking home from work.

The police never found his killer. A week after that, Elizabeth, who was in medical school in Johannesburg at the time, led a march through the city in protest of her father's death and called for an investigation of the company that he had worked for.

She and several others were arrested.

A group of American human rights lawyers got her released the next day. A few days later, Elizabeth convinced the gold miners at her father's company to walk out of work and stay away for twenty-four hours. The company owners went ballistic and hired toughs to beat up several of the workers.

An enterprising reporter for a Soweto newspaper actually caught one of the company's thugs beating up a worker on video. It was shown on every television station in South Africa. Shortly after that, the company came under investigation, and was forced to comply with everything that Edward Mbeki had asked for before his assassination.

However, it wasn't over for Elizabeth. Her family's

house mysteriously caught fire and her mother and younger sister perished in the flames. She began receiving death threats. Her college friends tried to help by concealing her in their homes. They tried to raise her spirits, but she became despondent, and contemplated suicide. That was when a black woman with a tattoo of crossed spears on her upper arm came to her and told her she was taking her to America where she would be among friends and she could continue her education.

Elizabeth told the woman she wanted to die. She had no family anymore, only distant relatives whom she didn't know well. "I promise you," said the woman. "Where you're going you will form a new family, and when you continue your work, you will find a new purpose. Your family will not have died in vain. You will live on and grow strong, Elizabeth. The name Mbeki will live on because of you."

She had been living in Sara's home now, for four weeks. She was still kind of shy around Sara and Frannie, but she had come to trust them.

Sara gauged her success by the number of smiles on Elizabeth's face each day. She knew that from personal experience, the only thing that could vanquish suicidal thoughts was a reason to live, a purpose. That's why she'd recently written Eunice and told her that the organization needed to find Elizabeth a job at a local hospital, preferably a job in which she would be working with children. Elizabeth was going to become a pediatrician before her life had been turned upside down.

That morning, when Sara checked her mail on the organization's site, she had found a message from Eunice saying that everything had been arranged: Elizabeth's new identity papers were ready, and she would begin work as a nurse's aide the following Monday. Eunice also added that it was taking longer than she had anticipated, but she had it on good authority that in a couple of months, Elizabeth would be admitted to the University of California College of Medicine on full scholarship.

Sara had the pleasure of relating all of that to Elizabeth over breakfast this morning. The expression of pure joy on Elizabeth's face made Sara tear up. Elizabeth immediately leaned forward and grasped Sara's hands in her small ones. "Don't cry, Miss Sara, you and Frannie have brought me back to life these past few weeks. Last night, I didn't dream about the fire. It was the first time I didn't dream about it. Instead, I dreamed my family and I were having dinner together on a Sunday, and we were all happy to be together like it was when I would return home from being at school for a long period of time. We all held hands and Father said the prayer. Then Mother served us all, herself last, as she always used to. Finally, Father looked us all in our faces and said, 'This is heaven to me.' Then, I woke up with such a warm feeling inside. I know, now, that they want me to go on. They want me to live well so that one day, hopefully when I'm old and worn out, I'll join them in Heaven."

Frannie got up to get paper towels for herself and Sara. Handing Sara hers, then sitting back down, she said, "How would you like to go shopping with us after work? Melissa Sutherland's turning sixteen, and we're going to help her celebrate."

"I would love it," said Elizabeth, her eyes shining with pleasure.

* * *

Jason got a rude awakening that day. He and Claude were in the southern vineyard pruning the vines when Claude, working several feet ahead of him due to the slowness with which Jason worked, uttered an expletive.

Jason looked in Claude's direction. He didn't think in all the years he'd known Claude Ledoux, that he'd ever heard him swear. Squinting against the bright sunshine, in spite of wearing shades, Jason said, "What's the matter?"

Sweat rolled down the sides of his face. It was seventy degrees today. Nice for October, but he was sweating like a horse ridden hard and put up wet.

Claude was speaking rapid French now, and holding out his hand with withered grapes in his palm. Jason didn't know what he wanted him to do with a handful of dried-up grapes, but he walked over to his foreman and took the grapes from him.

Claude began walking around the vines in the area where he had been working pointing out the raisining of several other grapes on the vine. After a while, Jason started seeing what Claude was seeing: the vines in this area were characterized by stunted shoots, dwarfed leaves, wilting and shriveled grapes hanging listlessly from them. They were sick.

Jason's heart skipped a beat.

Root rot. He'd heard of it, but as far as he could remember, his parents had never had a major case of it. Dead or severely damaged grapevines would have to be dug up and replanted after the soil had been completely cleared of the infected roots.

The problem was, it was extremely hard to get all of

the root, and if any survived at all it could thrive and reinfect the healthy vines.

He was trying not to panic here, but all he could think about was the fact that his parents had run the winery without losing it for many, many years and he'd been in control for under two years and could possibly lose everything.

He looked at Claude, who was still muttering in French. "What do we have to do?" he asked plaintively.

"Root collar excavation," Claude said with a dire expression on his dark brown face.

"Do I need to rent equipment for that?"

"No, you've got a mini backhoe in the storage shed."

Jason had done an inventory when he'd taken over, but he didn't know what half of the equipment was called that he'd encountered in his look around the place. "Then, let's get started."

Claude shook his head in the negative. "No, first we need to dig up a test root and have a plant pathologist diagnose which kind of root rot we have. Then we'll know how best to eradicate it."

"A root pathologist?"

"Yeah, it's kind of like CSI for plants. They can tell you what killed it."

"Oh, my God," said Jason. He had a lot to learn. "You mean I'm going to have to take the infected root up to U.C. Davis?"

"That would be your best bet, yes," said Claude.

"Okay, I'll go get a shovel."

Melissa took a photo of Sara, Frannie and Elizabeth as the three of them were sitting at a tiny round table in the food court. She quickly sent the photo via her phone to her nosy father. He was on the line now. She was standing around the corner near the restrooms where she'd told her friends she was going when she'd gotten up five minutes ago.

"Satisfied?" she asked sarcastically.

"The other two work at Sara's bookstore?"

"Yes! Now, I've got to go."

"Melissa, don't you have any white friends?"

"If you must know, no I don't. And those kids you've invited to my party tomorrow night will only come because you're filthy rich, not because they're my friends. The only person coming tomorrow night who is my friend will be Frannie."

"It's not healthy for you to hang out with black people all the time, Melissa. Do you have something against your own race?"

"You don't get it, do you?" Melissa asked, exasperated. "Unlike you, I don't care what color my friends are, just that they're my friends. I'm ashamed of you."

Erik sighed on his end. He really stank as a parent. Now his daughter thought he was a bigot. "Melissa, don't you think you're going to be ostracized by the white kids in town if you're always hanging out at that black bookstore?"

"I really don't care, and Sara sells all kinds of books at Aminatu's Daughters, not just books written by black authors. Maybe if you'd come in sometime you'd see for yourself, but all you want to do is complain. I'm going now. Bye!"

She hung up quickly and stuck the phone in her jacket pocket.

Rejoining her friends, she asked, "What did I miss?"

Before she had gone to the bathroom, they had been

boy-gazing. The mall was packed with teenagers. They were theoretically picking a boyfriend for Melissa.

Two tanned boys who looked like they might be high school seniors were sitting on a bench near the waterfall a few feet to the left of them. "The boy in the blue football jersey is *very* cute," Sara said. "Do you know him, Melissa?"

During their selection process, Melissa had known several of the boys by name. They went to her high school. They totally ignored her as a matter of course, but she knew them from class or by reputation.

The boy that Sara had pointed out was in her advanced Algebra class. He sat in front of her, and he'd never once turned around to say hello to her. She could have been a piece of furniture for all he cared.

"The boy in the football jersey is Danny Keener, the other guy is Tyler Gaines."

"Is Danny smart?" Sara wanted to know. He had the kind of dark good looks that reminded her of the actor who portrayed Clark Kent on *Smallville.*

"He makes A's in Advanced Algebra, so he must be," said Melissa.

"Do you think he's handsome?" Elizabeth asked. She had never played this game of observing males simply for their beauty. When she thought of dating a fellow student she wanted to know if he was a good student, if he was a good son, and if he was a spendthrift or not. Dating, to her, was a means to an end. The end was marriage.

This notion of dating for fun was intriguing, though.

Melissa's face turned red when Elizabeth asked her if she liked Danny's looks. She had secretly been in love with Danny Keener for two years now. She held out absolutely no hope that he would ever notice her. He dated girls like Sherry Newcastle who was beautiful *and* a cheerleader. Plus, she had thighs that didn't touch. Thighs that were trim and toned. Melissa knew she'd never have thighs like that. Therefore, she would never be noticed by Danny Keener.

She didn't lie to her friends, though. "I think he's adorable," she said. "But he's never even looked my way."

"Well," said Sara. "He's looking your way now."

Tyler Gaines, a tall, gangly boy with too-long blond hair that fell in his eyes and Tarzan's style of communicating was pointing at Melissa, then back at his chest.

Sara, Frannie, and Elizabeth had no idea how to translate his sign language, but Melissa immediately knew that, "He wants to come over and talk to us."

"Tell him to come on," said Frannie. "And to bring the cute one with him."

Melissa smiled shyly at Tyler and motioned for him to come on over.

Tyler got up and loped over with Danny beside him. "Hey, Melissa."

"Hey, Tyler."

"This is Danny Keener."

"And this is Sara Minton, Frannie Anise, and Mary Makebo," Melissa said. Like everyone else besides Sara and Frannie, Melissa knew Elizabeth by an alias.

"Ladies," said Tyler with a respectful nod. His eyes lingered on Elizabeth. Then he looked at Melissa. "I think it's cool that your dad's giving you a sweet-sixteen."

"I nearly gagged when he suggested it, but it's growing on me," said Melissa.

"Cool!" said Tyler. That word was apparently his favorite in the English language.

"I was wondering if I could bring Danny. The invitation said I could bring a guest. It doesn't have to be a person of the opposite sex, does it?"

Melissa was momentarily struck dumb. What could he possibly mean by that? He and Danny weren't gay, were they? "No, Tyler. You can bring whomever you want to. Danny's welcome."

"Cool, 'cuz, see Danny just broke up with his girlfriend and he's kinda down right now and I figure you're gonna have lots of ladies coming to your party tomorrow night. Maybe he'll meet someone."

Danny looked as if he wished the floor would swallow him whole. But his parents had obviously instilled good manners in him because he smiled at Melissa and said, "Thanks for having me, Melissa. I'm looking forward to it."

"Sure, anytime," said Melissa, smiling nervously.

"Well," Tyler said, yanking on the sleeve of Danny's football jersey. "See you tomorrow night, Melissa. Ladies, it was nice to meet you."

Danny smiled at Melissa before turning to leave.

When they'd gone, Melissa heaved a sigh of relief and said, "I almost peed my pants."

To which her friends burst out laughing.

Chapter 5

On Saturday afternoon at five, the bookstore's closing time, Sara was ringing up the purchases of a last-minute customer when Rosaura Ledoux came through the door. Sara had met Rosaura a year ago during harvest. Rosaura had patiently shown her how to snip the grapes from the vine without damaging the parent vine. Since then, Rosaura had joined the Wednesday Night Book Club there at the bookstore, and on occasion Sara babysat Rosaura and Claude's children, Claude, Jr. and Katrina.

Rosaura went to check out the new arrivals on the shelves while Sara finished. But as soon as the customer left she approached Sara. "Claude doesn't want me to interfere but I think you ought to know that they found root rot in the vines and Mr. Bryant is terribly worried. I wouldn't mention it but you know I sometimes help with the housework at the Hacienda and I overheard Mr.

Bryant talking to his sister and he said he had not said a word to you about it. And he wasn't planning to."

Sara was stunned to hear that Jason hadn't wanted to confide in her.

Rosaura, a petite woman in her late thirties with smooth chocolate skin, gray eyes, and beautiful long jet-black hair, wavy hair that she wore down her back, smiled at Sara encouragingly. "Men can be so stubborn," she said.

"And bullheaded," Sara added.

She felt like crying. If Jason didn't want her to know something as vital as this then maybe he was emotionally distancing himself from her. Formerly, he'd confided in her about things as mundane as choosing a new label for a variety of wine. Now, when the entire vineyard could be in jeopardy, he was leaving her out of the loop!

But she couldn't rush over there accusing him of wanting to hurt her by keeping her in the dark. That wouldn't be very mature.

Besides, she had her pride.

"What are they doing about it?" she calmly asked Rosaura.

"He has an appointment to see a plant pathologist at U.C. Davis in two weeks."

"Two weeks!" Sara cried, disgusted. "The damn rot could spread to the rest of the vines in two weeks' time."

"That's the earliest they can see him."

Sara knew Jason must be climbing the walls by now. He had reluctantly come back to run the winery and he wasn't yet confident in his ability to make it work. He was probably riddled with a whole new set of doubts.

She had to see him. But she couldn't let him know she knew what was going on.

"Rosaura, let's pretend you didn't tell me a thing, shall we?"

"That's fine with me," said Rosaura, smiling. "Claude would not be happy if he found out I'd done the exact opposite of what he told me to do."

"He won't hear it from me," Sara assured her. "And, thank you!"

"We girls have to stick together," Rosaura said with a smile before leaving.

The store was empty now except for Sara. She had let Frannie and Elizabeth go home early. Frannie to start fretting over what she could possibly wear to Melissa's party that could qualify as sexy but would not make Erik Sutherland's tongue hang out of his mouth. And Elizabeth had plans to go to a movie with one of the other bookstore employees, Linda Ramirez. Sara was both surprised and delighted when Elizabeth had told her she was going out. It was proof that she was coming out of herself more every day and was making a real effort to be happy.

Sara *wanted* to rush over to the Hacienda and offer comfort to Jason.

However, she made herself go through all of the steps of closing the bookstore for the day in order to give herself time to think about her actions before she did something she would regret.

An hour later, she left the bookstore, locking the door behind her, and hurried to the bank down the street to deposit the day's receipts. From the bank, she went home, showered, put on her robe, then sat down at the computer on the desk in her bedroom.

She went to the organization's Web site and went through the profiles of her sisters, looking for a plant pathologist. Whatever that was! One of the advantages of being a member of Aminatu's Daughters was the rich sources of life experiences the other sisters had to offer. Whenever a sister was in need of help, all she had to do was ask and she received.

This was the first time she'd had to ask any of her sisters for a favor, but if there was indeed a plant pathologist in the sisterhood, she was going to request her help.

It took a few minutes, but she finally came up with a name: Dr. Willow Quigley.

Unfortunately she worked at a university in the Pacific Northwest. She wasn't right there in California. Sara sent her a message explaining her predicament, anyway.

At that precise moment, at the Hacienda, Jason was standing under the spray in the shower, letting it rain down on his head. In the last twenty-four hours he'd castigated himself over and over for not being more thorough. When his parents had handed him the reins, they had specifically told him he needed to read the winery's log books. His parents kept a record of every important occurrence on the farm. There was a book for every year the winery had been in operation, dating back to the sixties. Last night, he hadn't been able to sleep, and he'd found an entry about his parents finding root rot in the southern field. His father had made a note in his careful handwriting: "We believe we got it all, but you can never be sure with root rot. Be sure to keep an eye on the southern vineyard. If it comes back, we'll have to be more aggressive."

But his father hadn't said what kind of root rot they'd discovered in 1978. Maybe there had been no plant pathologists to name the culprit back then.

Jason shampooed, and rinsed. His hair was cut short and close to his head. Black and naturally wavy, he usually just washed it, dried it with a towel, put a little moisturizer on it, and he was set. Tonight, he didn't even bother with the moisturizer.

Who cared if he had soft hair?

For one selfish moment, he thought about Sara. She used to sit him down and oil his scalp, massaging the oil in with her long, talented fingers. He trembled slightly. Was the act of oiling his scalp as sensual as he remembered? Or did he just miss her so much every memory had become a tactile experience bordering on the erotic?

Yeah, he missed her that much.

He should call her and tell her about the root rot.

After he'd dried off, he grabbed his robe, wrapped it around him, tied the belt, and sat on the bed. He picked up the phone to call Sara. He put it down again. The clock on the nightstand read 7:32. What did Sara do without him on a Saturday night?

Go out to dinner with friends? Go to a movie with friends? Soak in the tub? Read a good book? She was a voracious reader. She had almost as many books on her shelves at home as she did in her bookstore, the nutty woman.

God, he missed her.

But if he called her she would consider it a coup in their war of wills. Yes, she would count this battle as her victory.

He didn't care.

He dialed her home number. The answering machine clicked into operation after the fourth ring. Sara's voice said, "This is Sara. I'm unavailable at the moment.

Please leave a message and I'll get back to you as soon as possible."

Frannie's voice then chimed in with, "Hey, it's Frannie. You know the drill. Leave the digits or don't leave the digits. No skin off my nose!"

Jason didn't leave a message for Sara. She would see that he'd phoned because his number would be on her caller ID.

He hung up the phone, and dialed her cell's number.

Sara was standing at the front door of the Hacienda when her cell phone rang.

She rang the doorbell, then fished in her shoulder bag for the phone.

Jason walked to the front door with the cordless phone to his ear.

She said hello into the mouthpiece just as he swung the door open.

Sara wasn't wearing anything special, just her favorite kicking-around clothes, a full, flowing long-sleeve cotton shirt in purple and her favorite button-fly jeans which she'd worn so much, they were the shape of her hourglass figure.

The jeans hung low on her hips, so her bellybutton was visible due to the fact that she'd left the last three buttons of the shirt unfastened.

Smiling at Jason, she closed her cell phone and put it in her shoulder bag.

Grinning back at her, Jason clicked off the cordless phone.

She stepped inside. Jason closed the door and turned to face her. He set the cordless phone on the foyer table. Sara dropped her bag into the chair beside the table.

The air was electric around them. They circled each other warily.

Jason spoke first. "I wanted to tell you that I missed you."

"Okay, tell me."

"I need you."

"I thought you said you missed me, not needed me." Her eyes danced with happiness.

"In my mind they're one and the same."

"I need you, too. Should we establish this night as neutral ground? Whatever we do tonight will not be used as ammunition in case of further fighting."

Jason's heart was pounding excitedly. His voice cracked when he said, "I agree to your terms."

Sara smiled wider and said with a mischievous note to her voice, "Okay, what do you want to do tonight, play pinochle?"

Jason laughed, quickly closed the space between them and kissed her hard on the mouth. "Girl," he said between kisses. "You drive me crazy!"

Kissing him back, Sara said, "Let's not get into a debate about who drives whom crazier right now. I want you naked in two seconds flat."

Jason opened his robe, untied the belt, and let it fall to the floor. "Done!"

His thick-lashed eyes swept over her body, daring her to match his boldness.

Sara sucked in air, released it and stood looking at him with her mouth open. She wasn't about to get naked with all the living room blinds wide open.

She bent and picked up the robe. Handing it to him, she said, "I'd rather not give the Ledouxs an eyefull in case they're looking up the hill tonight." She turned and hurried to his bedroom where the curtains could be drawn and no one would be the wiser to anything that went on behind its walls.

Jason put the robe back on and followed.

Sara removed her shoes and began peeling off her clothes immediately upon entering his bedroom. She unbuttoned the shirt and Jason took over, pushing it off her smooth shoulders and pausing to kiss the side of her fragrant neck. She was wearing a scent that left her skin smelling faintly of a flower with a light head to it. Jason wrinkled his nose. He couldn't quite place it, and he was thinking that he should be able to. He had a talent for wine and could discern the many underlying fragrances and tastes in a certain variety of wine. But this he couldn't identify, possibly because it was combined with her own unique fragrance. It was confounding him.

"What's that scent you're wearing?" he asked. "It's very sexy."

"It's something I bought at a fragrance shop in Santa Rosa. They'll mix anything you want. It's mainly gardenias with a few spices that I won't name."

Jason smiled as he licked her earlobe. "I'll have to taste you, then, to find out what they are."

The shirt was then hastily dispensed with and he turned his attention to the buttons on her jeans. The robe stood open all the while he was undressing her, and Sara enjoyed the view. A runner, Jason had a lean, muscular body, powerful leg and thigh muscles and wonderfully delineated calves. At six-one, he was four inches taller than Sara which was a near-perfect fit as far as she was concerned. She didn't have to tiptoe too much to reach all the good parts and he was tall enough and powerful enough to make her feel protected, which she occasionally liked to feel. As a tall woman there weren't that many men capable of making her feel that way.

Jason pulled the jeans down past her hips, gravity did the rest, and Sara stepped out of them. She stood before him now in just her panties and bra.

She pushed the robe off his shoulders and it fell to the floor.

Jason pulled her into his arms. He left her bra and panties on just to test how long he would be able to resist ripping them off her.

Sara's hands were splayed on his back. Her body seemed to relax with the satisfaction of finally being this close to him. He also smelled delicious. It was just the soap he'd used in the shower, a spicy masculine scent that was probably used by millions of men, but she wasn't in love with those men and no one could convince her that love didn't do something to your olfactory senses. At the very least the sense of smell worked in conjunction with every other sense that lent itself to sexual arousal. Jason's scent alone could awaken her sensory perception.

She sighed and threw her head back, offering him her neck. Jason rained kisses along the curve of her throat, then lower to her cleavage. All the while, his penis was thickening and lengthening until it pressed urgently against her crotch.

He moaned deep in his throat as pure pleasure began to course through him. Sara straightened and reached down, grasped his engorged penis and placed it between her thighs where she could feel it throbbing against her clitoris.

Jason reveled in the feel of her warm, moist sex. Their eyes met and held as he bent to kiss her mouth. As the kiss deepened, he thrust between her thighs. His penis grew harder and Sara's movements became more urgent as the climax building inside of her gained momentum.

She didn't want to climax in her panties, though, so she pushed him backward onto the bed. Jason smiled lazily as he lay on his back, his penis pointing straight in the air. He watched as Sara did a little striptease and a minute later her bra and panties lay on the floor next to the rest of her clothes.

"I take it you still keep the condoms in the top drawer?"

"Of course. Right next to that tape I made of us."

"Don't be funny. You're never going to get me on tape, buddy, so quit hoping."

She got a condom, opened it and straddled him. "So, you'd just as well be happy with the memories." She rolled the condom onto his penis, and positioned it at the opening of her vagina. Jason pushed slightly, but she was tight, which he loved, and they both took their time as they gazed into each other's eyes.

He reached up and simultaneously rolled her nipples between the forefinger and thumb of each of his hands. He loved the deep golden brown richness of her skin. In summer it took on an even darker golden tone underneath the medium brown hue. With her black glistening braids she looked like an African goddess born of the sun.

He yelled. While he'd been waxing poetic, his goddess had accepted him fully inside of her body and was riding him with abandon. Her nipples were distended, her eyes were closed in ecstasy and her thrusts were strong, rhythmic and relentless.

It took a minute for it to register in his fevered brain that he was no longer in control here. As if he'd ever been. Her vaginal muscles squeezed him and released him, bestowing on him such a riot of sensual gratification that all he could do was smile and roll with it.

Between intermittent kisses to his mouth, his chest, his chin, she took her fill of him and didn't seem to be anywhere near being done with him. It was as if she was making up for the three weeks they had been apart.

Surprisingly, though, her movements were not frantic, as if release were her only goal. No, she moved slowly and luxuriously, as if she were relishing every thrust of his body inside of hers, as if nothing had ever been more fulfilling.

He didn't know how much longer he could hold on without coming.

Sara, taking no pity on him, pumped harder. Then she opened her gorgeous eyes, looked into his, smiled at him and squeezed his penis between her vaginal walls. She held it firmly and then slowly released it by degrees.

Jason gave a little pant every time she let go. Then, he exploded. He sighed heavily.

Sweat moistened his forehead. It had been the best workout he'd ever gotten on his back. Coming down from the high, he looked into her eyes trying to gauge her level of satisfaction

Sara was smiling contentedly. He was her hero. He'd held on until she'd had two orgasms. She sighed and lay atop him, her head on his chest. Jason wrapped his arms around her.

Sara kissed his chin. "Got anything edible in the fridge? I skipped dinner tonight."

Jason smiled and reached up to brush her braids out of her face. "You jump in the shower and I'll go make roast beef sandwiches for us."

"Deal."

She kissed him again, and climbed off him.

He sat up in bed and watched her gather her clothes from the floor, then hurry into the adjoining bath.

Frannie experienced a moment of indecision when she saw the sprawling house in the middle of the woods. It was an architectural wonder of wood and glass, rising three stories, and probably had five thousand square feet of living space, she guessed.

She'd heard that Erik Sutherland had been one of the lucky Internet start-up geeks. He'd gotten out before speculation had cooled and so many others had hit rock bottom. Before that he'd played professional football. An injury retired him at twenty-eight.

That was the sum total of her Erik Sutherland information, and that had been gleaned from Sara who admittedly didn't have much interest in Erik's personal life so her information might prove unreliable.

The boom of a bass guitar could be heard on the air and the reverberation of the resulting sound waves could be felt on her skin as Frannie walked onto the huge front porch. Could Erik have sprung for a live band?

She rang the doorbell. The night was cool and she'd worn a leather jacket over her sleeveless black dress. The dress was short, but not a crotch kisser. The hem fell about three inches above her knees.

She was looking down at the tips of her toes in the high-heeled black suede sandals when someone opened the door.

"They're really nice shoes," a masculine voice said.

Startled, Frannie jerked her head up and Erik was standing in the doorway smiling at her. He was wearing jeans and a short-sleeve shirt, both black, and for some reason she thought the contrast between all that black and the dark red of his hair was very appealing. She peered at his black boots.

"What size shoe do you wear?"

"A fourteen," he said.

"Oh, then you can't borrow mine," she quipped and stepped inside.

Erik laughed. He liked her immediately.

He followed her inside and closed the door. She pulled off her leather jacket and handed it to him. Erik was busy taking in that tight little body and beautiful legs. She had mounds of black, curly hair and her skin was the color of (he had to think here) *toast.* Perfectly done toast that's taken out of the toaster just before it threatens to burn.

He was just about to introduce himself when his daughter came barreling into the foyer and threw herself into the beauty's arms, crying, "Frannie! You came. I was beginning to worry."

Erik swallowed hard. This couldn't be Frannie Anise. She was a black woman. Admittedly he didn't hear everything that Melissa said to him, but he couldn't have missed that.

"Am I late?" Frannie asked.

"Only an hour!" Melissa cried, not letting her off the hook.

Frannie laughed. "I'm sorry, sweetie."

Erik could have cussed. He loved the sound of her laughter, a sure sign that he was attracted to her.

"Oh, that's all right, you're here now," said Melissa happily.

She turned and saw her father standing aside with his hands in his pockets. With a great deal of pride, she presented Frannie to him. "Daddy, I want you to meet Miss Francesca Anise, book maven, world traveler, and, generally, a wonderful friend. Frannie, my dad, Erik Sutherland."

"What, no superlatives?" Frannie joked as she held out her hand to Erik.

"I'm afraid she takes me completely for granted," Erik said as he shook her hand. "I'm only her father, after all."

Melissa hadn't seen her father look at a woman with such interest in a long time. Satisfied that her plan was working, she said, "Well, I'll get back to my party while you two get better acquainted. Daddy, why don't you show Frannie your car collection? She loves old cars."

With that, she turned and fled in the direction of the loud music.

"Wow," Frannie said, watching Melissa's exit. "Do you think this is a setup?"

Erik laughed. He was definitely going to have to watch his P's and Q's with this woman. "I'm beginning to get that feeling," he said, gesturing for her to follow him.

They walked away from the sound of the music, down a wide, dimly lit hallway. Their footfalls echoed off the walls and on the hardwood floor. "Do you really like old cars?"

"I drive a 1965 baby-blue Ford Mustang convertible with its original paint job, and it's in cherry condition."

"You're kidding!"

"No, it belonged to my mom. She kept it in a garage for twenty years and when I turned thirty she had it refurbished and gave it to me as a birthday gift. I'd always lusted after that car."

Erik's ears turned red when she said the word *lusted*. It was an apt description of how car lovers felt about their cars, but he didn't have cars on the brain right now. He was wondering how anyone could smell as good as Frannie Anise did.

Frannie wasn't immune to his charms either. Her keen powers of observation told her that he was a big eater and probably downed too many beers during the course of a day. He had the beginnings of a paunch and a double chin. But he had a good, solid frame. Nice arm and leg muscles, and beautiful hands. Okay, she was a sucker for a man's hands. His were big and tanned, and they were hairless, a plus in her book.

She'd been prepared to dislike him on general principle because he'd hurt Sara in the past. But even Sara had said there was the possibility that he had changed his ways. Frannie was willing to give anyone the benefit of the doubt.

They turned a corner, and suddenly they were in the kitchen of the big house. A full catering staff bustled about. Frannie guessed that the party's guest list hadn't been limited to only a few friends.

"I apologize for being a poor host," Erik said. "Would you like something to drink?"

Frannie was looking around the gleaming kitchen and at the amount of food and drink that was being prepared, transported through the house to the guests, and the empty trays in the hands of returning wait staff coming through the double doors.

"No, thanks. I'm fine."

You certainly are, Erik thought. "Okay, then," he said aloud. "If you're interested, I'll take Melissa's suggestion and show you my car collection."

"Lead on," Frannie said pleasantly.

Chapter 6

Melissa stepped onto the deck that was accessed from the library. She had to get some fresh air. She had never seen so many phonies in one room in her life. Girls who had never spoken to her were coming up to her saying, "Happy birthday, Melissa. You look hot tonight!"

Melissa was wearing the dress that Frannie had picked out for her. It *was* cute. It was short, sleeveless and cut so that it minimized her midriff, which was less than flat, and emphasized her shoulders and her legs, two of her best features. Frannie had insisted on her wearing green, a dark green that was almost black. Melissa had thought the color would be too dark for her because she wasn't exactly tanned. But instead the color had brought out the green in her eyes and her dark red, wavy, shoulder-length hair looked more lustrous than ever. She had never cut her hair before and it had hung past her butt before she'd had it styled yesterday. The effect was, she looked less like a kid and more like a woman.

But no matter how good she looked, she couldn't help thinking that no one would be here tonight if her father hadn't been rich. Everyone wanted to get on his good side. She supposed they reasoned that if they did him a favor by coming to his pathetic daughter's sixteenth birthday party then somewhere down the road he would owe them a favor in return.

Inside, one of her favorite bands, a heavy-metal group from Seattle called Liquid, was doing their level best to bring the house down. Nearly a hundred teenagers were throwing themselves around the dance floor, looking disturbingly like dying fish flopping on the ground. Waiters and waitresses maneuvered around the headbangers balancing trays laden with shrimp, hot egg rolls, and several other delicacies she didn't recognize.

Everyone was having a blast. Including Danny Keener whom she'd spotted backed into a corner by three skinny, high-cheekboned creatures with "next-girlfriend" written all over them.

And Tyler Gaines was a rapt hanger-on, just waiting to scoop up Danny's leftovers.

A couple of minutes ago Hillary Jacobs, editor of the school paper, had walked up to her and said, "Your dad must really love you. I've never been to a party quite this—" she searched for the right word; after all, she was the editor of the paper "—ostentatious."

Melissa must have had a blank look on her face because Hillary added, "That means a vulgar display of wealth and success designed to impress people."

"I know what it means, Hillary," Melissa calmly told her. Surprisingly, Hillary's comments had served to make Melissa appreciate her father more. Sure, he was clueless most of the time, but he loved her. He'd wanted to give her a special day. One that she would always remember.

Too bad he didn't know that a special birthday celebration for her meant simply spending it with him. Nevertheless, Hillary Jacobs had done her a favor, so she smiled at Hillary and said, "I *do* believe my dad loves me. Thanks for pointing that out, Hills. Do have a wonderful time. Try the shrimp, it's to die for."

The sky was clear tonight. The best thing about living way back in the woods was that there were no other houses nearby and no lights to obstruct her view of the sky on a night like this. There was a telescope on her bedroom's balcony. Sometimes when she couldn't sleep, she'd spend hours out there looking at the constellations.

She heard someone opening the sliding glass door behind her and turned to see Danny coming outside. "I hope you don't mind," he said. "I saw you leave the room and followed you."

Melissa hid her surprise very well. She was used to concealing her emotions.

"Oh?" she said. "Is there something I can help you with? I hope you're enjoying yourself."

Danny stood beside her, his hands on the redwood railing. He looked skyward. "Do you remember when you and your dad moved here four years ago, and somebody left wildflowers on your front porch step?" he said quietly.

Yes, she remembered. She was twelve then. It was a few months after her parents' divorce and abandonment by her mom. She was an emotional mess, arguing with her dad all the time because she resented him for forcing her mother to give him custody. At the time she had thought her parents had busted up because he'd cheated. She knew now that it had been the other way around. While she had selfishly thought she was the only one suffering her dad was nursing a broken heart. What's more, he had not had to put up much of a fight to gain sole custody of her. Her mother had simply given her up. One day she got into her father's safe and read every word of the divorce agreement. He'd given her mother everything she'd wanted in the split. All he had wanted was Melissa.

Nervousness in Danny's presence had made her remember all of that. She forced herself to turn and face him. "That, that was you?" she asked, incredulously.

"I left a note, too," he confirmed. "In it I asked you if you liked me and if you did, to call me."

"I never saw a note," she said regretfully. "Where'd you leave it?"

"Next to the flowers."

"Underneath a rock?"

"Nah, just next to the flowers on the step."

"Anything could have happened to it. The wind could have blown it away!" She couldn't believe how irritated she was to learn after four years that Danny Keener had written her a love note and she had never gotten it!

"Give me a break, I was only thirteen."

Looking into each other's eyes, they laughed at the absurdity of it.

After she'd gotten her laughter under control, Melissa, still smiling happily at him, said, "Why didn't you ever ask me about it?"

"I was devastated. You were this beautiful new girl

in town. Rumors were going around that your dad was super rich, not just rich, and that intimidated me. I figured you had gotten the note and you didn't phone because you didn't like me."

"Oh, this is so weird," Melissa cried. "I always liked you, Danny. But I thought you didn't even see *me.*"

Danny inclined his head toward her. Melissa had never been this close to him before. His eyes were hypnotic. She could feel his body heat, and suddenly her face was hot with embarrassment. Of course, this wasn't the first time she'd felt physical attraction for Danny. She felt it every day in Algebra.

"Why would you think that?" Danny asked.

"We've been in the same advanced Algebra class all year, and you've never uttered a word to me."

"You've never uttered a word to me, either," Danny said. "But I sit next to you every day in that class."

Melissa had to admit that was true. Mrs. Klaus didn't require you to sit in alphabetical order. You could sit anywhere you pleased. It had never occurred to her that it pleased Danny to sit next to her. She arrived before he did every morning. She assumed that by the time Danny arrived there weren't that many desks left to choose from, so he sat in front of her.

Melissa grinned. "I can't believe I never noticed that."

"Because you never noticed *me,*" said Danny.

"You're wrong there. Every day was torture for me. I would hope that you would turn around and say something, anything, even, 'Hey, have you got an extra pencil?' anything! But it never happened. So, now, you're telling me that—" she was afraid to say the words "—you *like* me?"

"That's what I'm saying," Danny said softly.

As if by mutual silent agreement, they each turned back to the redwood railing and placed their hands on it. Gazing up at the stars, Danny slid his left hand over and grasped Melissa's right hand. She held on to him firmly, but not too firmly. She didn't want him to think that she was desperate or something.

"Do you think you'd like to go out with me sometime?" Danny asked.

"Like on a date?"

"Yeah, just like a date."

"Uh, okay."

They stood there holding hands and looking up at the stars.

Below them, in the garage, Frannie and Erik were having a picnic atop the trunk of a 1967 Ford Thunderbird. After an hour of talking cars and examining all of Erik's classic cars, (ten of them), Frannie decided she was ravenous. Erik went to the kitchen and came back with a tray of everything on the menu plus a bottle of Moët, which was not on the menu. He was not going to be accused of sending high school kids home from Melissa's party full of booze. He'd told the staff to watch the kids to make sure no one spiked the punch. He'd been a kid once and was usually the one doing the spiking.

Frannie limited herself to one glass of the champagne. She was driving. However, she packed the food away as prodigiously as Erik did. After popping a mini egg roll in his mouth, Erik said, "You're so tiny. Where do you put all that food?"

"I'm really into sports," Frannie told him. "I jog with my friend Sara practically every day. I have a black belt in judo. That's really good exercise. And I love to swim when I can."

"Back up," Erik said. "A black belt in judo? What got you interested in martial arts?"

"Look at me," said Frannie, biting a jumbo shrimp in half with beautifully strong white teeth. She chewed and swallowed. "I'm five-three and I weigh one hundred and fifteen pounds. I used to be a hundred and five until I started eating Sara's cooking. But, I like the extra weight. Gives me heft. Anyway, I'm a little woman. Unsavory men like to pick on women they think will be an easy mark. I didn't want to make it easy for them so I started going to judo classes when I was fourteen. I've been practicing it for twenty years now."

"You're thirty-four?" Erik said, disbelieving. "You don't look over thirty."

"That's 'cuz black don't crack, honey," Frannie said with a smile. Her intelligent eyes observed him closely. She had had a sneaking suspicion all night that he had no idea she was black. It was true that sometimes it was hard to tell. Her skin color and facial features had fooled others into thinking she was Italian, Hispanic or, once, from India. But she had never claimed to be anything except African-American and Jewish.

Her hair, which could be very frizzy when left to air dry, was tamer when she took the time to condition it and dry it using the diffuser attachment on the hairdryer like she'd done tonight.

Erik was quiet for a record five minutes. The longest lull in their conversation all night. Frannie continued to eat her shrimp and sip her champagne, but she would meet his eyes every now and then just to let him know she was waiting for some kind of a response. She truly didn't care what it was. Race was not an issue with her. She was at ease with being biracial. If it made someone else uncomfortable, then so be it. But as far as she was concerned, it was way cool being in her skin.

"Melissa told me you were black," Erik finally said, looking intently into her eyes. "But when you showed up tonight, I really didn't see it. I thought you must have been somebody else she'd invited."

Frannie smiled at him. "Yeah, I thought so."

"Forgive me, I didn't mean to offend you."

"You haven't offended me. You were honest. I appreciate that. You weren't what I expected either."

His green eyes held an amused glint in them. "What did you expect?"

"From what I'd heard you were a bully."

He laughed shortly. "Will I ever live down my high school days?"

"Not if you insist on living in your hometown. Some people will always think of you the way you used to be. Never mind how you turned out."

"Well, I'm not a bully. I'm still somewhat of a buffoon, though."

Frannie laughed. "In what way?"

"I can't seem to give up the notion of ruling this town. You see, when I was growing up my old man was the king around here. He raised me to follow in his footsteps but I've never lived up to his high expectations. Instead of going into business with him, I went to school on a football scholarship and then went pro. Even after I injured myself and couldn't play anymore I didn't come home and go into business with him. Instead I invested in an Internet start-up company and made a bundle. He died five years ago. My mom died two years before that."

"You don't have any brothers or sisters?"

"No, you?"

"No, I'm an only child," Frannie replied.

"Your parents?"

"Doing well. Still married to each other. They live in San Francisco."

"You grew up there?"

"Yes."

"Are your parents both…"

"Black?"

"Yeah."

"My mother is. My father's Jewish."

"Oh."

"Yours?"

"My father was British. My mother was Italian."

"You mean his ancestors came from England? Or he actually came over himself?"

"He actually came over himself."

"Where'd you get the red hair? Your father?"

"Yes, although his was brighter red. Mine is darker, so I suppose that comes from my mother's genes."

Frannie leaned closer to him. "Your parents had nice genes."

"So do yours," Erik told her, smiling foolishly.

Frannie straightened back up and regarded him more soberly. "This rule the town thing you have—does it have anything to do with your wanting to be the mayor?"

"Absolutely," Erik said. "It has everything to do with it."

"And your platform—keeping illegal aliens out. What do you suppose your immigrant father would think of it?"

"He would probably be very ashamed of me. That's where the buffoon part comes in. That wasn't thought out very well."

"Does that mean I can safely vote for you?"

"I would rather you go out with me, than vote for me."

"Can't do that," Frannie told him, after which she finished off the champagne and set the glass back on the tray.

"Why not?" Erik looked sincerely disappointed by her announcement.

"Because Melissa is my friend, and she's been hurt enough for one lifetime. It would never work out between us. You're not ready to date a sister. And when it blew up in our faces, Melissa would be very disappointed."

It was Erik who looked disappointed. He thought he'd been making headway with her and all the while she'd been judging him and had determined that he wasn't right for her. He didn't know whether to be angry or shocked, or both.

She slid off the trunk, smoothed her dress, then leaned over and kissed Erik on the cheek. "I'm going to go find the birthday girl and tell her good-night. It was a pleasure meeting you."

Erik followed her like a lost puppy. "Two hours together and I've been tried, judged, and sentenced to life without you?"

"It's a free country," said Frannie. "You can always try to change my mind."

Erik considered that a challenge.

Jason moaned, "Oh, God, don't stop. It feels so good." Sara was sitting on the bed and he was sitting between her legs. She was oiling his scalp and smiling at his exaggerated exclamations of pleasure.

"If anyone was listening, they'd think we were having sex."

"This feels almost as good as sex."

Sara laughed. "Not from where I'm sitting."

They had showered together and, afterward, eaten the sandwiches Jason had made.

Now they were simply enjoying each other's company.

Finished massaging the light oil into his scalp, Sara put the lid back on the jar. She playfully tapped him on the back of the head. "Let me get up, I need to wash my hands."

She got up, went into the adjacent bathroom where she returned the hair oil to its spot in the medicine cabinet, then washed her hands at the sink.

Jason came up and hugged her from behind while she was drying her hands on a towel.

She was wearing his robe. He was wearing boxers. She looked at their reflection in the bathroom mirror.

Their skin tones were quite similar, but that's where the similarity ended. He had near-perfect features, a well-shaped nose that was long but not too long. A wonderfully full mouth with bow-shaped lips. Large, thickly-lashed brown eyes that were looking at her right now with sensual intensity. His cheekbones accented a gorgeous square-chinned face, that, because he'd maintained his athletic body since high school didn't have many fat pockets.

As for her, she was happy with her face, although she'd always thought her nose resembled a ski slope with a dip in it capable of launching tiny imaginary skiers into the stratosphere.

Jason kissed the side of her neck and said, "I need to talk to you about something I should have told you yesterday."

She met his eyes in the mirror. "Okay."

They went back out into the master bedroom where she sat on the bed and Jason sat down beside her. He turned toward her and took one of her hands in his. "When my parents turned over the running of the winery to me, they gave me all of the journals they'd kept over the years that had everything that'd ever happened to them while they ran the place. I never got around to reading them. I don't know why. Maybe I thought they weren't important, and I already had my hands full with the day-to-day running of this place."

He paused and let her hand go. Sighing, he ran a hand through his hair. "That was a mistake. If I had read them, I would have known to keep an eye on the southern field. Yesterday, we found root rot in the vines over there. Do you know what that is?"

Frannie nodded in the affirmative. "I've heard of it. It can destroy the vines if it's allowed to spread."

Jason's face was a mass of frowns. "Right. If not controlled it can devastate a vineyard. To get rid of it you have to dig it up, destroy the infected roots entirely, and then replant. That's why it's important to catch it as soon as possible."

"It sounds like you did catch it in time," Sara said, trying to offer encouragement.

"No, I didn't, Sara," Jason disagreed. "Because I was too lazy to read those books, I missed the signs. And I couldn't rely on Claude to clue me in about the southern field because he wasn't even here in 1978. If we lose the southern vineyards it will be my fault. It was my responsibility."

"Your parents saved the field once, it can be saved again," Sara said. "What's the first step?"

"We dug up some vines. I phoned to make an appointment to take them to U.C. Davis to be analyzed by a plant pathologist, and I was told they couldn't see me for two weeks."

"U.C. Davis isn't the only place with a plant pathologist on the staff, is it?"

"It's the closest, and the best."

Upset because he was apparently very worried about losing the southern field, Sara got up and started pacing as was her habit when something was on her mind. "In two weeks we'll be in the midst of the rainy season. Even I know how fast roots spread in wet weather."

Jason closed his eyes and rubbed his temples. "Yeah, I thought of that. I was hoping we'd get the excavating done before the rain set in."

Realizing that she'd added to his tension, Sara went and hugged him. Still sitting, Jason wrapped his arms around her waist and lay his head on her stomach. "We'll get through this," Sara said soothingly.

She sent up a prayer that Willow Quigley would get her message and come right away. How she would explain how she'd come to know a plant pathologist to Jason, she didn't know. She'd worry about that later.

"Damn!" Willow Quigley, 47, cried as she stepped into a pile of manure. A harrowing six-week expedition to the Amazon jungle on behalf of a pharmaceutical company had left her yearning for some good old American food and her own bed.

The American food craving had been satisfied at a restaurant in Seattle twenty minutes after her plane had landed. Her belly was full. Now, all she needed was a bath and to climb into her wonderful bed. But, no, that wasn't to be because first she had to clean the dog poop off her living room floor, then clean it off her perfectly good hiking boots, then find Elvin and kill him.

Elvin was her live-in lover, not the dog. Although killing the dog did cross her mind. That wouldn't do, though. She could not abide cruelty to dumb animals. Cruelty to Elvin, however, was permissible.

The dog, a lovable big old mutt who answered to Rufus came padding into the room probably looking for something eat. From the smell of the house, poor Rufus had had to relieve himself repeatedly in his master's absence.

"Elvin!" Willow bellowed. She'd phoned him and told him when she would be home. He had no excuse for not being here. It was after nine on a Saturday night. He definitely wasn't working at the aquarium. Elvin cleaned the tanks at the aquarium. Willow had met him a year ago when she'd taken her niece and nephew, who'd been visiting with their parents from Florida, to see the dolphins. Elvin had moved in two weeks later.

Willow didn't mind the fact that he made a lot less money than she did. She didn't mind that he came with a dog. She liked dogs. She did mind that Elvin let the dog pee and poop all over the house, though. It showed a lack of respect.

"Elvin!" She received no reply to her summons.

Going into the bedroom they shared, she noticed clothes strewn all over the floor.

Wait a minute. She bent down and picked up a ratty purple lacy bra. It certainly didn't belong to her.

She heard a noise to the left of her and stood very still, listening for it again. It had sounded like it had come from the closet. Oh, God, she hoped Elvin hadn't brought another animal in here while she was in South America.

She went and yanked the closet door open, and Elvin was huddled inside, naked as the day he'd been born, with a strange woman, also naked.

"I can explain!" were the first words out of Elvin's mouth.

Willow grabbed the baseball bat propped in the corner of the closet and brandished it. "You can explain to this Louisville Slugger."

The woman screamed and fled, her flabby buttocks shaking like jelly. Elvin eased out of the closet with his back pressed against the wall and slowly moved past Willow.

"Now, honey, you wouldn't hit me with that thing, would you?"

Willow was so mad she didn't trust herself to actually start swinging with the bat. She might not stop until he was a bloody pile of manure. Just like that pile she'd stepped in upon coming through the door.

"Take your crap, and your dog, and get the hell out of my house!" she shouted.

Elvin was pulling on clothes so fast he tripped and fell twice. But he was out of there in under five minutes, jerking on Rufus's collar because the dog didn't want to go with him.

Willow shut and locked the door. Then she got busy cleaning up her house.

"The story of my life," she muttered. "Cleaning up after some man."

Chapter 7

Willow was glad she'd slept on the plane. It took four hours to get her house back to some semblance of order. Anger infused her with a tremendous amount of energy. She didn't start feeling fatigued until after three in the morning. By that time her entire house smelled clean and fresh.

She dragged herself to one of the spare bedrooms and fell into bed. She didn't know if she'd ever again be able to sleep in the room she and Elvin had shared. She was definitely getting rid of the bed. The sight of him and that woman buck naked in the closet was going to take a long time to fade from her memory.

Willow had survived two bad marriages and the death of a child, though, and Elvin's infidelity was small beans compared to that. She slept like a baby.

On Sunday morning, right after breakfast, she set her

wireless laptop on the kitchen table and logged on to the organization's Web site. After reading the newsletter that told members which clients had been relocated and also gave updates on clients who had been relocated some time ago, she checked her messages.

She had several. Her eyes were looking for the words *new assignment* in the subject line. She could use a new assignment. Something to occupy her mind. She would not go back to work at the University of Washington until January and it was only October. Research had the potential of keeping her busy but an assignment would really get her juices flowing.

She came to the bottom of the list. No luck today!

She began reading the messages from fellow members, beginning at the top. When she came to a message whose subject line read, I need help only you can give, her curiosity was piqued.

After she'd read it, she reached for her cell phone sitting next to the laptop. The person she was calling answered after only a couple of rings, and she sounded as if she'd been awakened out of a deep sleep.

"Hello?" she mumbled.

"Sara Minton?"

"Yes."

"Willow Quigley."

In Glen Ellen, Sara sat straight up in Jason's bed. She'd given Willow her cell phone number. She had not expected to be contacted so soon. She'd sent the message only last evening. She looked over at Jason. He was sleeping soundly.

Climbing out of bed naked, she grabbed Jason's robe from the foot of the bed and hurried from the room. "Thank you for calling!" she half whispered as she walked through the bedroom door and headed to the kitchen, slipping into the robe on the way.

"Sorry I woke you," Willow said. "But your problem sounded urgent, and I wanted to tell you that I'll be there Tuesday afternoon more than likely. I have to get the locks changed tomorrow. But after that I'll be making my way to Glen Ellen, isn't it?"

Still walking, Sara said, "Yes, it's in Sonoma County, in Northern California. You're coming? I've never asked for a favor before, I wasn't sure how it worked."

"Well, I have," Willow told her. She had a deep authoritative voice that Sara associated with college professors. Which was what Willow was. From her voice Sara could tell she was a black woman and originally from the South. "And it works like this—If it is at all possible to grant your request, we do it. No questions asked, and no payment either. I will come to Glen Ellen under my own steam. I would like you to find me somewhere to stay while I'm there, though. That would save me time."

"No problem. Please stay with me while you're here. There are three people living in my four-bedroom house. Two members and a client."

"Great, I can let my hair down at the end of the day," Willow said. "Thank you."

Sara breathed a sigh of relief. "Thank you! Which airport will you be flying in to? If you'll phone me I can come pick you up. San Francisco International?"

"How far is that from you?" Willow asked.

"It's not a bad drive at all," Sara told her. "I do it all the time."

"It's settled, then. Goodbye for now, little sister."

Sara laughed. "How do you know I'm younger than you are?"

"I just pulled up your profile," Willow told her. "You're thirty-one."

"Oh," Sara said, feeling foolish.

"I'm eccentric, but I'm not psychic," Willow said, laughing. "Goodbye."

"Goodbye," said Sara. She closed the cell phone, placed it on the counter and went to put the coffee on. When she had looked up Willow's profile she had not thought to look at her vital statistics. The only thing she had been interested in was her field of expertise.

She wondered what Willow looked like. She also wondered why she had to get her locks changed tomorrow.

She switched on the under-the-counter TV so that she could listen to the morning news while she prepared breakfast.

The weather was on. Since it was a Santa Rosa station, the meteorologist was more concerned with their local weather. However, during the course of his delivery, he said something that made her ears prick up.

"Sonoma County may be in for some severe weather this year," he said. "The Weather Service reports that El Niño may cause extreme shifts in weather systems. So, the area's normal rainy season may be extreme this year." He laughed. "I'm sure the vintners in Sonoma Valley don't want to hear that." Then he continued with his report on the local weather.

Sara changed the channel, hoping to catch another morning report that would give a detailed Sonoma County forecast. She switched the TV off when she couldn't find one.

Maybe Mrs. McClarin and the other ladies had been right, after all. The area might very well be in for some bad weather in November.

She was folding over scrambled eggs in a skillet when Jason came into the kitchen. He was barefoot and wearing a pair of jeans and a white sleeveless T-shirt. He went over and briefly kissed her lips. She could smell the toothpaste on his breath, which reminded her that she hadn't brushed yet.

Turning the gas flame off under the eggs, she handed Jason the spatula. "They're done. Would you put them on the plates while I go freshen up and dress?"

Smiling at her, Jason accepted the spatula. As soon as the spatula was in his hand he pulled her hard against his chest and bent to kiss her. A real morning greeting, not a dry, chaste kiss like before.

Sara moved her head so that his mouth connected with her cheek. Jason tried to kiss her again. Sara avoided that kiss, too. He was laughing now because he knew precisely why she was playing dodge-the-kiss with him. She hadn't brushed this morning.

"Girl, we shared all kinds of bodily fluids last night, and you're not gonna kiss me this morning?"

"No, I'm not!" she vehemently cried, twisting out of his embrace. She hurried from the kitchen.

"You're nuts, you know that!" he yelled after her, still laughing.

The doorbell rang.

Jason glanced at the digital display of the clock on the stove. It was only 9:15. He put the spatula on the counter and trotted to the front door.

After a quick peek through the blinds of a nearby window that afforded a view of the portico, he quickly went and opened the door.

His parents stood on the other side, looking travel-weary but very healthy.

"Mom, Dad!"

His mother was squeezing him tightly in a matter of seconds. "We were in Reno when Erica phoned last night, and we got right on the road!"

Jason was instantly incensed. But he smiled for his mother's benefit. "I told her not to bother you. That I would phone after we identified the type of infection the roots have. But I see she went right ahead and phoned, anyway."

His father had his head in the refrigerator. He came out with a pitcher of orange juice.

Walking over to the cabinet to get a glass, he said, "Don't blame Erica. She called us because you sounded panicked over the phone. She got upset. You know she's eighteen months pregnant."

"Honey!" Simone scolded him, but couldn't help laughing. She went and took the pitcher of orange juice from him, got the glass he seemed to be having trouble finding, and gestured for him to sit down at the table.

She did the same with Jason.

Jason sat across from his dad.

"We're not here to take over," his mother told him as she poured juice into the glass and handed it to Eric. "In fact, this is just a stopover to lend you a little moral support. Then we're heading to Santa Fe, New Mexico to attend a friend's wedding."

Jason calmed down a little. He should be used to Erica sticking her nose where it didn't belong by now. She'd been doing it all her life. "It *is* good to see you," he said with a smile. "And I *was* panicked when I phoned Erica. I should know by now not to phone her when I'm upset because she goes directly into 'fix-it' mode."

"Fixing it, in this case, meant calling us," his father

said. Eric Bryant was in his late sixties, six-three, and had nearly been six feet under (to hear Simone tell it) almost two years ago when he'd had a heart attack scare. Scare him, it did. He retired, bought an RV with his wife and had been enjoying himself ever since. He regarded his middle child with warmth. "Besides, we wouldn't have missed your first crisis for the world. You'd been handling things so well, I thought you'd never come up against something really challenging."

Jason laughed shortly. "You sound like you're glad we have root rot."

"Hell, no," said Eric. "I wouldn't wish root rot on my worst enemy. But I am happy to see you in the midst of it, and handling your business."

"I'm not handling my business too well," Jason said. "If I were handling it, I would have spotted the symptoms of root rot sooner and done something about it before now."

Simone was standing behind him with her hands on his shoulders. "Farmers are at the mercy of Mother Nature, sweetheart. What happened wasn't your fault. It wasn't anybody's fault." She looked at Eric. "Remember when we found it? We didn't know what it was. Old man Santini, bless his heart, had to tell us what it was and how to repair the damage it had done to our crops."

Eric nodded, remembering Carlo Santini. "He was one of the finest vintners I ever met. His sons sold the place after he died. A real shame."

"How did you get rid of it, then?" Jason wanted to know. He had nothing against reminiscing about Carlo Santini, but he wanted to get to the bottom of the root rot mystery.

"We had to dig up the affected vines, allow the field

to lie fallow for a while, and replant later on. These days
some vintners opt to fumigate. But we don't use anything that would detract from the quality of our wines.
So, we'll still have to dig."

"Now you've got backhoes and other equipment to
make it a little easier, but not much. It's still one of the
most physically grueling jobs a vintner has to do," his
mother told him.

Then, in a quick mood change, she thumped him
upside the head and said, "Where are your manners? Go
and tell Sara that you have company before she comes
out here in the altogether."

Jason had to think hard for a moment. His mother
sometimes used such archaic forms of speech. What did
she mean by "the altogether"? Then it came to him. She
meant Sara might come into the room naked.

He jumped up. "I'll be right back!"

His parents laughed at him as he hurried from the room.

"When are those two going to get married?" Eric
wondered after Jason had left.

"Don't be greedy," Simone admonished as she sat
down at the table, took his glass of orange juice out of
his hand and finished off the contents. "Two of our
children are happily married. So what if Jason decides
to be a bachelor the rest of his life? We have one grandchild on the way, and knowing Franklyn and Elise,
another one not too far behind. Bask in the blessings
you've already been given."

"Yeah, but, we're going to be living here in Glen
Ellen, not in San Francisco or Healdsburg. I want some
grandchildren I can spoil right here."

Simone looked heavenward. "You hear him, Lord?
The man is never satisfied."

"I didn't hear you complaining about satisfaction last night," Eric said roguishly.

Simone narrowed her eyes at him. "Not in the Lord's presence, heathen."

"The Lord knows man can't live by bread alone."

Jason and Sara's return saved Eric from a sharp rejoinder because Simone was getting ready to lay into him when Sara cried, "Oh, my God, the vagabonds have returned!"

She received generous hugs from both Simone and Eric after which Jason watched as she wrapped them around her little finger. "Sit down, sit down," she said happily, her eyes bright. "You've got to tell us how life is on the road while we have breakfast together."

Simone, a seasoned storyteller, launched right into several road tales. One of which was about Canyon de Chelly National Monument in Chinle, Arizona. "It might not be as big as the Grand Canyon, but depending on the time of day the walls of the canyon change into an array of amazing colors. And there is such a strong spiritual vibe there. I felt very close to God when I was there."

"What I liked best were the cliff dwellings," Eric said. "They're the oldest houses in the United States. A tribe called the Anasazi built them, archaeologists believe. The dwellings were mysteriously abandoned in the 1300s. No one knows why the Anasazi left them to this day."

"Maybe they were a nomadic people," Sara suggested as she set a platter of bacon and sausages on the table. "Several Native American tribes were."

"Could be," said Simone. "Anyway, today, the canyon is part of the huge Navajo Indian Reservation. You can't simply go out there on your own. You have to have a guide. Eric and I went on what the locals call a 'shake and bake' tour because you ride in an open Jeep over bumpy roads under the blazing sun. It was fabulous!"

"Fabulous is not the word for it," Eric begged to differ. "I nearly cooked. You on the other hand got a nice tan and flirted outrageously with our guide."

Simone laughed. "He *was* good-looking. But I wasn't flirting with him, he was flirting with me. There's a difference."

Sitting beside Jason, Sara leaned over and whispered. "I love your parents."

Later, when he accompanied her out to her car, she told him, "I have a confession to make. Someone came to the bookstore yesterday afternoon and told me about the root rot. I knew about it when I got here last night."

"What? Who?"

"I promised I wouldn't tell," Sara answered. "But that's not important. The fact is, I heard about it and I got online and contacted someone I know. Well, I don't really know her. She's part of a service organization I belong to. Anyway, she's a plant pathologist at the University of Washington. She has a doctorate in botany and she's a professor at U of W. I told her about your predicament and she's agreed to come examine your vines at no cost to you. She'll be here on Tuesday. I'm going to pick her up at San Francisco International."

Jason was stunned. His emotions wavered between irritation at her taking matters into her own hands and sincere gratitude. He controlled the baser emotion and pulled her into his arms. "Thank you."

Sara looked astonished. She had been prepared for him to bellow at her and assert his male right to fend for himself in the big, bad world. His pride often got in the way of common sense, but she loved him anyway.

"You're welcome," she said softly, gazing up into his eyes.

"Really, thank you," Jason said. "You had my back, and I won't forget it."

"I love you, Jason. I'll always have your back."

She kissed him on the chin, and he kissed her brow. "I love you so much," he said tenderly. He hesitated. "I love you, that's all."

Sara's gaze had never left his. His eyes had glazed over with pain. He'd wanted to say so much more than he loved her.

She knew that no matter what she did to prove her love, nothing would be enough until she agreed to marry him. And now his parents were here as a constant reminder of what true love could be like, and what sharing a life meant.

She kissed him goodbye. "Be patient a little longer. That's all I ask."

He smiled sadly and opened the car door for her. "I'm trying my best."

Jason hadn't told anyone in his family that Sara had rejected his proposal. He knew them well enough to know they would hound him until he went nuts, seeking reasons why she would turn him down. What could he have possibly done to make her have second thoughts?

He was busy wracking his brain about that himself.

So, when he and his parents walked out to the site where he and Claude had found evidence of the dreaded root disease and his father had asked him how he and Sara were faring, Jason, already irritated, had said tightly, "Can we just concentrate on one problem at a time?"

Now, why did I have to say that? he wondered, too late. He tried to cover up by laughing and quickly saying, "I mean, we're doing just fine, Dad. Nothing to worry about there." He gestured to the hole in the ground where he'd dug up a root sample to give to the plant pathologist at U.C. Davis. "That is our main concern."

His mother stepped in front of him. Jason could not bear it when his mother cried. Yet here she was, tears in her eyes, regarding him with a great deal of sympathy.

She grasped one of his hands in both of hers and continued to look into his eyes.

"I knew something was wrong. The air around you two just didn't feel right. You've argued about something, haven't you?"

Jason couldn't withstand the emotional assault of his mother's tears. Put him in front of a firing squad, and he would not spill his guts. Pull his fingernails out by the roots and he would not utter a word.

But he saw a tear roll down his mother's cheek, and told them everything. When he was finished he felt cleansed, as if telling someone about the humiliation he'd suffered at Sara's hands had helped to release the residual pain he'd been coping with.

He expected commiseration from his parents. At least acknowledgement of his being wronged by Sara when she had told him she couldn't marry him. However, what he got was: "Stop whining, boy. Soldier up. Be a man. If the woman said she can't marry you right now, she has a perfectly good reason why she can't. Give her room. Give her time to settle her affairs, whatever they may be. But don't chase her away by acting hurt by her decision. Get a grip. Get a clue. And get a backbone!" This, from his mother.

His father was even rougher on him. "Sara's a strong woman. The only kind of woman worth having. Are you strong enough for her? Because if you can't handle this so-called rejection, married life is going to whip you, but good!"

"Tell him, Eric," Simone cried, cheering her husband on.

"Instead of showing her that you would support her through anything, you're trying to bend her to your will, like some petulant child who can't have his way. That ain't how we raised you, Jason. If you want that woman, take her, damn it! Be her man through this crisis, whatever it is. Let her know that you trust her to always do what's right. Do you trust her, son?"

"Yeah!" Jason said with conviction.

"Then what's the problem?" Simone asked. "You don't know everything there is to know about her? Is that what's bothering you?"

"She has so many secrets," he said, in a halfhearted effort to defend his actions which he was beginning to realize were indefensible.

"Eric," Simone said, looking up at her husband. "Do you know everything there is to know about me?"

"Hell, no."

"Do you want to?"

"I like to sleep at night, thank you" was her husband's reply to that.

Simone laughed shortly and once again turned her attention to her son. "The point is, Jason. No spouse anywhere knows everything there is to know about his or her partner. We are human beings. And human beings, by their very nature, do not reveal everything about themselves. Either out of shame or self-preservation or any number of reasons. I love your father, but to this day I've never asked him what he does at those lodge meetings he attends. I don't want to know!"

"We smoke cigars, drink whiskey and look at skin flicks," said Eric.

"I wouldn't be surprised," Simone said, and walked off, leaving the men alone. "I'm going to make some phone calls."

"Mom!" Jason cried, figuring she was about to call in the troops about his and Sara's problem.

"Don't worry," she assured him. "Your dad and I aren't going to tell anybody. I'm going to check on your grandmother. I phone her every Sunday, remember?"

In his mother's absence, Jason turned to his father. "I've been a wimp, huh?"

"I ain't gonna lie to you," Eric said. "I'm surprised Sara hasn't told you to hit the road. But I'm not really surprised by the way you've been behaving toward her."

"Why aren't you?"

Eric paused a moment, choosing his words carefully. "It's like this, son—you were on a steady diet of hamburger, then you got a taste of filet mignon. Hamburger was cheap and you had to show it practically no concern in cooking it. Throw some patties on a grill and you're good to go. But filet mignon requires talent, finesse in preparing it. Plus, it's expensive, dear, if you will. The women you were used to dating meant nothing to you. You showed them no concern and they threw themselves at you. Sara is different. She will not throw herself at you. You have to be worthy of her. You have to use finesse. You actually have to work at it."

"Am I good enough for her?" Jason asked.

"No, son," Eric told him frankly. "No man on earth is good enough for the woman he wants. That's just a fact. But you don't have to be good enough. You just have to love her with everything you've got. Luckily for us, that's usually good enough for them."

Monday morning found Jason running down Arnold Drive in the middle of town. He usually ran all the way from the winery to town and back, which was a little over four miles. Today, as he passed the building where The Olive Press was located, Erik Sutherland suddenly appeared beside him, also attired in running clothes and huffing and puffing as though he hadn't run in years. Which, Jason thought, looking over at the sweaty multimillionaire, he probably hadn't.

"Mornin', Jake," Erik said.

"It was," said Jason.

"Come on, don't be like that. You and I used to practically be best friends."

"You were two years ahead of me, and you bossed everyone around like you owned them. We weren't that close."

"Yeah, but who got you on the football team?"

"I did. I worked my ass off to get on first string."

"Yeah, but I was the one who asked Coach Thompkins to give you a shot."

Jason blew an exasperated breath out and inhaled. "Okay, I'll give you that."

"Then you owe me a favor."

"A small one," Jason allowed, and picked up his pace a little. Maybe he could lose him. "A very small one."

Erik groaned a bit at the extra effort of keeping up

with Jason, but he pushed himself and kept up. "Okay. You know Frannie Anise?"

"Sure, she's Sara's best friend."

"What's your opinion of her?"

"What has that got to do with anything?"

Erik thought for a moment. Jake was being none too cooperative. If he could have only one favor out of him, albeit a small one, he had to make his request count. "Okay, listen, what does a man have to know about dating a black woman? I asked Frannie out and she told me it wouldn't work. I'm not ready to date a sister. What did she mean by that?"

Jason laughed loudly. His laughter echoed up and down Arnold Avenue. "Good God, man, how would I know?"

"But you're dating a black woman."

"Women are individuals, Erik. Black, white, red, whatever. Frannie only told you that to confuse you."

"Why would she do that?" wondered Erik.

"Because women like to keep us off-balance. Women are deadly serious when it comes to affairs of the heart. I'm learning that myself. What she meant was, she sensed in you a desire to play without suffering the consequences. It's okay if they tell you they don't want any strings attached. But they have to be the ones to say that. Not you."

Erik actually got it. "So, she thought all I wanted was a good time, that's why she told me I wasn't ready to date a sister."

"Wasn't that all you wanted?" Jason asked.

"At the time," Erik admitted. "But I've given it a lot of thought since Saturday night and I want more than that now."

"You asked my opinion of Frannie a minute ago,"

Jason said. "Well, the fact is, I like her. She's smart. She's a loyal friend to Sara. And from what I've seen, she's a good person. People tend to get attached to her. Like your daughter, for instance."

"And you're saying this because?" Erik wanted to know.

"Think before you start pursuing Frannie. Not just you and she could get hurt if it doesn't work out. Your daughter could, too."

"That's the reason she wouldn't go out with me."

"Told you she was smart."

"Who says anybody has to get hurt?" Erik asked optimistically.

Jason shook his head, pitying his old teammate. "I'll have that put on your gravestone after you get creamed on the highway of *love*."

Chapter 8

Franklyn and Erica and their spouses descended on the Hacienda the next day.

To be there, Franklyn had left Lettie Burrows, his sous-chef, in charge of the restaurant. His wife, Elise, had asked for and been granted a week off from taping her cooking show on the Food Network.

Erica and Joshua Knight owned a vineyard in Healdsburg in the Russian River Valley. It would still be a couple of years before they harvested their first grapes. The vineyard would be fine without them for a few days.

Both couples got there relatively early Tuesday morning, Erica and Joshua at around eight and Franklyn and Elise at around nine. They breakfasted together. Franklyn and Elise, both professional chefs, did the cooking, while everybody caught up on each other's lives. They were killing time while they awaited Sara's arrival with the expected plant pathologist. She and Frannie had left at six that morning in order to be on time to meet Willow's plane at 9:20.

Simone and Eric were sleeping late.

"How do they look?" Erica asked Jason about their parents. She paused long enough to take a sip of orange juice. "All that traveling isn't taking a toll on them, is it? I worry about them."

"They look healthy," Jason told her. The five of them were sitting around the big oak table. They were casually dressed. Bright sunlight was streaming through the windows and the temperature outside was cold enough to cause condensation to gather on the panes. It was going to be another clear, cool October day.

Erica, who was eight months pregnant, wore her short black hair in natural twists. She'd stopped having her hair relaxed when she'd found out she was pregnant, wanting to be chemical-free for the duration of her pregnancy.

Sitting next to her, her husband, Joshua, also had natural corkscrews, although his hair was several inches shorter than hers. "Lately, you worry about everything," he said. "You need to relax more."

Franklyn, the eldest at thirty-seven, laughed. His light brown eyes lit up when he did. Unlike his sister and brother who had black hair, his was dark brown with red highlights like their father's. "You've been married two years now," he told Joshua. "It's time you faced the fact that Erica is never going to quit worrying about everybody. Or trying to fix everybody's lives. That's who she is."

He had a deep-timbered voice that was compassionate and wholly pleasing to the ear. Elise, sitting beside him, laughed too. "But she does it out of love, not because she's a busybody."

Jason nearly choked on his coffee. He looked at Elise. She was a beauty with long black wavy hair, big, brown eyes and the personality of a saint. She had to be a saint in order to have said that about his sister! "You're too kind, Elise. But then you didn't grow up with her. She's most definitely a busybody."

Instead of being offended, Erica's eyes sparkled with excitement. No one liked a debate better than she did. "If not for my interfering ways, you and Sara would not be together today. I practically twisted your arm to make you pursue her."

"She certainly did have to light a fire under *Franklyn*," Elise put in. "I thought I was going to die of old age before he would ask me out!"

"Thank you, Elise!" Erica cried triumphantly. She bounced on her chair, she was so excited. Her huge belly made it difficult for her to sit close to the table.

Joshua reached out and placed a protective hand on her arm. "Careful, you're gonna shake my son loose."

Erica's hand went to her abdomen. The baby was moving inside her. "He sure didn't like that." She placed Joshua's hand on the moving fetus. "Feel that."

Joshua was always happy to track the movements of his son. Smiling, he said, "He's gonna be a soccer player like his dad."

"Soccer?" Jason said. "In this country? He'll be a football player like his uncle."

"Let's not get into another argument about the superiority of soccer over American football," Joshua, who had lived in France for ten years and had been on a soccer team over there, said. "The relative merits of American football do not compare to the unrivaled universal appeal of soccer."

"Hey, buddy, in America, football rules," countered Jason. He looked to Franklyn for support. "Right, bro?"

"I like both," Franklyn said. "American football is a contest of strategy and brute force. Soccer requires stamina and agility. But, personally, I prefer rock climbing." His muscular arms and legs attested to the fact that climbing was an effective sport.

"There is no competition in rock climbing," Jason protested.

"Sure there is," said Franklyn. "You're competing with yourself every time you go out there."

"I have to say, it makes you use muscles you never knew you had," Joshua said. "The only time I ever went climbing with you I was sore for a week. Erica had to give me a massage every night."

"That's how I got in this condition," Erica joked. "So, thank you, Uncle Franklyn."

Everybody laughed.

Eric and Simone entered the kitchen at that instant and Franklyn, Elise, Erica and Joshua got up to hug them hello.

"How long are you going to be staying?" Erica wanted to know. She was being hugged tightly by her mother.

"Only a few days, then we're off again for a while. But we'll be back in time for Thanksgiving."

"You'd better be," said Franklyn. "Elise and I want to have you all at our house."

"Great," cried Erica. "I won't have to worry about cooking. Cook plenty so I can take home lots of leftovers."

"She's not fond of cooking now," Joshua explained. "She says her hormones turn her into a walking furnace, anyway, and slaving over a hot stove is hell."

Simone actually had her ear pressed against Erica's

protruding belly. "Don't worry, honey," she said. "This rascal will be here in about three weeks."

"Three weeks!" Erica exclaimed, none too happy to hear her mother's prediction. "My doctor says he's not due until November fifteenth."

"My guess is as good as the doctor's," Simone told her. "If you're anything like me, that baby will come at least two weeks earlier than your doctor predicts."

"I'm not ready! I thought he was going to cook a while longer." Erica sat back down.

Joshua stood behind her, massaging her shoulders. "Of course you're ready. You've been hoping he would come on out so you can sleep better at night."

Simone sat next to Erica. She was petite and slightly plump with golden brown skin and dark brown eyes. In her early sixties, she had the kind of youthful facial features that would always confound those who tried to guess her age. "Sweetie, no matter when the baby arrives, you're going to be ready. That's a quality God gives us, at least if we love our children, and you love this baby, don't you?"

"With all my heart," Erica said.

"Then, stop worrying, because you will handle it. And no matter where your dad and I are, when we hear that little Joshua, Jr. has made his way into the world, we're gonna haul ass to Healdsburg to make sure that you and he are all right. Depend on that."

Erica threw her arms around her mother's neck. She always knew just what to say to make her feel better.

The phone rang, and Jason went to answer it.

It was Sara. "She's here," she reported. "She's collecting her bags now and we'll be on the road in a few minutes."

At San Francisco International Airport, Sara was standing near the luggage carousel looking at Frannie and Willow as they grabbed two large black bags. One looked like a garment bag while the other was bulky and lopsided. She guessed that the plant pathologist had the tools of her trade in that one.

"Great," said Jason. "Thanks for calling. Everybody's here waiting. Drive carefully."

"Always," said Sara. "Love you. See you soon."

"I love you, too," Jason said.

After hanging up, he related what Sara had said to his family. But his family was too busy smiling at the fact that he'd told Sara that he loved her to pay much attention to what he was saying.

Erica, who lately cried at the drop of a hat, went and hugged him, fresh tears in her eyes. "My brother's in love!"

Sara's curiosity about how Willow looked had finally been satisfied.

She was an Amazon. Jason would be delighted to add her to his long list of the fabled warriors whom he said invariably wound up working at Aminatu's Daughters.

Willow stood at least six feet. She had to weigh two hundred pounds because she was solid. Not fat, but toned and kind of thick, as the fellas liked to say nowadays. Healthy.

She had skin the color of roasted chestnuts, widely spaced brown eyes, a small nose and a full mouth that was completely free of lipstick. In fact, she wasn't wearing any kind of makeup. Her black hair was about an inch long and it was naturally wavy with a gray streak in the front.

Sara thought she was beautiful, and told her so. "You're gorgeous, Willow."

Willow, who had just walked up to them after she saw Sara and Frannie standing in her carrier's waiting area, looking exactly as Sara had described them over the phone, beamed her pleasure. "Ditto, darlin'."

They hugged. Then she hugged Frannie, too.

Willow was wearing khaki slacks, a short-sleeve khaki shirt, and brown hiking boots. Sara easily spotted her crossed spears tattoo on the inside of her right arm about two inches above where her arm bent.

"How was your flight?" Frannie asked as they began walking toward the luggage carousel.

"Excuse me a moment while I make a call," Sara said. That's when she phoned Jason to tell him Willow had arrived safely.

After the phone call, she walked over to Frannie and Willow and insisted on taking the bag that Willow had in her hand. "Okay," said Willow. "It's heavy."

She handed the bag to Sara. It must have weighed nearly a hundred pounds. "What have you got in here?"

"A portable soil analyzer, among other things," Willow said. "I like to be prepared."

They were soon at Sara's Mustang. Frannie climbed in the back while Willow sat up front so that she'd have space enough to accommodate her long legs.

After Sara had started the car and was backing out of the parking space, she smiled at Willow and asked, "Are you hungry? I'd be glad to stop for something to eat before we get on the road."

"No, I'm fine. I'd like to get to Glen Ellen and take a look at the site. I'm intrigued. Do you know if the site used to have oak trees on it?"

"No, I don't," Sara said. "But the whole family, including Jason's parents, is waiting for you. I'm certain they'll be able to give you the history of the site."

"Good, because I've been reading up on the area. There was an occurrence of Armillaria mellea, causal agent of Armillaria root rot, in the Sonoma Valley not too many years ago and there used to be a copse of oak trees on the affected land. The problem with Armillaria is that it can survive on host roots long after the host dies. It kind of lies dormant underground, waiting to come back to life, if you will."

"Kind of like a vampire," Frannie joked.

Willow laughed. "Yeah, something dead that's reanimated."

"You're kind of like a plant detective," Sara observed.

Willow smiled at the analogy. "Curiosity drives me. I can't rest until I solve the mystery. Enough about me, I want to hear your recruitment stories. Whenever I'm fortunate enough to meet new sisters, I want to know how they were tricked into joining up."

Sara laughed. "Tricked into joining up?"

"That's what I call it," Willow said, not equivocating. "I was at the lowest ebb of my life when I was contacted. My son, David, had drowned two months earlier and my husband, unable to cope, had walked out on me."

"I'm so sorry," Sara cried. "How old was David?"

"He was three. We had a house near a lake and I was working inside. He wanted me to come play with him, but I had just a bit more work to do, and I asked him to give me a few more minutes, and I would take him for a walk by the lake. He loved going down there. I continued to work and, then, all of sudden it occurred to me that the house was too quiet. You know that preternatural kind of quiet that tells your psyche that something's wrong?"

"Oh, yeah," said Sara. "I know exactly what you mean."

Frannie sat on the back seat, listening raptly, with tears in her eyes.

"Well, it was at that point that I got up and called for David. He didn't answer, and I started frantically searching the house. I couldn't find him anywhere. Then, I came to the back door, and the damned thing was cracked. Not standing open, just cracked a little. A large enough space for a little boy to get through. And I knew. I felt weak because the knowledge of something terrible awaiting me out there was so strong. But I went anyway. I found him near the dock underneath an overturned rowboat that we kept there. He'd dropped his ball in the water, bent over to retrieve it, and had fallen in."

Sara wiped the tears away as she drove. "How long ago?"

"Seven years now," Willow answered. She also had to wipe tears away. "After that Michael couldn't look at me. He blamed me for leaving the door unlocked. He wasn't there at the time, you see. He was on a business trip, and when he returned his child was dead. I can understand why he left me, why he couldn't live with me anymore. But, the fact was, the door was locked. David simply knew how to unlock it. He was smart and he was always learning new skills. I didn't know he could get the dead bolt undone and open the door. If I had known, I would have gotten better locks. But it was too late for self-recriminations. David was dead and he wasn't coming back."

She paused long enough to dig in her bag, get a tissue, and blow her nose. "I've always been the type of person who works hard to keep the demons at bay. I threw myself into my work after David's death and Michael's departure. And I started doing foolish things to invite my own death. No, I would have never considered suicide. It wasn't in me to do it. I can sympathize with those who think of it, though. Instead of suicide, I was looking for ways to get killed. I started hanging out at some of the seedier Seattle bars and, honey, when I say seedy I mean nasty. I'm not much of a drinker. A couple of drinks and I'm three sheets to the wind. One night, I went home with this guy who tried to beat me after I wouldn't give it up. I say tried because my self-preservation mechanism kicked in as he was hitting me and I turned the tables on him and kicked his butt. The person in the apartment next to his called the police and I was hauled in for assault. I tried to explain that he was the one who jumped on me but the police didn't believe me. I was three inches taller than the guy and was thirty pounds heavier." She laughed. "Yeah, big women get no breaks. Anyway, while I was in jail this sister came to me and told me she had a proposition for me. I got the usual spiel about helping others in order to get over your grief. It sounded good to me at the time, so I signed up."

Sara was quiet. Willow's story was very similar to her own. Grief had been the impetus for both of them joining the organization. Frannie's story was different.

"Frannie, why don't you tell Willow what made you join," Sara said after a couple minutes of complete silence in the car.

"It was ten years ago," Frannie began, her voice a little thick from crying. "I suppose I should give you a bit of back story before I begin. My dad's Jewish and my mom's black. I grew up a privileged princess in Nob Hill, the snootiest neighborhood in San Francisco. My father's family had so much money they didn't know what to do with it. Growing up I was sheltered so well that I had never heard the *N* word. I was exposed to it when I entered the private high school my parents sent me to and encountered a clique for the first time. Remember the movie, *Heathers?* Well, these witches were worse. My dad could buy their dads ten times over but money didn't matter, skin color did. That truly baffled me."

"Honey, I grew up in Alabama," Willow said softly. "I was called the *N* word so many times I started considering it an endearment. It started to roll off my back with little lasting effect."

Frannie laughed. "I didn't know how to do that. I turned their hatred inward and by the time I went to college I'd developed an inferiority complex that my mother the psychiatrist probably could have written books about if I'd confided in her. I felt so worthless that I would befriend anyone who showed me the slightest affection. Enter Chaz Devlin, career college student and con artist. By the time I'd met him he'd used countless coeds to finance his lifestyle, but I didn't know that. All I knew was that he made me feel beautiful for the first time in my life. So what if he needed a little cash every now and then? I had plenty. A little turned into more and more, though. My parents got suspicious and started insisting on knowing how I spent my money. I couldn't tell them that I was giving it to some guy. So I lied to them. That was my first step down the path of degradation. Next, he convinced me that the pressures of college could be eased if I smoked a little marijuana with him. Sure, the pressures of college eased after that because I quit going to class! My parents were livid when they found out I'd skipped a whole semester. They held an intervention for me. My mother was big on those. They had to get to the root of my problem. By that time, though, I'd become insensate. No emotions reached me. My mother cried and it didn't affect me at all and I used to hate to see my mother cry. All I wanted to do was smoke dope and hang with my friends, who weren't really friends, but I was too doped up to know that. My parents cut me off financially. I drifted from low-paying job to low-paying job. I'd dusted Chaz off. I didn't need him anymore. I'd *become* him. From twenty to twenty-four I led a life only one paycheck from the streets. I lived with friends, anyone who could loan me their couch or their floor. Didn't matter to me. Then one night, I was walking home from a restaurant where I washed dishes and a guy grabbed me, pulled me into the alley, and raped me. At fourteen I'd started doing martial arts and felt confident I could somewhat defend myself. But, no, he *brutalized* me. I had to stay in the hospital for a week. I was too ashamed to call my parents. I hadn't seen much of them since I'd moved to NYC. It was on the last day of my stay in the hospital that a woman doctor, a blonde in her thirties, walked into my room and said, 'Little sister, are you ready to stop getting stomped on by life?' Just those words, and she stood there looking at me, and I lay there looking at her. Her stare was so intense, and my brain was so bent out of shape that I thought I must have imagined her. I closed my eyes and opened them again but she was still there waiting for my reply. Tears sprang to my eyes, and I said, 'Yes, yes I am.' I joined about a month later."

"What happened to the guy who attacked you?" Willow asked.

"He was killed a few months later when he tried to rape a woman who happened to be armed. By that time I had connections at the NYPD, and I read the report. She shot him four times, twice in the groin area."

"Okay, Sara," said Willow. "It's your turn. Tell me they didn't recruit you at the lowest ebb of your life so that my theory can be disproven."

"I can't," Sara said. "Frannie recruited me and if she had been a few minutes late the day she came calling, I might have slit my wrist and bled out before anyone found me. But she did, and I didn't, and I'm still here." Then, she told Willow all about Billy and how despondent she'd been after his death.

When she'd finished, Willow said, "We're a bunch of sad sacks, aren't we? All with tragic stories."

"Yes, but we're all stronger because of what happened to us," Sara said.

"Stronger in some ways," Willow allowed. "But I still have a habit of choosing the wrong guy to take home." She told them about Elvin and what she'd found upon returning home from South America three days ago.

"The good thing is," Frannie said. "You didn't hit him with that bat. You'd be in jail now instead of here."

Willow nodded in agreement. "Hallelujah!"

To which they laughed. Sara, who had had the CD player on very low the whole time, reached over and turned up the volume. Mary J. Blige was singing "One" with U2.

"That's my favorite song on the CD!" she exclaimed.

"Yeah, girlfriend, got down on that song," Willow agreed, and she closed her eyes and swayed with the music.

So, they drove and listened to Mary J. Blige's entire CD, commenting on every track, and generally enjoying each other's company. After all, they were sisters.

Chapter 9

Once at the Hacienda, Sara made the introductions and after expressing her pleasure at meeting everyone Willow told them she wanted to see the vineyard right away. They were all standing in the foyer: Willow, Sara, Jason, Eric, Simone, Franklyn, Elise, Erica, Joshua and Frannie.

Sensing she was not a woman who didn't know her own mind, Jason was fast to offer to take her to the site. "I'll go get the truck and pick you up out front."

"Thank you, Jason," said Willow.

She went to grab her equipment bag and go wait for him. Franklyn stepped forward and lifted it as if it weighed next to nothing. "Let me get that for you, Dr. Quigley."

Willow smiled up at him. "Please, call me Willow, Franklyn."

She and Franklyn led the way outside, everyone else bringing up the rear.

The day was bright and clear, and the temperature in the low sixties. Willow looked at the sky. "Do you all have beautiful weather like this all the time?"

"Pretty much," Franklyn said. He set the bag on the porch next to his jeans-clad leg. "Although, November and December are usually wet months."

Willow laughed. "Only November and December? It must be heaven to live here. Seattle seems to get rain year-round. I'm not complaining, mind you. My livelihood depends on rain. If not for rain there would be no plants. If not for plants, I might have become a professional wrestler."

Willow guffawed, after which the others felt comfortable enough to laugh with her. Willow usually was the one to break the ice about her size. She'd been big from birth and had learned to crack the first joke because it was inevitable that others would follow.

They spread out on the huge portico, some taking seats on the patio furniture, others standing near Willow. "I suppose I should be asking a few questions while I'm waiting for Jason to bring the truck around," she said, looking at Eric and Simone. "I was wondering if oak trees were ever on the property where the root rot was found."

"Yes!" Simone said immediately. "We had to cut down several oak trees. Hated doing it. But it was the ideal spot for the southern vineyards."

"Mmm," said Willow, thinking. "I thought that might have been a possibility. Did you know that root rot occurring on sites previously inhabited by oak trees has been documented since the 1880s?"

"Honey, if we had known that, we wouldn't have planted in that field," Simone said with a short laugh.

"When Eric and I started the vineyard we were as green as green can be. We were used to growing vegetables."

Willow laughed softly. She liked Simone Bryant and was pleased Sara was going to have her for a mother-in-law. From the first moment she saw Jason and Sara together it was obvious to her that they were in love. "Well, you've done a wonderful job converting it into a splendid family business. I don't drink much, but when I do I drink Bryant Chardonnay. Your Zinfandel is good, too."

That comment sparked a vigorous conversation about wine which everyone there felt passionately about even though their individual knowledge on the subject varied widely.

They were still deep in conversation when Jason parked the truck in front of the house and got out. He ran up the steps of the portico. "Dr. Quigley, your chariot awaits."

"Do I have to keep telling everybody to call me Willow?" Willow asked. She looked at Sara. "Are you coming, Sara?"

Sara, who was sitting next to Frannie on a chaise longue, was surprised to be asked. She figured Willow would find it irritating having too many people looking over her shoulder while she worked.

"I'm going to need someone to take notes for me while I'm digging."

"I'd never stand by and let a lady do any digging," said Jason.

"What a gentleman," Willow said, smiling. "Thank you, but I need to get down in the dirt in order to see the soil stratum by stratum. It's just how it's done."

Soon, Sara, Willow and Jason were in the truck. Willow's equipment bag had been stowed in the truck's bed. As they pulled away, Eric said, "She seems to know her stuff."

"Yes, I like her," said Simone. She turned to go back into the house. "I think we ought to get dinner started. They're going to be ravenous when they get back."

Jason had never seen a woman know her way around a shovel as well as Willow Quigley did. She had declined the use of his shovel, pulling her own from the equipment bag and locking the segmented handle into place.

Then she handed Sara a thick notepad and a ballpoint pen with black ink.

She picked a spot in the middle of the defoliation, the place where the leaves of the vines were withering and the grapes turning into raisins before their time. She talked while she dug, and Sara soon had two full pages of notes.

When she was sufficiently deep enough to see the root structure, she got down on her knees in the hole and started digging in the soil with her bare hands. Jason had stood and watched all this time, wondering what she would find. He did not understand half of the botanical jargon she'd been feeding Sara.

After several minutes during which Willow had not said a word, and he was becoming tenser by the moment, Willow slowly got off her knees, brushed the sand from her khakis and looked up at him. "It's definitely *Armillaria mellea*. It was here before your parents planted the vineyard. Even though they cut down the oak trees the infection survived by feeding on the woody roots that once belonged to the oaks. Obviously, when your parents tried to eradicate it in…what year was it?"

"1978," Jason said.

"1978," Willow continued. "They did not dig deep enough to get all of the root. You're going to have to dig deep, remove all the symptomatic grapevines and let the land sit for a while to be sure you've got it all before replanting. And I suggest you get to work on it early in the morning. You're going to need backhoes and several people with strong backs to help you."

Jason nodded his agreement. He had known the news wasn't going to be good. The thing to do was to jump on it as soon as possible to prevent further damage.

"How much of the vineyard do you think has to go?" he asked, confident in her knowledge now.

"Everything within a forty-foot radius, to be safe," Willow advised. "I'll mark off the area for you early in the morning." She reached for his hand. He helped her out of the hole she'd dug. Once on her feet, Willow stomped her feet to knock the black soil from the sole of her boots, then she brushed off her clothes. "Right now, I want to walk through the vineyard looking for any more signs of decay."

"We've already done that," Jason told her. "This is the only area."

"If you don't mind, I'd rather see for myself," said Willow, her tone light. "It's not that I don't think you did a good job, it's just that my eyes are trained to see the signs."

Jason smiled. He was learning to accept help when it was offered. "Thank you."

Willow playfully punched him on the shoulder, which hurt, and laughed. "Just part of my routine."

Sara and Jason walked with her. She would pause near a clump of grapes, bend to peer closely at them.

She didn't pick any of the unripe fruit, she simply observed. She also paid close attention to the leaves close to the ground, which, Jason remembered, he and Claude had paid no attention to.

It took them two hours to walk through the vineyard, whereas it usually only took Jason fifteen minutes. That's how thorough Willow had been. However, after her inspection he was happy to hear, "I don't see any signs of further infection. Clear the area I've pointed out and you should be all right."

Jason sighed heavily. "Thank you, Willow. Thank you so much!"

"You're welcome," Willow said. "This has been interesting, kind of like a mini-vacation for me. I got to meet two of my sisters in the service organization I belong to and I got to see the vineyard where my favorite wine comes from."

"Digging holes is a vacation to you?" Jason asked jokingly.

"You should have seen what I was doing in the Amazon jungle," Willow said. "This was a walk in the park compared to that."

As she had promised, Willow was there to mark off the area to be excavated early the next morning. While she and Jason were pushing the stakes into the ground, Erik Sutherland drove up in his Land Rover.

It was barely 6:00 a.m. The other men, Eric, Joshua, Franklyn and Claude, weren't expected until seven. From a distance, Willow and Jason, both around the same height, and both attired in long-sleeve shirts and jeans, looked like two men to Erik.

"Hey, fellas," he said as he walked up.

Then, Willow turned in his direction and he saw at once that she was definitely a woman. "Sorry, ma'am," Erik said, chagrined.

Willow smiled. "Blame it on the fog."

The fog was clearing, but there was still a good deal of mist in the vineyards.

Erik stepped forward and offered his hand. "I'm a neighbor, Erik Sutherland. I haven't had the pleasure of meeting you, but I've heard good things about you."

Willow's brows rose in curiosity as she shook his hand. "This is a small town if news of the great Willow Quigley has spread so fast," she said self-deprecatingly.

"Glen Ellen *is* a small town, and your reputation precedes you," said Erik pleasantly. "My daughter, Melissa, is close to Frannie. They spoke on the phone last night. Melissa told me about the excavations this morning. Since I don't have a job to speak of, I thought I'd come over and let you-all put me to work."

"Between jobs, huh?" said Willow sympathetically.

"Sort of," Erik said.

Jason, who was tying string around one of the stakes, said, "The more the merrier." He wasn't about to turn down the offer of free labor. As it was, the job was going to take them all day long. With an extra pair of hands, they might be able to shave off some of that time.

He glanced at Erik's attire, an expensive long-sleeve denim shirt, designer jeans and designer hiking boots. Jason knew fashion because he had a closet full of designer suits he no longer had any use for. "Didn't have any old clothes?"

"It's been a long time since I dug ditches," Erik said.

"All right, then," Jason said. "We get started at seven."

* * *

"What's the brother situation like around here?" Willow asked Sara as they, along with Simone, Erica, Elise, Frannie, Rosaura and Melissa stood on the sidelines watching the men work. Sara had left Elizabeth and Linda Ramirez in charge of the store. Melissa had arrived a little after seven armed with a camera in order to get evidence that her dad had actually done physical labor at one time in his life. She couldn't stay long. She had to be at school by nine.

"You're looking at it," Sara told her.

"And they're all taken," Willow fumed. "I suppose a sister has to wait until she gets back to Seattle to go on the hunt. I do like a hunt outside of my normal territory, though."

"I'll invite all of the eligible bachelors in town to your going-away party," Sara said. "But I hope you'll stay on a while after this is over. You say you don't have to go back to work until January."

"Yes, but I don't want to wear out my welcome, and I have a sneaking suspicion Elvin is going to try to get into my house while I'm gone. I had the locks changed, but he left in such a hurry that I'm sure he forgot to grab a few important things," Willow said, laughing.

"Possession is nine-tenths of the law," Sara quoted. "Give his things to the Salvation Army."

"I would, but I doubt they would want them. Elvin wasn't exactly ready for *GQ*. He cleaned the tanks at the aquarium. His idea of dressing up was putting on a shirt over his sleeveless T-shirt and putting on clean black socks with his sandals. The next guy I date will *not* wear socks with sandals. I just won't tolerate it!"

Laughing, Sara said, "Maybe his feet were cold."

"Could be," Willow agreed. "He even wore them to bed." She groaned. "Oh, my God, I just realized something. The whole time we were together, I never saw Elvin's feet! He wore black socks all the time. How could I have missed that? He could have had fungus between his toes."

"Or webbed feet," Sara suggested gleefully. "He worked at the aquarium. Maybe Elvin was a merman, and he could not let you see his feet because you would have found him out!"

Laughing uproariously, Willow said, "No, honey, he was definitely not a merman. He didn't turn back into a fish when he got wet. But he could have had a condition like hammertoe, for all I know. I could have been sleeping with a man who had hammertoe for the past year. I'm swearing off men until I can start being more discriminating."

"Or at least see their feet first," quipped Sara.

"What are you two giggling about?" Frannie wanted to know. She'd been deep in conversation with Melissa about Danny, Melissa's favorite subject these days since they had started dating, but Melissa had had to leave in order to make it to Santa Rosa in time for her first class.

"Men," Willow told Frannie. She turned and glanced over at Erik who was busy assisting Jason by pulling up a stubborn network of roots. "For example, Erik told me that you and Melissa are very close, and after she told him about today's excavations he came because he wanted to lend a hand. That's wonderful. But I suspect he's also here so that he can get his fill of looking at you. The man's attention has been on you more than on what he's doing, which can be dangerous if he doesn't watch where he puts the blade of that shovel."

Frannie looked concerned as her eyes raked over Erik's face. "You really think so?"

"She likes him, too!" Willow crowed triumphantly. She smiled down at Frannie. "I was just testing a theory. Unless he's a complete klutz, you have nothing to worry about. He won't lose a toe."

Simone, with Elise, Erica and Rosaura, walked up and jumped right into the conversation. "Who's gonna lose a toe?"

"Erik is if he doesn't stop looking at Frannie," Sara explained.

Simone smiled at Frannie. "You could do a lot worse. I knew his parents. Good people. He was kind of a bully in school, though. But I'm sure Sara has already filled you in on that. But people do change. Look at Jason. That boy rarely showed an interest in the winery at all. He liked designer clothes, expensive cars and elegant surroundings. Only the best of everything for him. I wouldn't be exaggerating if I said he was spoiled rotten. Not by his father and me, but by himself. He was making money hand over fist and didn't deny himself anything. Now, look at him, worried to death that he's going to lose the winery and he's sweating and working like a dog to prevent it. Erik Sutherland can't be all bad if he's out there assisting his old teammate. Besides, Melissa's a sweet kid. Must be from his influence. I've never met her mother."

"I think I remember hearing that Erik met Melissa's mother while he was in college," Erica, looking beautiful in a light blue caftan with gold thread shot through the fabric and navy slacks, put in. "She's not from around here."

"Yeah, you're probably right," Simone said, calculating the years between Erik and Melissa. "Erik was a couple years ahead of Jason in school, so that makes him around thirty-six, and Melissa just turned sixteen. That means he became a father at twenty. Takes a special kind of guy to take responsibility at that age. A lot of men would run."

They had Frannie reconsidering her no-dating-allowed stance with Erik. Stubborn, though, she wasn't going down without a fight.

"I know what you all are doing," she said, looking at Simone and then Willow. "But I can't date Erik. If it doesn't work out between us, Melissa would be heartbroken. She looks at me as a mother figure. She's already lost one mother."

"Her mother is dead?" Willow asked, alarmed.

"No," Frannie answered quietly. "Her mother gave her father full custody without a fight, and Melissa sees it as proof that her mother doesn't want her."

"That poor kid," Willow said with a sympathetic sigh. "Yes, little sister, I can see why you have to be careful. But, I'm warning you—the way he looks at you it's going to be hard to resist him. I'll pray for you."

"Pray hard," Frannie requested.

When the men broke for lunch, each of them was made to feel special by the woman in his life. It had been Simone's idea for the women to pack picnic lunches and find comfortable spots so that their men could eat, relax, and have stimulating conversation.

Sara could see why she and Eric had been married for so long.

Willow and Frannie wound up sharing Erik Sutherland.

Sara tried not to wonder if Willow was good at sharing as she spread the thick blanket on the ground for her and Jason to sit on. She had found a secluded spot a few yards behind the others.

Jason was a little tired, but he was in good physical condition. That morning's labor hadn't taken much out of him. His eyes were on Sara as she opened the picnic basket and withdrew sandwiches, fresh fruit and Gatorade in his favorite flavor.

He'd worn work gloves, so his hands were not dirty, although he knew he'd have blisters on them for a few days. He cursed his time as a lawyer when having soft hands wasn't a disadvantage in the courtroom. Having soft hands when you were digging in the hard earth definitely made you feel less than a man. He bet his father wasn't going to have blisters on *his* hands for a few days.

"How's it going?" Sara asked as she opened a bottle of Gatorade.

"Dad thinks it's going pretty fast compared to the last time. I think he likes operating that backhoe."

"According to your mother, a little too enthusiastically," said Sara with a smile. "She nearly passed out from fright when he backed it too close to a hole. He could have toppled over."

"I'll tell him to watch that."

"Eat," Sara encouraged him.

Jason picked up a sandwich but set it back down again. "I can't eat anything until I tell you how wrong I was about you. I've been a fool, Sara."

Sara was wary of his apologies because, lately, they were soon followed by inexplicable behavior like the other night when he'd invited her for dinner, and more, and had then decided they should become celibate. Plus, she was under the impression that nothing had been settled between them and when they had recently made love it had been under cease-fire conditions. The war was still on.

She looked at him with a "prove-it" expression in her eyes.

Jason laughed shortly. "You don't believe I've been a fool?"

"That part's not hard to believe. But what exactly have you been a fool about?"

As far as Jason was concerned, her tone was justifiably cynical. He'd behaved erratically. He'd told her he was cool with her needing more time before she could commit to marriage. Then he'd gone back on his word and tried to bend her to his will.

That kind of behavior wasn't conducive to trust in a relationship.

Yet, she'd gone out of her way to help him even though she wasn't certain they still had a relationship. She had been faithful. She had been a true friend.

"Everything about you points to the fact that you're a truthful person. I lost sight of that," he told her quietly. He was looking directly into her eyes. "You are innately honest, Sara. My problem was, in my former life I didn't often encounter people like you. Practically every woman I knew had something to hide. It got so bad I started to believe that no one was capable of real honesty."

"You mean no woman."

He nodded in the affirmative. "Yes."

"Then, when I told you I couldn't agree to marry you until I settled my affairs, you thought I was reluctant to marry you because I was trying to hide a shameful secret. So shameful that I couldn't even talk about it."

"My imagination tortured me!" he said with a laugh.

"But now you realize that it can't be too awful because I'm innately an honest person." She still sounded skeptical.

"That's right. I have faith that whatever you have to settle will be settled soon and then you and I can get married."

"That's what I've been telling you all along," Sara said, exasperated.

"Yes, but I was too hurt by your rejection to see straight then. We'd been seeing each other for a year and a half. I thought you *wanted* to get married."

"I did! I mean, I do!"

"So when you said you couldn't, it threw me. That's when the suspicions began. It occurred to me that every time you went out of town, you either got a new book-store employee or you let one go. I thought maybe you were part of a smuggling ring."

"A smuggling ring!"

"Smuggling people into the country. Everybody you hire has an accent."

"Yeah. Linda Ramirez is Mexican-American."

"That's not what I'm talking about, and you know it. Your last hire, ah, *Mary*. She sounds like Nelson Mandela. Tell me she's not from South Africa!"

"She *is* from South Africa. She's over here because she wants to be a doctor. She starts school at the University of California in a couple of months, premed. I like helping young women who know what they want out of life. You know that. When Billy died he left me financially sound. I bought the bookstore just to have something to do with my time and, hopefully, to have a way to help others. Aminatu's Daughters, as you've said many times before, could be the haven of modern-day Amazons. The women who work there are all working toward a goal, their own empowerment. And once they're on their feet, they reach back down and help another sister onto hers. That's how the organization I belong to works."

"Now, Willow," Jason said, smiling, "*looks* like an Amazon. You and Frannie just have the spirits of Amazons."

Tears sprang to Sara's eyes. Could he actually be getting what she had been trying to tell him for the longest time? "Then you're okay with the fact that I still need time to settle matters before I can accept your ring?"

Still smiling, Jason nodded. "Yeah. I'm with you, baby. I've got your back from this moment on."

They leaned in and kissed briefly, then he reached up and gently wiped her tears away with the pads of his fingers. "Eat your lunch," he said. "You're going to need lots of energy to handle me tonight."

Sara laughed shortly. "Yeah, right. You're gonna be so sore you won't be able to move even the good parts."

Jason was not sore that night, but when he went to get up on Thursday morning his body was so stiff and sore he lay in bed a few minutes more. He wanted to get out of bed because his parents and siblings were leaving after breakfast, and he wanted to see them off. If he could only get into a hot shower he was sure his muscles would loosen up and, as an added benefit, he'd be in less pain.

He was still lying there in his pajama bottoms when someone knocked on the door.

Luckily, he rarely locked his bedroom door and could call, "Come in" without having to move a muscle to go open the door.

The door opened inward and Sara strode in with his breakfast on a tray. Startled by her presence, but very glad to see her, Jason tried to sit up. Wincing, he managed to pull himself upright and swing his legs off the bed.

Laughing, Sara quickly put the tray down on his desktop and went to him. Catching him by the upper arms, she said, "I think I should rub you down with alcohol first, and then you'll be able to get in the shower."

"I'm okay," Jason said.

"Like hell you are," Sara countered. "Your mother told me exactly what to do."

"My mother!"

"She's doing the same thing for your father right now, and he didn't do half as much as you and the other guys did yesterday."

"Yeah, but he's in his sixties. We're young."

"You sound like an old man this morning," Sara told him matter-of-factly.

"I'm gonna get you for that remark as soon as I can raise my arms to spank you."

"Promises, promises. I'm going to get the alcohol. I assume there's some in your medicine cabinet?"

"No, I keep it under the sink."

Sara left the bedroom, went into the adjacent bathroom and returned with a bottle of rubbing alcohol and a thick towel. She set the alcohol and towel on the nightstand beside him, and then helped him lie on his stomach.

Jason closed his eyes when she began massaging the alcohol into the muscles of his shoulders, arms, and back. The coolness of the alcohol soon gave way to the friction of the effort she put into it and then her hands felt warm on his body. It felt so good, he sighed with satisfaction.

After fifteen minutes or so, Sara said, "All right, turn over and let me do the front."

"Not this minute," Jason said.

"Come on, Jason, we haven't got all morning. Your parents are getting on the road at ten, and it's nearly nine now."

"Okay," Jason said in warning tones.

He turned over and Sara could see why he'd wanted to wait a while. He was fully erect. Smiling at her, he said, "You know you can't touch me without turning me on."

Determined to get on with the massage, Sara looked away and picked up the bottle of alcohol. "It isn't as if I've never seen you aroused before."

"Yes, but before we were usually about to make love. This time we can't do anything about it except let it go down. Unless you'd like to…"

"Are you crazy!" exclaimed Sara, keeping her tone low. "With your entire family in the house?"

She had screwed off the cap of the alcohol in preparation for pouring some into her palm but now she closed it again and set the bottle on the nightstand. "For that, you can get in the shower by yourself. I'm out of here."

She turned and quickly left the room.

"Sara!" Jason called, laughing. "Come back, I'll behave myself."

In the hallway, Sara paused to lean against the bedroom door. She smiled and pushed away from the door. He could always make her smile. But she was not going anywhere near him while his family was in the house.

When Jason came downstairs, he was moving with more alacrity. He was still sore, though. His family was gathered in the kitchen. He could tell by the general lethargy of the men sitting at the table that they were also hurting. They looked sapped of energy.

The women hovered around them, putting plates on the table, refilling a coffee mug here and there and encouraging them to eat to build up their strength.

Jason sat down stiffly. "Thank God we don't find root rot every year!"

His father, brother and brother-in-law laughed between winces of pain.

Chapter 10

Since Willow had been staying with them Sara and Frannie had enjoyed her company on their morning runs. Although, *technically,* they were walking out of deference to their guest who had told them that due to her height, weight and age, she didn't jog. Jogging was too hard on the joints.

She certainly walked fast, though. Sara and Frannie were winded this morning trying to keep up with her. Must have been those long legs of hers.

It was Saturday. Willow had been talked into staying another week. Next Friday Sara was giving her a going-away party at the Hacienda at Jason's insistence.

As was their habit, they were talking as they walked. At present the topic was men. Specifically, the best man they'd ever had in their lives. Frannie started the ball rolling with, "Now, we're not talking about sex, are we? Because sex often doesn't figure into how good a man is. I mean I've known some really good men who were lousy in bed. And some men who were good in bed, but were lousy men."

"Just a good, decent man who treated you well," Willow said.

"Do fathers count?"

"No!" cried Willow. "It has to be a man you could have sex with if you wanted to. No relatives." She laughed. "Come on, you must have known one man that you'll always remember was good to you."

Frannie laughed too. "Okay, okay, I've got you now. I would have to say Adam Malone. I met him right after I joined the organization. I moved into his building and we met at the elevator. I dropped a box of books and he helped me pick them up. He truly was the kindest man. We dated for six months, but I still had a lot of trust issues and I never let him get close to me. I wouldn't go to bed with him. It took me two years after the rape to go to bed with anybody. But he was really good to me. I sometimes wonder what might have been."

"You've still got trust issues if he was the last kind man you've ever met," Willow said bluntly. Sara and Frannie had come to accept that Willow said what was on her mind, holding nothing back.

"I'm not denying it," Frannie spoke frankly. "After I got raped all I could think about was revenge. I mistakenly thought the organization would help me with that but that isn't what they're about. I was getting ready for it, though. I stepped up my training in judo. I bought a gun and learned how to use it. Like a fool I would walk through the alley where he had attacked me. I was really disappointed when it was some other woman who got the chance to blow him away."

"You were in a bad place," said Sara.

"Yeah, damaged goods," said Frannie.

"Is that how you think of yourself," asked Willow. "As damaged goods?"

"No, not really. Some days I don't think I'll ever get past it. When I date a man I put up walls between us. As soon as he starts getting possessive and wants to make us exclusive, I run. I'm still working on it."

Sara knew that about Frannie but had never thought she would admit it. "The basketball player you dated in New York. He fell in love with you, didn't he?"

"Shelton," Frannie said almost nostalgically. "I take it back, Adam Malone wasn't the last kind man I met. Shelton was very good to me."

"Then you were not exactly truthful when you said you couldn't go out with Erik Sutherland because you don't want Melissa to be hurt if you two should break up," Willow surmised. "You won't go out with him because he touches something inside of you. You're afraid he's going to be one of those men who'll want to protect you. And you're Frannie Anise. You don't need their stinkin' protection!"

"That's right, I don't!"

"And you say your mother is a *psychiatrist?* Why haven't *you* ever been on her couch?"

"Well, go on and speak your mind!" Frannie shouted.

"I will!" Willow shouted back.

Sara stopped in her tracks and stared at them. "Stop it! Stop shouting like that. You're sisters, and this is a public road."

Willow and Frannie laughed.

"She's letting her life slip away without taking the risk of falling in love," Willow accused Frannie. "She's only half living."

"What has taking risks gotten you?" Frannie asked. "Two divorces!"

"Two divorces and a dead child," Willow said uncompromisingly. "But hell if I'm going to quit trying altogether. I'd sooner go to bed with the next man that comes along rather than give up on trying to find love."

"Hello, ladies, who's the doll with the beautiful gams?" Joe Rizzo called as he slowed his pickup next to them. Joe smiled, showing good white teeth in a tanned face. His thick, wavy dark brown hair had gray streaks throughout but it hadn't lost its luster.

The ladies trained their eyes on him. Sara and Frannie were amused. Willow was intrigued. Sara laughed and said, "Good morning to you, too, Joe."

"Good morning, good morning," Joe cried. "Now that the niceties are over with, introduce me to the goddess."

Sara gave Willow an askance look. Willow smiled her consent.

"Joe Rizzo," Sara said. "This is Dr. Willow Quigley of Seattle. She's staying with us for a few days."

Joe held out his big paw to Willow. She stepped up to the driver's side door and shook his hand. "Pleased to meet you, Dr. Quigley," Joe said. He'd cleverly offered her his left hand to shake so that she would be induced to offer *her* left hand. He got a good look at it. There was no wedding band on the ring finger.

"A pleasure, Mr. Rizzo," Willow said.

Joe smiled broadly. He loved the sound of her voice. "Say that again?"

Willow thought he might be hard of hearing. A

shame because he was definitely good-looking in a weathered cowboy kind of way. He had laugh lines around his brown eyes, a nice size honker which she liked, and a nice mouth, the lower lip fuller than the top. "I said, it's a pleasure to meet you, Mr. Rizzo."

"You don't have to shout," Joe said. "I heard you the first time, I just liked how it sounded so much, I wanted to hear it again."

He finally let go of her hand, but didn't seem in any hurry to get going. "It's Saturday night."

"Not yet, it's still morning," said Willow.

"It's going to get dark sometime," Joe said. "How about you and I going dancing?"

Sara and Frannie were having a hard time controlling their laughter. Here was the biggest senior Casanova in the county asking a six-foot-tall black woman out on a date while widows who'd been waiting to snag him for years were left high and dry!

Willow must have heard them snickering behind her back because she turned sharply and gave them a withering look. They immediately snapped-to and put on straight faces.

"I don't know you from Adam," Willow told Joe. "How do I know you'll be safe with me?"

Joe had to think for a second. Then he laughed with gusto. "I'm hoping that I won't be, pretty lady."

"Okay," said Willow. "Pick me up at Sara's house at eight."

"You've got it." Joe sighed with contentment before taking his foot off the brakes. "Have a nice day, ladies!"

"You too, you old pervert!" Frannie yelled.

They could hear Joe's laughter as he sped up.

"You're really going out with a man you just met?" Frannie asked Willow as they continued their walk.

"Look," said Willow. "You two obviously know him. He's picking me up at Sara's house so you'll know whom I'm with and where we're going because I will tell you before we leave. Plus, he has a full head of hair, clean teeth and fingernails, and a great smile. How tall is he, by the way?"

"About your height, give or take an inch," Sara told her.

"That's good enough."

"But we won't hold you to your word," Frannie said, smiling.

"What word?"

"You said you would sooner sleep with the next man who came along rather than stop trying to find love," Frannie reminded her.

"Hey," said Willow. "It's been three months since I had any. He'd better watch out!"

"I've never seen him in black socks and sandals," Sara offered up helpfully.

"That cinches it," Willow said. "He's *mine.*"

Later that day, Elizabeth, who had begun working at a hospital in Santa Rosa and was no longer helping out at the bookstore, came in unexpectedly to talk with Sara. Frannie was busy doing children's hour in the children's section while two other employees worked in the coffeehouse area and the bookstore area, respectively.

Sara took Elizabeth into her office and closed the door. She gestured for Elizabeth to have a seat, leaned against the corner of the desk, and gave Elizabeth her attention.

"I received an e-mail from a friend in Johannesburg,"

Elizabeth told her. "He said he was e-mailing me using another person's computer because someone broke into his house and stole his computer. I might have thought nothing of it, but this is a special friend."

The girl glanced down as though she'd done something shameful.

Sara's voice was calm when she asked, "Someone you were dating?"

"Yes," Elizabeth said softly, her eyes still downcast.

"Elizabeth, please look at me. Is there more you want to tell me?"

"I think I might have told him where I am," Elizabeth said regretfully. "But I can't check my old e-mails because I used the computer at the public library when I wrote him."

"How long ago was this?" Sara asked, keeping her tone level.

"Five days ago."

"Five days since you e-mailed him with what could possibly be your location, or five days since he wrote to tell you his computer had been stolen?"

"Five days since he wrote *me*."

Sara panicked, but she schooled her features so that Elizabeth wouldn't know how upset she was. She didn't want two panicked people on her hands. Speaking softly, she said, "Listen, Elizabeth, you stay right there. I've got to go talk to Frannie for a moment."

Elizabeth nodded her acquiescence. There was a sad aspect in her dark eyes.

Once Sara was in the corridor, she shut the door and hurried to the outer store where Frannie was sitting in a bright red rocking chair reading a story to around fifteen children whose ages ranged from two to six.

Sara was always touched by their rapt faces when Frannie read to them. She was the one who usually entertained them so she didn't often get the opportunity to simply watch.

She had no patience for it this afternoon, though. Elizabeth's whereabouts may have been compromised and they needed to act quickly in order to safeguard her. However, normalcy was also important. She thought it best not to interrupt Frannie. She knew the story, and Frannie was very close to finishing it.

Five minutes later, Frannie was hugging tykes and receiving compliments from parents who were always grateful when their children sat still for more than thirty minutes while they perused the bookstore's shelves.

As soon as Frannie extricated herself from tykes and parents, Sara walked up to her, took her by the arm, and whispered, "I believe that someone might know where Elizabeth is." While they were walking across the store to the office, she explained the situation and by the time they reached the office it had been decided that they needed to get Elizabeth out of town right away.

Elizabeth was still sitting in the office, a worried expression on her face. "I've done wrong, haven't I?" she asked.

"Negative thinking isn't good for women of action," Sara told her. "It makes our legs leaden. We need to move."

"I can pack in under five minutes," Elizabeth said.

"We're not going back to the house," Sara told her. "We're getting in my car and leaving right now."

She was picking up her shoulder bag with her cell phone in it, and her laptop as she spoke. "Frannie, you'll sit up front with me. Elizabeth you'll lie down in the back. Let's go."

Frannie collected her shoulder bag from the locker in the office and, with Elizabeth between them, they walked down the corridor to the outer store. "Linda!" Sara called to the attractive twenty-five-year-old woman. Linda Ramirez was standing behind the counter in the coffeehouse section, but she was not serving anyone at the moment. She hurried over to her boss.

"Yes, Sara?"

"I need you to close tonight."

Linda smiled. She was eager and competent, two things Sara liked in an employee.

"No problem," Linda said.

"Thank you," said Sara. "Enjoy your weekend."

At the car, Sara unlocked the doors, and everyone got in as she'd earlier instructed.

Elizabeth, truly nervous now, had started crying silently. "I should have told you as soon as I heard from him," she said, sniffling. "But I didn't think anything of it. Things get stolen all the time. Then, I read a novel about a physicist's computer getting stolen with all of his files on it. They stole the modem, and everything was on it. I don't know, I thought that if somebody was really looking for me, and they found out Samuel and I were lovers, they might steal his computer to see if I'd contacted him."

"You came to us," Sara said as she pulled the Mustang onto the main street. "That's what counts. With any luck, no one is looking for you. What we're doing now is only a precaution."

"I'm sorry," Elizabeth said, inconsolable. "You and Frannie have been so good to me and I return your kindness like this."

"Listen to me," Sara cried vehemently. "You're a twenty-two-year-old kid who's just trying to live her life. You didn't do anything to be in this predicament in the first place. None of this is your fault! Now, I want you to relax and close your eyes. We're taking you to a safe house in San Francisco. From there you will be given another identity and your life *will* be your own again, soon. Do you trust me?"

"Yes, Sara, I trust you," said Elizabeth in a tearful voice.

Sara gripped the steering wheel. Inside, she was a mass of nerves but control was something she'd learned a long time ago. First, you dealt with the situation at hand, then, in your leisure, you could fall to pieces.

Frannie was on the phone to the safe house in San Francisco. As she drove them out of town, Sara heard her say, "This is Francesca Anise. My partner is Sara Minton. We believe that the identity of our charge has been compromised. We're bringing her in." Frannie paused, listening. "It usually takes an hour and fifteen minutes." After another pause, she said, "A 2007 red Mustang convertible with a white ragtop."

She hung up the phone. "They'll meet us halfway and escort us in."

"Good," said Sara. She concentrated on her driving. She knew that the organization already had her chosen route to the safe house. Someone was probably getting into one of those black SUVs they were so fond of and hitting the road. She felt a boost of confidence from that image, alone.

"Willow's going to be upset that we didn't swing by and pick her up," Frannie joked.

"And have her miss her date with Mr. Smooth?" Sara said, smiling.

In the backseat, Elizabeth was somewhat comforted by their chatter.

A silver Mercedes stayed three car lengths behind them. The two men in the car wore twin mirrored sunglasses, black jackets, jeans and black motorcycle boots. The outfit reminded them of the getup Arnold Schwarzenegger had worn in *Terminator 2: Judgment Day*. It was their favorite movie in which the California governor had starred.

"I told you it was her," said the driver.

"She," his partner said. "The correct word is 'she'."

"Who gives a damn. We've got her now."

"Where are they going?"

"We'll know soon enough. It was tough tracking her down with just the name of the bookstore. But I knew if we were patient, she would show up here."

"She kept a low profile. No one we asked had ever heard of her."

"Of course she kept a low profile. She knew Mr. Oswald wanted her head on a pike. I would lay low, too."

The driver turned to smile briefly at the man in the passenger seat. It was like looking into a mirror. They looked very much alike. If a plastic surgeon were to place them side by side on matching operating tables in order to make them perfect matches he would not have to do a thing because they were already identical in every way except one: Sean was a quarter of an inch taller than John.

Sean, the driver, was six-two. He and his brother,

KIMANI PRESS™

An Important Message from the Publisher

Dear Reader,

Because you've chosen to read one of our fine novels, I'd like to say "thank you"! And, as a special way to say thank you, I'm offering to send you two Kimani Romance™ novels and two surprise gifts – absolutely FREE! These books will keep it real with true-to-life African-American characters that turn up the heat and sizzle with passion.

Please enjoy the free books and gifts with our compliments...

Linda Gill

Publisher, Kimani Press

Peel off Seal and Place Inside...

...d like to send you two free books to introduce you to our ...line – Kimani Romance™! These novels feature strong, sexy women and African-American heroes that are charming, loving and true. Our authors fill each page with exceptional dialogue, exciting plot twists, and enough sizzling romance to keep you riveted until the very end!

KIMANI ROMANCE ... LOVE'S ULTIMATE DESTINATION

Your two books have a combined cover price of $11.98 in the U.S. and $13.98 in Canada, but are yours **FREE!** We'll even send you two wonderful surprise gifts. You can't lose!

THE EDITOR'S "THANK YOU" FREE GIFTS INCLUDE:

▶ Two NEW Kimani Romance™ Novels

▶ Two exciting surprise gifts

YES! I have placed my Editor's "Thank You" Free Gifts seal in the space provided at right. Please send me 2 FREE books, and my 2 FREE Mystery Gifts. I understand that I am under no obligation to purchase anything further, as explained on the back of this card.

PLACE
FREE GIFTS
SEAL
HERE

168 XDL ELWZ   368 XDL ELXZ

FIRST NAME   LAST NAME

ADDRESS

APT.#   CITY

STATE/PROV.   ZIP/POSTAL CODE

Thank You!

The Reader Service — Here's How It Works:

John, were blond with ice-blue eyes. Whippet-thin, they did not buy into the Hollywood image of pumped-up males even though their hero was Schwarzenegger. They believed the streamlined body was the perfect form for ease of movement. In their line of work, assassination, they were often called upon to move quickly after the deed was done. A lumbering muscle-bound body would be a hindrance to a quick getaway.

They were also very health-conscious and put only whole foods in their bodies. Holistic medicine was used in the case of illness, and their lips never touched wine. Their mother, the dietician, whom they had poisoned with strychnine when they were fifteen, would be proud of them.

After they had been following the red Mustang for fifteen minutes, it was apparent that its driver was leaving town. "This could be problematic," said Sean, worried.

"It certainly isn't in line with our original plan to murder her in her bed," John agreed. "Speed up. You're too far behind."

"I am not too far behind!" Sean was upset because John invariably complained about his driving, as if *his* license hadn't been revoked in two countries. "And if you want to drive, you can as soon as you get your driver's license."

It was a bone of contention between them. They were murderers and yet Sean who was older by fifteen seconds insisted on their obeying the laws of the countries they worked in. You can never be too careful, Sean often warned. You don't invite the attention of law enforcement agencies. What if you were pulled over for speeding and the officer learned you don't have a license? You would be locked up and then they would learn that you're wanted in four countries. That wouldn't be good, little brother.

John hated it when he called him little brother.

"She drives like a bat out of hell," Sean complained.

"It's her country, she can get away with disobeying the laws," John said testily.

The Mustang led them through several small towns and then they got on US-101, going south toward San Rafael. "She's headed to San Francisco," Sean predicted.

"We can't let her get there, she's going to ground again," John said frantically. "I don't want to waste another day looking for her. We've got to take her out before she gets there."

"On a public highway?" Sean said skeptically. "Highway Patrol are all over the place. We just passed a patrol car, or didn't you notice?"

"We don't have to run into her, you idiot. If you drive steadily, I can shoot a tire out. The crash will probably kill her."

"I don't like it," Sean protested. "You can never be sure it took. It's not as if we can stick around to make certain she died."

"We don't have to stick around. We can read about it in next day's news or see it on TV on the nightly news."

"No," was Sean's final answer. "I want to get close and personal. Make sure it's done to Mr. Oswald's satisfaction. The old geezer won't pay us if it isn't done right."

"Done correctly," John said, peevishly.

Sean's lips tightened in irritation, but he didn't say anything.

* * *

Jody Easterbrook and Caryn Dodd left the mansion in Pacific Heights as soon as they received their orders. Jody drove the black SUV with the bulletproof windows and enough horsepower under the hood to give the racers in the Indy 500 a run for their money.

Both were African-American women in their late twenties who had past histories with the armed forces and civilian police. Unlike Sara and Frannie who had not been trained in combat, Jody and Caryn were experts in hand-to-hand, weaponry and reconnaissance. They belonged to an arm of the organization that the other operatives hoped they'd never have to call upon but were thankful to have at their disposal when they needed them.

In the Mustang, Sara checked her rearview mirror once more and announced, "There's a silver Mercedes that's been behind us ever since we left Glen Ellen."

Frannie didn't turn to look behind them. She used the mirrors. "Yeah, I noticed it. Don't get paranoid yet. We're not the only ones on 101 that are headed to San Francisco. It's a big city."

It was too late to tell Sara not to be paranoid. She'd been way past that ever since Elizabeth had confessed she might have told someone where she was. This was new to her. Over one hundred missions, and none of the charges had revealed their location to anyone. She didn't blame Elizabeth. She was sure that it had been a slip-up on her part. She had known she was supposed to be very careful. Anyone could make a mistake. Unfortunately, this mistake could get them all killed.

In the silver Mercedes, Sean prepared to slow down. Ahead, cars were entering the toll booth.

"Here's our chance," John said. "If she gets across the bridge she can get lost in the city. Sean, let me shoot a tire out now before she slows down."

"No, John!"

John withdrew his gun, an automatic with an elongated barrel. He'd paid a pretty penny to have it custom-made. It was highly accurate and packed quite a punch. He could feel the recoil all the way up his arm to his shoulder.

"I'm doing this for you, Sean," he said as he took aim.

Coming in the opposite direction, Caryn spotted the red Mustang. Taking her field glasses, she identified Sara Minton as the driver and Frannie Anise in the passenger seat.

"Got 'em," she told Jody. She scanned the area, and that's when she saw a man with a gun leaning out the window of a Mercedes, preparing to fire. However, the driver of the Mercedes started swerving, and the shooter could not get off a shot.

"Perp at twelve o'clock," Caryn said as she smoothly raised a rifle with a scope on it and aimed at the shoulder of the shooter. She fired and scored a solid hit with one round. The man dropped the weapon out the window.

Bedlam in the Mercedes. Seeing his brother shot, Sean panicked and ran into the RV in front of him. He reached for his brother, but since John had taken off his seat belt to get a better aim he went headfirst through the windshield and died on impact.

Sean, in agony now because his brother was dead, nonetheless had to move fast in order to escape before the authorities came to investigate the crash. He'd been wearing his seat belt and except for some minor cuts from flying glass, was not hurt.

He got out of the car and ran.

In the Mustang, Frannie's phone rang.

"Hello, Frannie here."

"Frannie, the way has been cleared. Come on in," said Jody.

In the black SUV, Caryn was shaken. She had meant only to disable the perpetrator, not kill him. She could reason that the accident had killed him, not her marksmanship.

However, the man was still dead. Even from here, she could tell that.

Chapter 11

The mansion in Pacific Heights had been built in 1917. The entry was through a two-story atrium that had meticulously carved sandstone columns and an Italian marble floor. Its owner was the media magnate Sara had met at the Amsterdam Avenue apartment six years ago when she'd been recruited by the organization.

She allowed the organization to use it as their Northern California headquarters.

Sara, Frannie and Elizabeth, who had been kept waiting for nearly two hours in the living room, were trying to digest what operatives Jody Easterbrook and Caryn Dodd were telling them. "He had you in his sights, and he was preparing to fire when the driver of his car started swerving as if to prevent his being able to shoot," Caryn said. She was of medium height and weight and wore her light brown hair in a sleek ponytail.

"That's strange," Sara said. "If they were working together, why would the driver try to interfere with his aim?".

"The dead guy's name is John Gamble. He goes by several aliases in several countries. But that's his true identity. We've been told that he worked with his twin brother, Sean. Siblings are not known for peaceful co-existence. Maybe they disagreed on methodology. At any rate, when I shot the gun out of John's hand, the driver, Sean, we believe, lost control of the car and ran into an RV. Physics did the rest. Immovable force, and all that. John went through the windshield. He was pronounced dead on the scene."

"Sean got away," Frannie said.

"Yes, but don't worry, we have several operatives on it. We'll find him," Jody said. She was tall, dark-skinned and muscular. She was almost bald, her black, natural hair was cut so close to her scalp. "If he's smart he'll go to ground, mourn his brother and give up any hope of getting to Elizabeth."

"He is an evil man," Elizabeth said of Horace Oswald, owner of the gold-mining operation her murdered father used to work for and the man responsible for his death.

"Why can't he just let it go?"

"Because you made him look bad," Jody said. "It's not the money he had to get up off of in order to comply with the government's new regulations regarding the treatment of his workers. He's filthy rich, and he won't even feel it. But he did feel the humiliation of being called on the carpet by a slip of a girl like you. He'll never live that down."

"Evil is incomprehensible," Sara said. "Don't tax

your brain trying to understand evil men's motivations. What counts is that you're safe and now that we know where the threat originated, we can do something about it." She got to her feet. It had been three and a half hours since their flight from Glen Ellen. It had been four in the afternoon when Elizabeth had come into the store and given them the bad news. Now it was almost 8:00 p.m., the time Jason was supposed to pick her up for dinner at Gary and Kat Pruitt's home.

"Are we done here?" she asked Jody and Caryn.

Jody and Caryn rose, too. "Yeah, you're free to go," Caryn said.

"What about Sean Gamble?" Frannie wanted to know. "He's still at large."

"We'll have operatives watching over you 24-7 until he's caught," Jody informed her. "You will be escorted home. From there, just follow your normal routine. We don't think he has a reason to target you. He must know that Elizabeth has been relocated. She's his target. He will look for her here in San Francisco. That is, if he even continues to look. He must know that the authorities are after him."

"And I'm the one who shot his brother. He had to have noticed that the gunfire didn't come from the Mustang," Caryn added.

Sara, whose brain needed time to absorb everything, wasn't sure of anything at this point. However, she realized that Jody and Caryn were being optimistic so as not to panic them further. She was still slightly shaky inside from the thought that someone had had a gun trained on her and if not for Caryn and Jody's timely arrival one of them, she, Frannie or Elizabeth, or all of them, could have been killed.

All she wanted right now was to be in Jason's arms.

She went and hugged Elizabeth. "Take care, honey. And don't worry, I'll pack up your things and send them to this address."

Elizabeth had tears in her eyes. "I don't know how to thank you for looking after me."

"No thanks needed," Sara said softly. She let go of her so that Frannie could hug her goodbye. Elizabeth thanked Frannie as well.

"If you want to thank me," said Frannie, "just be happy."

The two of them were about the same height and weight, and Elizabeth was able to look her straight in the eyes. "I will try."

On the drive to Glen Ellen, Sara and Frannie were both pretty quiet at the beginning of the journey. Sara simply concentrated on her driving. Frannie sat looking down at the cell phone in her hand.

For some unfathomable reason, she had an overwhelming urge to phone Erik Sutherland. Why was it that when she was in need of solace, the first face that appeared in her mind's eye was his? It was ridiculous. But, then, her life was ridiculous. She'd gotten up this morning with nothing more exciting on her schedule than reading stories to small children and had ended up almost getting killed. Excuse her if she needed a little physical proof that she was still alive!

"You know what I want to do?" she said aloud.

"Go jump Erik Sutherland's bones?" said Sara.

Frannie laughed. "You're spooky sometimes, you know that?"

"Nah, I was thinking the same thing. All I want to do is be in Jason's arms."

"We're gonna look like a couple of hootchies to the operatives keeping an eye on us if we head straight for Erik and Jason once we get home," Frannie said.

"They said to go about our normal routines. Besides, they're women. They know how it is, and even if they don't, I really don't care. When I phoned Jason while we were stuck waiting on Jody and Caryn, he was adamant about my coming to him as soon as I got back, no matter how late it was. I'm going."

She had also phoned Gary and Kat and told them she wouldn't be able to make their dinner party. Gary had understood. He was one of the organization's attorneys there in Northern California.

"Well, I'm phoning Erik," Frannie said. She had to look in her wallet for the card he'd given her to get his number. She'd never phoned him before. "Try not to listen in," she joked as she dialed the number.

Sara smiled. She was happy to see Frannie taking a risk on love.

"He's probably not at home," Frannie said as the phone rang in her ear. "He's probably on a date with a blonde with legs up to here." She gestured to her chin.

Erik answered on the fifth ring. He must have seen her name on the caller ID because he said, "I don't believe it. Frannie Anise. To what do I owe the pleasure of this call?"

"I was wondering if you'd like some company tonight," Frannie said boldly.

"I'd love some. Melissa finally communicated with her mom and she surprised me by wanting to spend the weekend with her. So, I'm all alone."

"Good for her," Frannie said sincerely.

"Yeah, I think so, too," Erik said. "When can I expect you? Or I'd be happy to pick you up, if you want."

"No, I'll drive. See you around ten."

"I'll chill the wine."

"All right. Bye."

"Bye."

Frannie closed the cell phone and looked over at Sara. "He's thanking his lucky stars right about now."

"Probably getting out of his easy chair and getting into the shower. Your voice was dripping with sex."

Frannie smiled. "I'm gonna make him sing like choirs of angels."

Sara laughed.

At that very moment, in Glen Ellen, Willow was walking slowly to the front door of Sara's house to answer the bell. Not anticipating that she might begin a social life while on a mission of mercy, she had brought only one dressy outfit with her.

It was a sleeveless beaded tweed dress in pale brown with various shaped beads around the neckline and around the waist. At six feet and just under two hundred pounds, Willow had a long graceful line to her body. Very nice arms, a flat stomach, shapely hips and gorgeous legs from all the walking she'd done in her lifetime.

She was a beautiful woman. There was just a lot of her to go around, which intimidated most men. She hoped Joe Rizzo wasn't one of them.

Her fears were allayed as soon as she opened the door and saw him standing there.

He was wearing an off-white tailored blazer, a white cotton shirt open at the collar, a pair of jeans (ironed to submission with a sharp crease in them as evidence of his hard work), and a pair of polished brown cowboy boots. He held a dozen red roses in his right hand.

His eyes raked over her appreciatively. "I'm glad I took my heart medication before I left home."

Willow laughed delightedly. "So am I."

He handed her the roses. "You look beautiful. I hope you like roses."

"Love them." She briefly inhaled their heady fragrance, glanced up at him because he was a couple inches taller than she was in her flats, and said, "Come in and sit down for a few minutes. I want to put these in water. I would ask Sara or Frannie to do it for me but they had business out of town. And I don't want them to wither while I'm out dancing the night away with you."

Joe stepped inside and watched her turn and walk toward the back of the house. Now, that was a backside a man could grab hold of. Not that he would actually grab it without her permission. Frannie might jokingly refer to him as a pervert, but he was a gentleman through and through. No harm in looking, though. He looked so long he almost forgot to close the door behind him.

He was just closing it when Willow reentered the room with the roses in a vase she'd found in a cabinet above the refrigerator in the kitchen. She set the vase in the center of the dining room table then went to join Joe.

He was still standing by the door.

"Better take a jacket," he said helpfully, looking at her lovely bare arms. "It gets cold here at night."

Willow had already put her jacket and her purse on the foyer table. "Got it covered," she said brightly.

She walked up to Joe and kissed him on the mouth. Joe didn't waste time being taken aback. That wasn't his style. When offered something good, he accepted before the offer was withdrawn. He gently kissed her back. They fit quite well together. His strong arms went around her and pulled her closer. Willow tilted her head more to the left and the kiss deepened. When they parted they were a bit breathless, but neither of them had any doubts about their mutual attraction.

"I really hate to have to wait until the end of a date to find out whether the guy's a good kisser or not," Willow explained. "You know your way around a woman, Joe Rizzo."

Joe smiled. The crinkles at the corners of his eyes became more noticeable when he smiled. He hadn't enjoyed a kiss that much in a very long time. "I'm fifty-nine. It took years, but I finally learned."

"I'm forty-seven and I'm still learning," Willow told him. "I'm looking forward to finding out what you can teach me."

Joe felt like dancing a jig as they left the house, he was so happy.

When Sara and Frannie got to the house, they waved to the operatives in the van that had followed them from San Francisco. Then they hurried into the house and went straight to their bedrooms where they showered, dressed and headed back out.

Sara got into her Mustang. She'd left it in the driveway.

Frannie had to get her baby-blue vintage model out of the garage.

That's the only reason Sara beat her tearing out of the driveway.

Frannie watched the red taillights of Sara's car disappearing in the distance as she backed her car out of the garage. Once on the street, she tore out of there as enthusiastically as Sara had done.

The doorbell rang at the Hacienda at a quarter past ten that night. Jason was in his office doing some work on the computer when it resounded throughout the house.

Barefoot, wearing only a pair of jeans and a T-shirt, he got up at once and hurried to the door. He had been worried about Sara ever since her call. Didn't she know his imagination ran wild whenever she did something like that? Okay, so she couldn't tell him everything that she was up to, but come on! Throw a dog a bone. Something!

He snatched the door open, prepared to start in on her when he got one look at her and caved in. He could tell she was exhausted. Perhaps not physically, but mentally worn out. Her golden-hued eyes were appealing to him for comfort.

He pulled her into his arms, lifting her off the floor, kicked the door shut with his foot and carried her a few feet inside where he set her down and hugged her, really hugged her, until they were both groaning with pleasure.

"Baby, I was worried about you."

"I only phoned to cancel our date," she said softly.

"Yeah, but you know that's not all there was to it. After everything we've been through, a cryptic call like that is sure to make me nuts."

Sara peered up into his eyes. "It was Mary. She got the call from the University of California sooner than we expected and Frannie and I had to take her to catch a plane to Los Angeles." Luckily, she'd remembered he knew Elizabeth as Mary.

That was the cover story they had been told to tell

anyone who asked about their sudden rush out of town and Elizabeth's disappearance. She hated lying to Jason. Soon, though, she would never have to lie to him again. She was going to contact Eunice via e-mail as soon as she returned home and tell her she was quitting.

Jason, looking deeply into her eyes, didn't believe her, but he'd sworn he would try to be patient and he didn't intend to go back on his word. "Okay," he said, and bent to kiss her hard on the mouth.

His body no longer sore from the recent excavations in the southern vineyard, he had no problem picking her up and carrying her to his bedroom. He was in a scary mood. Scary because he felt angry with her for not telling him the whole truth and yet he wanted her so badly right now, he felt as if he could make love to her until they both passed out from exhaustion.

Sara clung to him, her nose in the side of his neck that smelled of the spicy aftershave she was so fond of. "I love you," she whispered. "I love you more at this moment than I've ever loved anyone in my life."

Jason's heart stood still at that statement. He knew now that something had gone terribly wrong. It wasn't the words themselves that had been so intense. It had been the sound of her voice. It made him ache inside with longing. He longed to ease the pain he'd heard in her voice. And dispel the fear.

In the bedroom, he put her down and while she stood at the foot of the bed, he went over and pressed a button on the CD player. Roberta Flack's "The First Time Ever I Saw Your Face" filled the air.

It was their song. The moment he had realized Sara wanted him as much as he wanted her it had been playing over the stereo system. They were at Erica and Joshua's wedding here at the Hacienda. That was two years ago.

Turning back around, he began removing his clothes and tossing them onto the chair next to the door.

Soon, he was down to his boxers. Sara watched his striptease with a smile on her face. Except for removing her leather jacket with her car keys in the outside pocket, she had not made an effort to undress. She knew he liked doing that for her.

Sure enough, Jason gave her a crooked smile as he approached her and immediately went for the buttons on the front of her clinging shirtdress. The sleeveless dress was black, made of linen, and its hem fell three inches above her knees. She wasn't wearing hose, and her panties were exceptionally brief.

She wasn't wearing a bra which Jason discovered as soon as he got down to the third button on the dress front. He speeded up the unbuttoning. She made a provocative picture as she stood before him, the tips of her full breasts pointing north and her hip-hugging see-through panties hiding nothing at all.

He removed his boxers in a split second and kick-dropped them somewhere behind him. The dress was tossed onto the chair and he dropped to his knees in front of her.

Kissing her warm, fragrant belly, he hardened further, as he got closer to his goal, her sex. He prodded her to stand with her legs apart. Sara willingly complied. Then he bent and kissed the top of her sex through her panties. Sara's vaginal muscles clenched and unclenched with sexual stimulation.

Jason pulled down her panties. She stepped out of them, still in her high-heeled black leather mules. So now they were both naked. Jason on his knees and she standing with her legs spread apart and waiting to see what he would do next.

Her legs were against the side of the bed. Jason pushed her backward with just enough force to induce her to sit on the bed. Then, he moved forward and feasted on her, her long shapely legs framing his head. He gently pressed her thighs farther apart and delved deeper.

The sensation was so intensely delicious to Sara that she could not help moaning as wave after wave of sheer unadulterated pleasure coursed through her with every lap of his talented tongue. Her shoes fell to the floor.

If the French invented this form of pleasure, then bless them!

She was thinking of learning the language to honor them. She thought of one expression that was appropriate to the moment, *sans souci,* peace of mind, or without worry. Even in the midst of hedonistic passions such as these she was at peace with Jason. In his arms she didn't worry about a thing because she knew she was safe.

Jason felt it on his tongue when she climaxed. He did not rise. He stayed with her until she came down, and then he got up, sheathed his penis in a condom and entered her. Still, that strange mood had hold of him and his thrusts were powerful and sure.

Her cries of amazement at being able to become aroused once again and peak once more fed his fever until he felt he could continue all night long. It had never been like this between them. It had always been exciting and fully satisfying but tonight there was an added dimension to their lovemaking that puzzled him. And frightened him a little. She wanted him to come close to hurting her. She was so needy of closeness.

He couldn't explain it, but he could definitely sense her emotions.

Down to the bone. That's how she wanted it, and that's how he gave it to her.

When he finally came, he screamed with release. Sara clung to him, her legs wrapped tightly around him.

She felt his release and exulted in it. For a moment, she wished he had not used a condom and he could have filled her with his seed. She craved utter closeness tonight and didn't want anything between them.

Spent, they turned to face each other. He pulled her into the crook of his arm and held her close. Looking into her eyes, he said, "One day soon you're going to have to tell me what happened to you today. You're not the same woman you were yesterday."

Chapter 12

By ten-twenty, Erik was sweating bullets and Frannie still wasn't there. He had showered, shaved, flossed and brushed his teeth, including his tongue, twice, and now he was wondering if he ought to phone her.

He paced the floor of the living room because it was the closest room to the front door. When she rang the bell, he could get to the door in a matter of seconds. Since she'd phoned he'd been wracking his brain trying to figure out what had made her call. He hadn't seen her since the day they'd done the root excavations.

She had been aloof but cordial when she and Willow brought him lunch and told him they were having it picnic-style. He was putty in their hands as they spread the blanket on the ground there in the vineyard, directed him to sit and then proceeded to unpack the picnic basket.

Frannie sat on his right and Willow on his left.

"What's your desire, honey?" Willow asked. "Are you a ham-and-cheese man, or a roast-beef fellow?"

"Roast beef, please," he said, and thanked her when she handed him the thick sandwich that was neatly wrapped in wax paper. There were also crisp dill pickles, fresh fruit and homemade lemonade.

They ate in silence a few minutes, with him stealing glances at Frannie, and Willow keeping a sharp eye on them as if she were there to chaperone or something. A few minutes later he would be grateful for Willow's wisdom.

"This is delicious," he said of the sandwich.

"Frannie prepared the meal," Willow told him.

He could have sworn that Frannie blushed when Willow said that. The golden-brown skin of her cheeks actually got darker and she looked at him demurely with those dark brown eyes of hers. Eyes he'd been dreaming about ever since the night of Melissa's party when they'd gotten along so well and then she'd announced she couldn't date him because she didn't want Melissa to be hurt if things didn't work out between them. Oh, and that he wasn't ready to date a black woman. Whatever that meant.

He'd still been ticked off about it the day of the excavations.

"Well, it's delicious," he said again.

"It's not as if I killed the cow and butchered it," Frannie said. She gave him a disarming smile. "I didn't even cook the roast beef, I got it from the deli. I'm really not much of a cook."

"I can cook," he'd said. "I enjoy cooking. You ladies should come to dinner sometime. I'll make you my special lasagna."

"What's special about it?" Frannie asked as she bit into her ham sandwich. He watched her chew and to his horror found that it turned him on. What's more, Frannie was aware of the growing bulge in his jeans. She lowered her gaze to it, smiled, and raised it to his eyes again.

He cleared his throat. "That's a secret. To get it you'd either have to marry me or torture me."

"Isn't marriage torture?" Frannie said jokingly.

"Mine was," he told her, smiling.

"It wasn't all bad, was it? She gave you Melissa."

"Okay, I'll concede that" was his reply.

Willow suddenly grabbed her sandwich and glass of lemonade, got to her feet and announced, "Sorry, children, I just remembered I need to make a phone call and I left my cell phone in my purse at the house. Carry on without me."

The expression in Frannie's eyes as she looked up at Willow was panicked.

Erik was happy to see he wasn't the only one who was feeling emotions. For a while Frannie's reactions had seemed too cool and detached to him.

But, now, in Willow's absence, and after realizing that Frannie was not entirely immune to him, he felt free to tell her exactly how he felt.

"I want you to go out with me," he said, looking her straight in the eyes.

She gave him an emphatic "No!"

Narrowing his eyes, he tried again. "Not only do I want it, but Melissa wants it. She's always talking you up to me. I couldn't forget you if I wanted to."

"You haven't tried hard enough," she told him.

"I think about you all the time. I dream about you, for God's sake. I wake up with your scent in my memory."

She had simply sat there looking at him as if he had lost his mind. After a minute or two, she said, "Grow up, Erik. You want me because I said you couldn't have me. If I had thrown myself at you, you would have been through with me by now."

"You wouldn't say that if you knew me. Contrary to what the rumor is around here, I didn't cheat on my wife. She cheated on me. I was faithful to her the entire time we were married. I don't cheat on the woman I love."

That had shocked her. He could see it in the depths of her eyes. Also in how she had stiffened, sat up straighter, and started fidgeting with the hem of her blouse. When she raised her eyes to his, he saw that she was fighting to regain her composure. "I'm not attracted to you, Erik."

"You're a liar," he said. "But, nice try."

She had refused to say anything else to him the remainder of their meal together but she didn't get up and storm off as he'd expected her to.

Now, she was supposed to be coming over here, for what? A booty call? He'd heard of them but had never participated in one. Her voice had sounded so sexy over the phone, and there had been no mistaking her intentions.

She wanted him.

He wanted her.

What could be wrong with that?

The doorbell rang.

On the other side of the door, Frannie nervously smoothed the skirt of her dress. It was short, red, long-sleeved, had a scoop-neck, and it clung to every curve of her body. She was not wearing hose. Under the dress she was only wearing a bra and panties. And being a good little girl, she had a change of underwear in her shoulder bag for later.

Over the dress, she was wearing her brown leather jacket. And on her feet were high-heeled brown leather mules.

Erik opened the door less than ten seconds after the bell stopped pealing.

"Hi," he said, reaching for her hand.

Frannie placed her hand in his, and he pulled her inside the house. He turned to face her as he shut the door. It locked automatically.

"Hi," Frannie said breathlessly. Erik looked devastatingly handsome. He was barefoot and had on a short-sleeve cotton T-shirt in pale green, and worn jeans. His biceps, chest and thigh muscles were bulging. She couldn't believe the transformation he'd undergone in two weeks' time. When she'd met him he had a soft belly and the beginnings of a double chin. Obviously digging holes and jogging had gotten rid of that. She hated men! Women suffered trying to lose weight and all men had to do was put in a bit more physical labor for a couple weeks, and look what happened!

Still holding on to her hand, Erik admired her in that dress. "Damn, you're beautiful!"

Frannie set her shoulder bag on the foyer table. "Thank you, you look pretty, too."

He helped her off with her jacket and took it and hung it in the foyer closet.

Frannie watched him walk away from her. He still had a conditioned athlete's behind. Slightly high and nicely molded on the sides. He was *wearing* those jeans!

She grabbed her shoulder bag from the foyer table

and put it on her shoulder. When he turned back around, she asked, "Where can I put this?"

His answer would tell her where his mind was. If he'd had many lovers he would know that a woman didn't want to have her purse too far away from her when she came over for more than dinner. There might be something in it she needed.

"There's no one else in the house," he said as he walked up to her and pulled her into his arms. "You can leave it anywhere you want to."

Wrong answer. He wasn't quite as sophisticated as she'd assumed.

Smiling up at him, she said, "What do you think this is?"

"It's our first date."

His reply shook her. The sincerity in his dark green eyes made her want to shake some sense into him. She thought she had better lay her cards on the table. "I want to make love to you."

Why did she have to say that? He looked happier than a fat cat in a fish market.

At that point, there was no stopping the big schlemiel. He swept her up in his arms and almost ran with her toward his bedroom. She wrapped her arms around his neck. "Erik, you haven't even kissed me yet."

He remedied that situation on the stairs. In the course of the kiss he gently set her down and she slipped down his body until he was bent all the way over, kissing her. She wound up lying on her back on the stairs with him on top of her, holding himself up with his powerful arms so as not to squash her like a bug.

She was pleasantly surprised by his ardor. She had thought that due to his eagerness he would kiss her hard and sloppily, slurping her up like some sweet treat he was only occasionally allowed to have. But, no, he kissed her with passion and gentleness. She melted. Melted!

As for Erik, he was in heaven. She tasted wonderful to him. So sweet that it made him want to cry. Their first kiss was everything that he imagined it would be.

They came up for air and looked intensely into each other's eyes. "I think I'm falling in love with you," he said softly.

Frannie, who had already been confused by his behavior, was now even more confused. What kind of male said that on the first date? She mentally shook herself.

This was supposed to be a one-night stand. All she wanted was sex. Did that make her a bad woman? She didn't want strings. She didn't want him declaring his love for her, or promising her the moon.

She squirmed out of his arms. "This was a mistake."

Her shoulder bag had fallen onto the stairs while they were kissing. She scooped it up and ran down the stairs, Erik right behind her.

"Frannie, what did I say? What did I do?"

She spun on her heels to face him. "Don't you get it, Erik? I came here to have sex with you, that's all! I didn't want romance. I just wanted to feel good for one night." Tears sprang to her eyes. "I can't use you like that. I like you too much."

He went to her and held her by the upper arms. "Why don't you want more from me? Is it because you don't think we'd be compatible? You're a hypocrite if that's what you think. You told me your parents were still together. Why couldn't it work between us?"

"Because I don't believe I can let a man get close

enough to me for real love after being brutalized by one. I was raped, Erik."

"Oh, God, no," Erik cried, and took her in his arms. Her body shook with sobs.

Erik held her as if he would never let her go, and when she peered up into his eyes she saw that he was crying too.

She pulled him down and gently kissed him. "I want you very much, but I'm afraid to get close to you. So, I'm going home." She let go of him, then collected her jacket.

He didn't try to stop her. However, he walked her to her car, held the door for her and securely closed it. Then he stepped back while she started the car, put it in gear and pulled out of his driveway. He stood and watched until the taillights of the Mustang disappeared.

The drama wasn't over for Frannie yet, though. When she was about a quarter of a mile down the road, her cell phone rang. She dug in her shoulder bag sitting next to her on the front seat. Once she got it open, she said, irritably, "Yeah, Frannie here!"

The voice was low, feminine, and fraught with tears. "Frannie, I'm sorry to bother you this late but I'm in trouble."

"Melissa?"

"Yeah."

"What's wrong? Has something happened to your mom?" Frannie couldn't imagine why Melissa would be calling her when she could have phoned her father if something had happened to her while she was with her mother. "Your dad told me you were spending the weekend with your mother."

"I lied," Melissa said. "I'm at a motel in Santa Rosa.

It's called the Pink Flamingo and it has pink Pepto-Bismol flamingoes everywhere. I'm standing near the front desk right now and there's a creepy man looking at me."

"What's the address?" Frannie didn't ask any more questions. She got the message loud and clear. Melissa had gone to a seedy motel with Danny Keener, wouldn't have sex with him and he'd abandoned her in Santa Rosa.

Melissa gave her the address.

"Are you all right?" Frannie asked after getting the address. She knew where it was. It was in the same part of town where she went to get her hair done. "Did he hurt you?"

"He didn't touch me," Melissa said, sounding stronger now, almost defiant. "I'll tell you all about it when you get here."

"Stay at the front desk in a well-lighted area," Frannie told her.

"I will, and thank you so much, Frannie. I love you!"

"I love you, too, sweetie. Hang tough." Frannie hung up the phone and pressed harder on the accelerator.

How could Erik have let his sixteen-year-old daughter pull a fast one on him? But a second later, she had absolved him of all wrongdoing. She had been sixteen once and had been as scheming and duplicitous as Melissa had been with her father. Parents did their best. Sometimes their best just wasn't good enough. Kids today were extremely sophisticated. She knew that Melissa had her own car, cell phone and a wallet full of credit cards. It was asking for trouble to provide a sixteen-year-old with all of those weapons of destruction.

To say nothing of Internet access. A kid could find

all kinds of ways to get into trouble on the World Wide
Web. She was just glad Melissa appeared to have her
head on straight. She had gone to a motel with Danny,
but had changed her mind about having sex with him
in the nick of time. Good for her.

Melissa was waiting exactly where she'd said she
would be. The motel was made up of several separate
units, all painted pink, and as Melissa had described, the
flamingo was its motif.

Frannie walked into the motel office and Melissa
flew into her arms. "Frannie, thank you for coming. I
knew I could count on you." They hurried out to the car,
Melissa talking all the way. "It was awful!" She paused
long enough until they were inside and Frannie had
started the car. "I thought I was in love with that creep.
Can you imagine?"

"No, not if you don't fill me in. Why is he suddenly
a creep? You were so in love with him a week ago."

Melissa turned toward her after she'd fastened her
seat belt. "Yesterday, Friday, I was getting my sixth
period books out of my locker when Tyler Gaines
walked up to me and told me not to go with Danny to
that roach motel. First off, I was shocked that he knew
what Danny and I were planning to do. I had Dad
fooled. I'd made up an e-mail from my mom in L.A.
over a week ago about how badly she wanted to see me.
Dad got the tickets for me online. Then I convinced him
to let Danny take me to the airport. It was easy. I think
Dad wanted me to feel like I was independent. After all,
I'm sixteen now. He doesn't want me growing up not
knowing how to take care of myself. I admit it, I used
his best intentions against him. Don't worry, I'm going
to confess everything when I get home." She breathed.

"Where was I? Oh, yeah, Tyler walked up to me and demanded that I cancel my trip to the motel with Danny because Danny wasn't the one who loved me, he was! He said he was the one who put those wildflowers on my porch step when I was twelve, not Danny. He'd been stupid enough to tell Danny about it and Danny had used it to convince me he'd been infatuated with me for four years!"

"Will you stop yelling?" Frannie said calmly.

Melissa breathed deeply and exhaled. "I didn't believe Tyler. I didn't want to. I was in love with Danny, I'd been in love with him for two years. Now, he was in love with me and I didn't want anything to spoil it."

"Did you buy condoms?" Frannie asked.

"What?"

"Did you even think about safe sex? Or did you leave it up to him?"

"I bought condoms," Melissa said. "I know about AIDS and sexually transmitted diseases and unwanted pregnancies. I didn't want any of those things. I just wanted Danny to be my first."

Frannie sighed. "Thank goodness."

"We didn't even get that far," Melissa said. "We were kissing on the bed and I told him about what Tyler had said. You should have seen his eyes. It was all in his eyes. I guess he's a liar, but not much of an actor. I knew then that Tyler had told me the truth, and I yelled at him to get off me. To take me home. He yelled back at me and told me I should be grateful that anybody like him wanted to touch me. I laughed in his face and told him to just leave, I'd call somebody to pick me up. Then I got dressed and left him in the motel room and went to the office. That's when I phoned you."

"It's nearly eleven-thirty," Frannie said. "What time did you leave for the 'airport'?"

"This morning at around ten."

"You've been with him all day at the Flamingo?"

"No, we had fun together in Santa Rosa. We went all over the place. I guess he was trying to make sure I was comfortable with him. After dinner, we went to the motel and that's when we started kissing and undressing. Then, because I had to hear his side of the story, I blurted out what Tyler had told me about him, and the argument started."

"Your dad's gonna want to kill him for leaving you stranded."

"He's gonna want to kill me first," Melissa said.

When they got to Glen Ellen Frannie didn't walk to the door with Melissa. Let her take her medicine like a big girl. She watched as Erik opened the door, still dressed exactly as she'd last seen him. Then he pulled Melissa into his arms and hugged her tightly.

That was Frannie's cue to leave.

She pulled out of their driveway for the second time that night.

In Santa Rosa at an Italian restaurant, Willow was having a much better night. She and Joe had had a wonderful meal and had danced to practically every song the four-piece band had played.

The candlelight cast a flattering shadow over both of them. And the wine they'd imbibed added its own special glow. However, what they were feeling was anything but artificial.

Joe was a splendid conversationalist. His life experiences rivaled her own in number and depth. He had traveled extensively and had lived in five countries. His family on his mother's side grew olives and made olive oil in the Peloponeese near the city of Sparti, Laconia. He was half Greek and half Italian.

His father's family, the Rizzos, originated in Romany. They were gypsies. Most of them lived in Sicily today. His mother and father had come to the United States when he was two years old. They spoke with thick accents till the day they died. He had never had an accent.

He married his wife, Lydia, when he was twenty-five and loved her until she'd died in a car accident five years ago. They'd never been blessed with children.

Then it was Willow's turn to tell him her life story. She told him everything, about her divorces, her son's death, even about the debacle with Elvin. Willow was of the opinion that everything should be put up front when considering inviting someone into her bed. Not only health histories should be shared, but life histories.

Joe sat gazing into her face with his elbow on the table, his chin resting in the palm of his left hand. She was mesmerizing. After Lydia he had never dreamed he would meet anyone this fascinating.

"How could he even think about another woman when he had you to come home to?" he wondered aloud. "He's a fool."

Willow laughed shortly. "I'm not going to contradict you on that point. But it was as much my fault as his. I traveled a lot. I bet Elvin and I weren't actually together six months out of the twelve months he lived in my house. The house was practically his. No wonder he took liberties while I was away."

"Why *do* you travel so much?" Joe asked. "Is it mandatory, or do you do it because you choose to do it?"

Willow knew then that she was in the presence of a very astute person. "I've got what I recently accused a friend of mine of having." She was thinking of Frannie. Dear, sweet Frannie, who'd suffered trauma at the hands of a male and therefore didn't have faith in them any longer. That wasn't her excuse. She'd let life itself turn her into an eternal pessimist. Outwardly, she was an optimist. But inside, she didn't believe she deserved happiness. So she kept creating scenarios in her life that were sure to provide her with unhappy endings. "I suffer from the runs," she told Joe. "If I recognize something as having the potential to be really good for me, I run from it, or him. I knew Elvin wasn't any good when I invited him into my life. And I knew it would end badly."

Joe took her hand in his and peered into her eyes. "I guess that means you're going to run away from me, too, because I would be very good to you."

"After everything I've told you, you still want to take this further?" Willow asked, a note of disbelief in her tone.

"Try me," Joe challenged her.

Willow had never been able to resist a challenge.

After they'd made love, Jason and Sara showered together then went and raided the refrigerator. The turkey sandwiches and white wine they'd consumed had made them sleepy but they were not going to bed when there was a *Twilight Zone* marathon on the sci-fi channel.

"I recognize this episode already," Sara said when actor Burgess Meredith's face filled the big screen on the TV. "He was in more than one episode, but in this there is a nuclear war and everybody's killed except him…"

"And he's depressed until he discovers the ruins of a library," Jason continued.

"A bibliophile…" Sara said.

"Someone after your own heart," Jason provided.

Sara laughed softly. "Yeah. The poor guy. After he discovers all of the books he would ever want to read in his lifetime he breaks his glasses and can't read anything. I felt so sorry for him."

Jason kissed the side of her neck. "This is nice."

"Watching *The Twilight Zone* together?"

"Your being here," he said. "I wish you were here all the time."

"You'd get tired of me."

"I'd never get tired of you," he vehemently denied.

"I read in bed."

"I'd keep you so busy in bed, you'd have to start reading elsewhere."

Sara smiled at the prospect. "Yeah, you're right. To get any reading time at all, I'd better maintain my own residence."

Jason looked serious all of a sudden. "Are you ever going to marry me, Sara?"

Sara's mind flashed back to earlier that day. She could have been dead now and would never have seen Jason again. Might never have gotten another chance to be in his arms.

"Yes, Jason, I *am* going to marry you. And soon."

"You'd elope with me?" he asked, squeezing her.

"No, never. Your parents would feel cheated out of a wedding. My dad would be hurt if he didn't get to walk me down the aisle."

"We could get married in Vegas and then have a ceremony for everybody else."

"You're in a hurry, huh?"

"We want children and I want to get started on them as soon as possible."

"You don't want to wait a year or so after the wedding before we start a family?"

"Wait?" Jason said, his voice rising in indignation. "For what? We already know what we want. Why wait?"

Sara turned in his arms to kiss his chin. "You're a strange man. I would say the majority of men would prefer putting off becoming a father. Marriage is scary enough without adding children in the mix."

"Tell me you don't wish you'd had a child with Billy."

"I do," Sara said. "And I want to have your children." She settled deeper in his embrace. She was wearing one of his white T-shirts and a pair of panties. The hem fell just below her crotch. He was also wearing a white T-shirt, and a pair of boxers.

He kissed her behind the ear. "They would hopefully have your temperament," he whispered. "And your beautiful skin color."

"And your lips," Sara said, dreaming with him.

"Your baby hair around the edges of their scalp," he said, getting specific.

"Your big, brown eyes," Sara said wistfully.

"Nah, I want them to have your summer-sunset-colored eyes," Jason told her.

"It doesn't matter how they look," Sara said. "As long as they're…"

"Healthy!" Jason finished for her. He leaned back on the big couch and pulled Sara on top of him. She bent and kissed him, ending it by momentarily sucking on his bottom lip. Jason loved it when she did that. It remindéd him of the feel of her mouth on other parts of his body.

Sara felt his penis getting hard. "Speaking of healthy," she teased.

"Hey, we're young. We can sleep when we're too old to have sex."

"You Bryant men never get too old to have sex. Look at your father."

"That's true," Jason said. "But I don't want to think of my parents when I'm about to get with you, girl, so quit talking about them."

Sara laughed. "What do you want to talk about?"

Jason reached up and began pulling down her panties. She helped by raising her hips a little. "I want to talk about this," Jason said, grabbing her bare bottom with both hands and gently squeezing while pressing her to his hardened member.

"How round, and firm, and juicy it is."

"Juicy?"

"Yeah, baby, it's shaped like a perfect peach. I just want to bite it."

Giggling, Sara said, "Talk dirty to me!"

Jason removed his hands from her butt and cupped a breast in each hand. "Let's not forget these."

Sara took off her T-shirt so that he could see what he was feeling. "I'm listening."

"Proverbs in the Bible said it best," he began. "'Let her own breasts intoxicate you at all times. With her love may you be in an ecstasy constantly.'"

Sara looked at him in wonder. "You didn't get that from the Bible!"

"I'll show it to you later," Jason promised. "But for

now, I'm going to let your breasts intoxicate me." And he took one of her nipples in his mouth and drove her to distraction with his tongue.

Chapter 13

Frannie and Willow were having lunch on the veranda in the back when Sara got home the next day. They were laughing when she strolled out there. "Good morning!"

Willow and Frannie peered at her with whimsical expressions on their faces.

"*Morning!*" said Frannie. "It's nearly one o'clock in the afternoon. I see at least one of us had an eventful night."

"Two of us," Willow put in. "Sit down, missy," she said to Sara. "I'll go get another plate."

"Don't bother. Jason made a big breakfast this morning," Sara, once again in her black dress of the night before, said as she sat down at the small, white, round table.

Smiling, Willow shook her head. "He's gorgeous and he cooks *too!*"

She was wearing a long, flowing multicolored caftan, and was barefoot. Sitting across from her, Frannie had on jeans and a yellow cropped top. She wasn't wearing shoes either, and her hair was especially frizzy this morning from all the tossing and turning she'd done last night.

Sara looked into her face. There were dark circles under her eyes. She wondered if Erik had kept her up all night. "You look terrible. Is he an *animal?*"

Frannie laughed and looked across the table at Willow who nearly fell off her chair laughing. Sara stared at both of them. "What happened last night?"

Frannie said, "Willow, since I've already gone over it once, would you kindly tell Sara what my night was like?"

"I'd be happy to," Willow said. She took a large sip of her iced tea before beginning.

"Our Frannie went there last night with every intention of rocking Erik's world!"

"Don't editorialize," said Frannie.

"Too exaggerated?" asked Willow.

"Yes, just stick to the facts."

"Okay," said Willow. "She wanted to hit it and quit it, and he wanted to hit it and wed it. Or something close to it. The boy was too gone on her for her to use him like that. So she canceled the mission. But not before telling him why she couldn't force herself to trust any man."

Sara turned to Frannie. "You told him about the rape?"

Frannie nodded. "Mmm-mmm. And if that doesn't get rid of him for good, I don't know what will."

"He may not be like most guys," Sara said, offering comfort.

Frannie's experience had been all negative when it came to telling a guy about her sexual assault. They couldn't handle it. At first, they would sympathize and assure her that they were there for her. But then, she supposed, the image of her being brutalized ate into their minds and they could not look at her without seeing her as less than desirable. Perhaps too damaged to seriously consider spending the rest of their lives with. Perhaps too violated to seriously consider her to be theirs to cherish.

"I just don't want to go through the motions with him," Frannie said. "I shouldn't have said anything but it was in the heat of the moment. It came out of my mouth and I couldn't take it back."

"No, you were right to tell him," Sara said with conviction. She got up and hugged Frannie. "I haven't seen you like this with a guy in years." She looked into her eyes. "You're falling in love!"

"God, save me, I am," Frannie said sadly.

Sara got back in her chair beside Frannie. Smiling happily, she said, "I admit I would never have imagined you and Erik Sutherland together. But God works in mysterious ways."

"This time it's a bit too mysterious," Frannie said. "In spite of all that money, he's about as sophisticated as Jethro on the *Beverly Hillbillies*. He can't even tell when his daughter is pulling a fast one on him." She went on to tell Sara about Melissa's stay at the Flamingo Motel.

Sara was laughing when she finished. "She's a smart girl, though. She found him out before it was too late. I can't believe a seventeen-year-old boy could be that deceptive."

"He's eighteen," Frannie said. "Age doesn't matter anyway. I wouldn't be surprised if his ultimate plan was to get her pregnant. You know Erik would have insisted on his little girl marrying the guy. She would have had the baby because Melissa couldn't kill a fly let alone a fetus. And then Danny would have been set for life. His father-in-law would be worth millions and when dear old dad kicked the bucket, Melissa would inherit everything."

"Stop!" cried Willow. "You're making the boy out to be an ultrasmart con artist or something. He just wanted to get into her panties. You're simply too emotionally involved with father *and* daughter. You already think of her as your daughter. I bet if Danny had still been at the motel last night when you got there, you would have kicked his butt."

"Probably," Frannie admitted. She smiled at Willow. "Enough about me. Tell Sara about the Casanova of Sonoma County."

Willow smiled and sighed wistfully. A dreamy expression came into her eyes. "If I don't find out whether or not extra-virgin olive oil really *is* an aphrodisiac before I leave here, I'm going to regret it for the rest of my life."

Sara and Frannie burst out laughing. They knew Joe Rizzo was an olive grower and made extra-virgin olive oil. Some of the finest restaurants in California used his oil exclusively, so the old boy was doing all right financially.

"When I got back home last night after picking Melissa up at the roach motel, guess whom I caught steaming up the car windows like a couple of horny teenagers?" Frannie said, looking at Willow the whole while.

Sara was delighted. "He's a good kisser, huh?"

"Not only is he a good kisser, he also had all the right

reactions to a good kiss, if you know what I mean," said Willow conspiratorially.

"Viagra-less?" Frannie cried.

"We were together for four hours in total and he wasn't out of my sight once. I don't see how he could have popped a pill without my knowing it. Plus, why would he? You don't think he assumed I'd sleep with him on the first date, do you?"

"I was going to sleep with Erik on the first date," Frannie said.

"That wasn't your first date," Willow denied. "You've known Erik a while. What you feel for him has had time to simmer. What he feels for you has had time to ripen. But I just met Joe Rizzo. I mean, I joke a lot, but I'm not a loose woman. If he thought he was going to get busy with me…"

"Willow, you're working yourself up for nothing. You can't know Joe's intentions. And you certainly don't know if his hard-on was natural or drug-induced, so let it go!" Sara said, laughing. "He's probably just a healthy guy with healthy reactions to sexual stimuli. You turned him on."

"Hell, yeah, I turned him on," said Willow proudly. "I haven't lost it."

The doorbell rang and they looked at each other as if to say, 'Who could that be?'

"I'll get it," said Sara, rising.

She hurried through the house, to the front door.

Jody Easterbrook stood on the other side of the screen door. "Hello, Sara, I've got good news," she said, smiling. "Sean Gamble has been apprehended."

"Come in," Sara said excitedly. This was the best thing that could have happened. She turned away, calling over her shoulder. "I'll be right back, Frannie's gonna want to hear this."

A minute later, Sara, Frannie, Willow and Jody were sitting in the living room while Jody related what she'd been told about Sean Gamble's capture. "Nobody really thought he would have the nerve to visit his brother's body at the morgue, but that's just what he did last night. We'd left a photograph of him with the city morgue just in case. When the attendant saw him, he played it cool, told him that he had to have an appointment to see his brother's body unless accompanied by law-enforcement personnel. He was visibly upset when he was told that. The attendant said he even started bawling like a baby, talking about how he'd just been told his brother was dead and he'd flown all day to get there. Said he lived in Canada and the trip hadn't been easy on him. He did everything in his power to get the attendant to let him in. No dice, though. The attendant wouldn't let him in. So, after a while, he left. That's when the attendant got on the phone and called security. Two security guards stopped him before he left the building and detained him until the police could get there. He's in lock-up now, still saying that he's from Canada, and he doesn't know why he was arrested."

"What a cool character," Willow said. "He had some balls showing up at the morgue."

Jody nodded her agreement. "Oh, yes, he's good. Unlike most hit men he had identification on him. Everything identified him as Jon Gamble. We looked up Jon Gamble. He's a dentist from Ontario and he's never been in trouble in his life. Sean must have stolen his identity."

"Identity theft is running rampant," said Frannie. "You would think an assassin would choose the identity of someone who died a long time ago, though. Doesn't make sense to me."

"To me, either," said Jody. "But killers like Sean Gamble love to keep the authorities guessing. It'll give him great pleasure for us to have all kinds of trouble figuring him, and his motives, out. That's how they get their kicks."

"Could he have been so overcome with grief that he wasn't thinking straight?" Sara asked. "That seems out of character for a cold-blooded assassin." She bit her bottom lip, thinking. "I'm deliriously happy that he's been caught. But it all seemed to go down too easily. Plus the fact that the person whose identity he stole shares his last name."

"Sometimes," Jody said, getting to her feet, "that's how it goes down. Not often, but it does happen. I'm gonna get out of you ladies' hair and head back to San Francisco."

The other three women rose, as well.

Sara shook Jody's hand. It seemed inappropriate to embrace a soldier, which was what Jody's demeanor shouted. "Thanks for looking out for us."

"My pleasure," said Jody with a brief smile. Then she was all business again. "In parting, while I was watching the place last night I noticed a few things you could be doing, security-wise. You need some really good security lights in the back of the house. And if you're going to park in the driveway, always lock your car when you get out of it. Always."

"All right, thank you," said Sara. "I appreciate that."

"Yes, thank you," Frannie put in, and she walked Jody to the door while Sara and Willow returned to the veranda.

When Frannie got back there, they all sat quietly for a

moment. Then Willow said, "Well, I guess I can get on back to Seattle now. I was prepared to stay until they found Gamble. Now that he's been caught, I should be going."

"Oh, no you don't," said Sara. "It's only Sunday, and your going-away party isn't until Friday night."

"Are you sure I'm not getting on your nerves?" Willow asked seriously. "I'm a lot to take on a daily basis."

"On the contrary," said Frannie. "You fit right in. Most of the time Sara is too nice to tell me my stuff stinks, but you feel free to blurt it out. I like that."

Willow laughed. "Now, I expect you to tell me when I'm smelling up the place, as well."

"I will, I will," Frannie assured her. "But so far you've been a breath of fresh air."

"Amen," Sara agreed. "How dare you think of cutting your visit short? Besides, Joe would be devastated."

The doorbell rang again.

"I'll get it this time," said Frannie, getting to her feet.

When she got to the front door and peered through the locked screen door, she almost spun on her heels and fled. Erik stood there holding an orchid plant in an ornate pot. Where he'd gotten it on a Sunday, Frannie couldn't imagine. She didn't think there was a flower shop in Santa Rosa open on a Sunday, nor one that would have in stock an exotic plant like that white orchid he was holding against his broad chest.

"What are you doing here?" she asked coldly. She wasn't about to be friendly. The first rule of appearing not to be emotionally attached was to be rude, she'd learned. To turn on the rudeness and not turn it off until they ran away with their tails tucked between their legs.

Erik ignored her rudeness. All he could think when he caught sight of her in that cute little yellow top and loose-fit jeans was that she looked adorable. To say nothing of the way her hair was sticking up all over her head.

She looked like she hadn't even combed it today.

"Thank you for what you did for Melissa. I'm glad she knew she could count on you. I'm sure I would have made matters worse, and blown up at her if she'd phoned me."

Frannie tried her best to maintain an antagonistic attitude, but his sincerity was getting to her. The only thing she could think to do was to attack him.

She opened the screen door and stepped onto the front porch, forcing him to quickly move backward or get his toes crushed underfoot. "You're too easy on her. Did you even *ask* to read the e-mail from her mother before you let her go traipsing off to the 'airport' with Danny Keener?"

Erik actually smiled. His green eyes sparkled in his tanned face. Frannie momentarily peered up at his thick, wavy, dark red hair and the sunbeams seemed to be turning it a burnished gold color. She silently cursed her hormones. Before she'd met him she hadn't known, or cared, what burnished gold looked like.

"What're you smiling at!" she snapped.

"You look like one of those troll dolls with the fuzzy hair that people keep on their desks," Erik said. "You're beautiful."

"Put the plant down," Frannie ordered him.

Erik set the plant on an end table that belonged to the set of white wicker patio furniture there on the front porch, and turned to face her. "It's down."

Frannie, being only five-three, had to get a running start to leap into Erik's arms. She did it, though, and he caught her and lifted her off the floor of the porch with ease. "Don't you have sense enough to stay away from me?" she asked as she rained kisses on his face.

"I guess I'm kind of dense," he told her.

Frannie kissed his mouth. Erik kissed her back with all the pent-up passion he'd been denied the opportunity to express last night.

Willow and Sara found them wrapped in each other's arms when they came to investigate what was keeping Frannie so long. With one assassination attempt behind them, they weren't taking any chances with their safety.

Sara laughed softly. "Oh, she's all right."

"She's more than all right," Willow said.

They turned and gave Frannie and Erik their privacy.

Of course, when Frannie and Erik finally came up for air, she firmly set him away from her and on wobbly legs went to pick up the potted orchid. "Thanks for the plant," she told him. "Now, go away and never come back."

Smiling contentedly because he knew she didn't mean it, Erik turned and began walking down the front steps.

"Wait!" Frannie cried.

She set the plant down again and went to him. Grabbing him by the shirtfront she kissed him roughly. "Okay, you can go now."

"And never come back," Erik added, smiling.

"That's right!" said Frannie fiercely.

Erik left, not turning around once. If he had, he would have seen Frannie standing on the porch holding the potted orchid in her arms, looking after him with longing.

* * *

"I thought she was joking when she told me never to come back," Erik told Jason Friday morning as they jogged down main street. "But she won't answer my phone calls, or my e-mails. Yesterday I went by the bookstore to buy some books and she pointedly ignored me. She was wonderful to Melissa, but wouldn't even acknowledge my presence. I've never known a more stubborn woman!"

"You think you've got it bad?" Jason said. "My parents came back home on Monday. I love that they're back but Sara won't sleep over when they're in the house. We can't go to her place because she has room-mates. And she won't go to the inn with me because she knows everybody who works there. We haven't had any privacy since last Saturday."

"Boo hoo," Erik said. "At least you know Sara is yours once you do find a place to be alone together. Frannie tortured me with those kisses last Sunday, left me with hopes of more to come, then turned around and killed those hopes by not communicating with me at all."

"So, what's her problem?" Jason asked. "She likes Melissa. But she won't give you the time of day. What's up with that?"

"She has her reasons," Erik said. He was not going to discuss what Frannie had told him with anyone. He instinctively knew it was privileged information. "Believe me."

Jason did believe him. He and Erik were becoming friends. Real friends. Not like the relationship they'd had in high school when Erik had been the most popular boy in town and everybody considered themselves lucky if out of the goodness of his heart he chose to associate with them.

They had both changed. Jason no longer craved popularity so much that he would ignore the suffering of a bullied girl simply to stay in the clique. And Erik had matured into a man who could rise to the occasion when a woman he cared about told him she could never love him because she'd been irreparably altered by brutality.

"I'm sorry, man," he said of Erik's situation with Frannie. Whatever it might be. "I hope you two can work it out."

"I'm not giving up on her," Erik said with determination.

"Well, you two will be in the same room tonight," Jason offered as consolation. "You *are* coming to the party, aren't you?"

"Yeah. Melissa would kill me if I didn't take her. She's very fond of Willow."

"Who isn't?" said Jason. "She's a riot."

Erik smiled, remembering how Willow had gotten up and left him and Frannie alone on the day of the root excavations. All of a sudden, he also recalled something else that had struck him as interesting on that day. Frannie and Willow had the exact same tattoo on their bodies. He'd seen Willow's on the inside of her arm when she'd handed him the roast beef sandwich, and later when he and Frannie were alone, he'd spotted hers on the top of her breast when she'd leaned over and presented him with a very nice view of her cleavage. He wondered if Jason had noticed the tattoos. Jason would have to admit he'd been looking down Frannie's blouse to confirm it.

He was willing to put his friend on the spot if it got him any closer to understanding Frannie, though. "Uh, Jake, have you noticed that both Frannie and Willow have tattoos of crossed spears? It's really tiny, only about half an inch long but it's done so well that you can distinctly see that it's crossed spears. You can see the blades' tips."

Jason nearly tripped on his own feet when Erik said that. But he maintained his balance and kept running. Willow and Frannie had the same tattoo as Sara? Sara had told him she'd gotten it on a dare when she was in college. "No," he said, his voice clear and strong despite how surprised Erik's comment had left him. "I haven't noticed. But I know they all belong to the same service organization. Maybe it's the result of some kind of ritual they went through when they joined. I've heard of some fraternities who do that."

Erik was nodding. "Yeah, me, too. Then, Sara has a tattoo, as well?"

"Yeah, she has one."

"That's it, then, it's a symbol of their sisterhood," Erik concluded. "Kind of like the Amazons. Except the Amazons would cut off their right breasts so that they could draw a bow better and throw a spear."

"African Amazons didn't mutilate themselves," Jason told him. "I know because I looked it up. I jokingly refer to Sara and her friends as Amazons. I wanted to know their history, exactly what they were. Anyway, African Amazons were mighty warriors who didn't see the need to cut off their breasts. And unlike the Amazons that the Greeks made famous, they didn't hate men. They took them as lovers and husbands."

Jason felt a slight chill even though he was definitely

warm after running two miles. What he'd just said was
how Sara had described the service organization she,
Frannie and Willow belonged to. She had said that the
women were working toward a goal, their empowerment. And once they were on their feet, they reached
back down and helped another sister in need onto hers.
What Sara's organization did could be interpreted as
fighting like warriors for the empowerment of their
sisters. Jason couldn't help wondering just how dangerous the fights could get.

Now, he was more worried about Sara than ever.

Maybe that was the reason she couldn't marry him.
Maybe the organization didn't allow their members to
be married. She had to quit it before she could marry him.

Perhaps there was something preventing her from
quitting.

He panicked further. What if the organization was
like the Mafia, and the only way out was through death?
Nah, he was being ridiculous. Sara was too savvy to get
hooked up with people like that.

He and Erik had reached the ballpark. Their normal
routine was to run around the ballpark and head back
out of town. Both of them lived on the outskirts of town,
Erik a bit farther than he did.

"Have you noticed," Erik asked, "that none of them
are married? Sara is a widow. Frannie never married,
and from what I hear, Willow is divorced. Do you think
it's an organization of single women? They can't marry?
If that's the case, then I'm up the creek without a
paddle."

"You want to marry Frannie?" Jason asked, unable
to keep the surprise out of his voice. After all, Erik had
not known Frannie very long.

"I'm the marrying kind," Erik said.

"You've been married *once*. And you've been divorced for four years. How can you say you're the marrying kind?"

"I'd known Melissa's mom for less than two months when she got pregnant and I didn't try to deny the baby was mine. I married her."

"Yeah," Jason agreed. "You're the marrying kind."

Chapter 14

Sara, Jason and Simone did the cooking for Willow's going-away party, which was going to be a sit-down dinner with dancing in the sunroom afterward. The Hacienda was well-lit so that the guests could see their way up the long walk and onto the large portico. Sara and Jason greeted them at the door.

Willow was holding court in the big family room where there were comfortable leather couches and deep armchairs. Joe was in his element at her side and he was pleased to note that their conversational style complemented each other. Entertainers at heart, they had everyone in the family room laughing until they cried.

Joe was also perfectly at ease because he'd known Eric and Simone for over thirty years. They had been here when he and Lydia had moved to Glen Ellen. They had made them feel welcome. Joe soon learned that Eric

Erik removed his hands from Melissa's ears.

"Okay, you win," Eric conceded.

To which everyone laughed except Melissa who looked puzzled by their hilarity.

"Come on, everybody," Sara said shortly afterward. "Dinner is served."

Sara had put a place card in front of all nine of the chairs at the table and could not help noticing the daggers Frannie threw her way when she learned she was going to be sitting next to Erik.

Erik didn't seem at all put out about it.

Melissa couldn't have been more pleased. She was going to be sitting way at the other end of the table between Simone and Eric whom she really liked.

Willow and Joe were already deep in conversation by the time the first course had been served; and Jason, who had not been alone with Sara for five days, was happy to have her, sort of, to himself.

They dined on grilled shrimp with mixed greens, followed by racks of lamb baked with a sweet and sour sauce, sweet potato soufflé, crisp whole green beans stir-fried with onions and sweet peppers, dinner rolls, and for dessert Elise had sent one of her red velvet cakes. Sara had asked Willow what her favorite cake was, and Elise had baked it and sent it next-day via UPS. Elise had packed it so well with the words This Side Up and Fragile on it that it had arrived without any icing disturbed.

Jason rose and offered a toast. He raised his glass of Zinfandel. "To Willow, who rode to the rescue at a moment's notice, saved the day, then commenced to win our hearts. May you always be the wonderful woman you are. *Salud!*"

Everyone toasted Willow with exclamations of well wishes and continued blessings.

"Speech, speech," Sara cried, encouraging Willow to say a few words.

Willow was visibly choked up. Tears shone in her eyes as she began. "You all are making me out to be some kind of hero. But the fact is, I would have gone to *hell* in order to put some space between me and Elvin. It was either that, or murder. I'm glad I came here instead!"

Everybody laughed, and once they'd quieted down, she continued. "All jokes aside, I've never met people before who were so warm and welcoming. I'll miss all of you when I'm back in Seattle wringing rain water out of my socks."

"The only thing separating us is Oregon," Joe joked. "And I can get across that in no time at all."

He might have said it in a jocular manner, but Willow could see by the determined expression in his brown eyes that he meant it. She smiled at him and squeezed his knee underneath the table.

"Yes, let this be the beginning of a long friendship!" Simone said.

Later, after dessert, they went into the sunroom where the men had moved aside the furniture to make space for a makeshift dance floor. Jason had put several CDs in the player and programmed it for continuous play.

He'd chosen music designed to appeal to everyone there, not just the jazz standards he knew his parents loved. Some standards, yes, but also hip-hop, pop, and soul. He'd asked Melissa who her favorite singer was and she'd told him Sheryl Crow, and he'd programmed a few Sheryl Crow tunes in.

The selection began with "Embraceable You" sung by the incomparable Sarah Vaughan.

Joe and Willow immediately took to the dance floor, followed by Simone and Eric. Sara and Jason were next, but Erik, Frannie and Melissa sat on the sidelines watching.

Melissa sat between her dad and Frannie. She was wearing the dress that Frannie had picked out for her and her thick, wavy hair was in a loose 'do on top of her head.

In the past few days she'd gained a great deal of confidence. She'd put the incident with Danny Keener behind her and was talking to Tyler, although she still wouldn't go out with him. She was swearing off boys until she knew herself better. She believed her desire to be loved, even seen, by Danny had caused her to take their relationship too fast too soon. She wasn't going to make the same mistake with Tyler, no matter how flattered she was that he'd punched Danny in the nose in spite of Danny being bigger than he was.

The relationship she was concerned about now was the budding one between her dad and Frannie. Her dad, the dope, had been looking at Frannie all night with something akin to hunger in his eyes. Melissa might have chosen to wait until she was older before becoming intimate with a boy, but her dad and Frannie were old. Ancient! What was keeping him from asking Frannie out? And Frannie wasn't fooling her, either. She had pointedly ignored her dad all evening. Girls didn't do that unless they were *really* interested in a guy. Melissa couldn't believe they were both behaving so childishly.

While she was ruminating on the problem, her dad turned to her and did something really stupid. "Honey, dance with your old man?"

Looking up at him disdainfully, she pursed her lips. "And die of embarrassment? If I've told you once, I've told you twice, I'm only going to dance with you on my wedding day. I still remember the twelfth birthday fiasco when you did the Funky Chicken. No, sir, thank you. No. Ask Frannie to dance. She's much braver than I am."

Frannie, pretending not to have heard the whole conversation, sat on her chair with her spine perfectly straight, sending hate messages to Erik through the air. *Don't you dare ask me to dance,* she thought. *Not if you value your* cojones.

She turned and smiled at Erik as if challenging him to defy her silent command.

In the middle, Melissa was gesticulating with head nods and rolling eyes for her dad to ask Frannie to dance. Erik, just about fed up with the both of them, decided to ignore them.

Instead, when the song ended, he went and tapped Joe on the shoulder to ask permission to dance with Willow.

Willow was happy to oblige, but Joe looked none too pleased.

Joe went and asked Frannie to dance. She immediately got up.

A song from the Swing era came on. Willow and Erik, both tall and athletic, got into it. Erik turned out to be a fairly good dancer, not half the terror that his daughter had accused him of being. He matched Willow's enthusiastic style and fervor.

Joe, who'd been dancing all his life, and enjoyed it, whipped Frannie around the floor like a pro. Frannie was amazed at his stamina. Then found herself remem- ·

bering what Willow had said about his reaction to her kisses, and blushed.

Both Frannie and Erik were watching each other out of the corners of their eyes. Observing how each other moved. They had never gotten the chance to dance together and longed to be in each other's arms.

As the couples moved closer on the dance floor, Willow winked at Joe and he instantly read her intent. When the song went on the down beat, Willow turned in Erik's arms, Joe turned with Frannie in his and they pushed the two young people into each other's arms. Frannie hadn't seen it coming. Neither had Erik. Once their bodies touched, though, that was it. They were done. They surrendered and held each other close.

Peggy Lee's sultry voice came over the stereo system with "Gee Baby, Ain't I Good to You." Frannie demurely laid her head on Erik's chest—she was too short to lay it on his shoulder. "Okay, you win. I'll go out with you."

Melissa smiled happily when she saw that Willow and Joe had accomplished what she hadn't been able to.

From across the room, Simone and Eric smiled their approval, too.

Jason and Sara missed it all because they had left the room five minutes ago.

"I'm crazy for letting you talk me into this," Sara said as Jason lifted her and set her on the heavy oak table in the wine cellar.

"Tell me," Jason said, his hands moving up her dress to grasp the waistband of her panties, "that you didn't wear this dress just for me. If you hadn't wanted me to seduce you, you would have worn something difficult to get out of."

"That's a blatant lie," Sara protested as she threw back her head so he could kiss her throat. "No matter what I wear, you find some way to get me out of it."

Kissing her neck while he continued to pull the panties past her hips, with some assistance from her in the form of a little wriggling, Jason sighed. "Five days, Sara. I would have died if I couldn't have you tonight. I've thought about it all day long."

"Then you undoubtedly have a condom stashed somewhere down here."

Jason paused to reach into his pants pocket. He placed the condom on the tabletop for later. Then he removed her panties and placed them next to the condom. "Don't want to lose those. Could be chilly later on tonight."

"Thank goodness this table is smooth. Otherwise I could get splinters in my butt."

Jason kissed her. Sara closed her eyes and kissed him back, slowly and with delicious intensity. Between his tongue, his hands, and his scent, she was lost in him.

Jason broke off the kiss long enough to unbuckle his belt, unzip his pants and release himself from his boxers. Sara took his penis in her hand. It was warm and very hard, the veins along the sides prominent. He throbbed in her hand.

She bent her head and kissed it.

Jason, watching her, had a hard time holding back the quick ejaculation that her mouth on him sometimes threatened. But he wanted to be inside of her and oral sex, no matter how pleasurable, was not going to cut it for him tonight. This might have to last him another five days, and he wanted to please her, as well.

Sara wet her lips, and he knew that was usually a precursor to her taking him into her mouth. "Not tonight, baby," he said, and bent to kiss her mouth.

During the course of the kiss, they straightened back up, facing one another. Sara opened her legs and Jason began to gently massage her clitoris with the pad of his thumb in slow, circular movements. He looked into her face the whole time. He never got tired of watching her in the throes of passion. Nor, the high he got knowing he was the one making her feel so good.

When she began to move with his rhythm, he knew she was enjoying it. He could feel her clitoris swelling, the wetness increasing. She was ready for him. But, he wanted to hear her breathing when she came. That always turned him on further.

He didn't increase his speed or pressure, he simply continued doing what he was doing, moved in a bit closer, and whispered, "Lean back with your elbows on the table, and spread your legs."

Sara gingerly did so. She didn't relish falling off the table onto the stone floor of the cellar.

Jason bent and performed cunnilingus on her.

Sara restrained herself from bucking on the tabletop. Of all the precarious positions he had had her in over the past year and a half, this one took the cake! Ah, but he made her grateful she was a woman.

She came with a loud sigh of release.

Jason waited a moment or two before withdrawing his tongue. Until after her contractions had subsided, then he kissed her inner thighs close to her sex, and straightened to pick up the condom, put it on, and step closer to her. Sara scooted forward as he grasped her by the backs of the legs and pulled her toward him.

He lay the tip of his engorged penis at the opening

of her sex and slowly entered her. Sara's vaginal walls contracted around him, accommodating him. Jason moaned softly. He didn't think he would ever tire of this singular sensation. Some men said sex with one woman was much like sex with any other. He disagreed. Sara was his equal in every way. She was his mate.

Sara wrapped her legs around his waist. He raised her hips off the table and thrust deeper. Up on her elbows, Sara met his fierce gaze. He looked half-mad with passion. Like some rutting animal.

The thought made her climax again. Shortly afterward, he came too, and threw back his head with a growl. Yes, a growl. Sara laughed. Jason laughed too. He bent and kissed her before withdrawing, holding his penis with the used condom on the tip. It had practically come off due to the violence of their lovemaking.

Turning to walk over to one of the barrels, he returned with a small light-blue box.

"Look what I have for you."

Sara was collecting her panties from the tabletop. She looked up. Jason was holding a box of Kleenex Cottonelle Fresh folded wipes. "I know how you like to freshen up afterward."

Sara gratefully accepted the box. "You're a man after my own heart."

The party broke up around midnight.

Three cars pulled out of the driveway, Willow with Joe in his truck, Erik and Melissa in his SUV, and Sara and Frannie in Frannie's Mustang.

Willow had told them not to wait up for her.

In Frannie's Mustang, Sara said, "I can't leave you alone for one minute. When I got back in the room,

Willow told me you and Erik had danced three dances together. I missed that!"

Frannie smiled. "I'm too old to still be hanging on to my fears. If I keep it up, I'll end up alone, childless and eventually friendless. If you can take risks, so can I."

"What kind of risk have I taken?" Sara wanted to know.

"To love again. I know how much you adored Billy. I knew both of you, remember? He was the love of your life."

"Yes, little did I know he would be the love of the first *part* of my life. We never think that way when we get married. We think it's going to last forever."

"We'd never have the guts to get married if we didn't think that way," Frannie said.

Joe reverently held Willow in his arms. They were standing at the foot of his bed and they were both completely nude. Her skin was satiny smooth and she smelled like cocoa butter and something else, some sensuous fragrance that made him want to inhale her even more.

He just wanted to stand there and hold her.

Willow's hands were on his backside which was firm and round from hard work. And although like most men his age, the skin over his muscles was slightly slack, he was in good shape. Nice pectorals, biceps, stomach muscles, and (her hand went lower) a nice muscle there, too.

"Willow," said Joe softly. "I want you. But if you're not sure. If you're with me now because you think this is it between us, then, don't go any further. I'm not letting you go. I aim to court you properly."

Willow smiled. That was the first time a man had ever said he wanted to court her. It was so archaic. So… Joe!

"Joe, don't make promises. Let's live for the moment and let the future take care of itself. If you make love to me with everything you've got and I return the favor then let that be sufficient. I'm not asking for more."

"I don't hear you asking for anything, Willow Quigley. I'm offering. And if you're as smart as you pretend to be, you'll accept it."

Willow went to say something and Joe stuck his tongue in her mouth. After that, she didn't want to talk, she just wanted to feel.

In the next couple of hours she found out that a man of fifty-nine definitely had stamina, and this particular man of fifty-nine knew his way around a woman's body.

Three condoms and a love hickey later, he drove her to Sara's house and kissed her good-night.

Willow would still be smiling in the morning.

As for Frannie, she didn't get anywhere near a physical culmination of her feelings for Erik that night. However, a short time after she got home, her cell phone rang. She'd put on her nightgown and was climbing into bed at the time, and didn't want to answer it. But something told her to pick it up.

It was Erik. "I wanted you to be the first to know," he said. "I'm not going to be the next mayor of Glen Ellen."

Frannie, sitting cross-legged on the bed, a smile curling her lips, said, "What, not enough illegal aliens to harass?"

Erik laughed. "There never were any illegal aliens here."

Frannie could think of several who had come and gone in the past three years. She wasn't going to tell him about them, though. "Then why did you drop out of the race? If you can call you and one other person a race?"

"I was running for all the wrong reasons. Some politicians run to serve the people. Some to serve themselves. I was in the latter group. I had no interest in the needs of the people. I was just interested in being called Mr. Mayor. Pitiful, isn't it?"

"Pretty pitiful," Frannie agreed. "Congratulations on quitting."

"Thank you. Now, of course, you know since I don't have to devote my time to my campaign, all of that extra time will be devoted to you."

"Uh-oh!"

"Uh-oh, indeed," Erik said, laughing softly. "I plan to wine you and dine you and generally spoil you rotten."

"Wait a minute, you already have one spoiled female on your hands. You don't need two. Wasn't she adorable tonight, by the way?"

"Yes, she was," Erik agreed. "She was especially adorable when she was calling me a doofus with two left feet!"

"Oh, she was only trying to get you to grow some *cojones* and ask me to dance."

"Now, who's being indulgent towards her?" Erik asked. "She wasn't the only adorable female there tonight. I wanted to kiss you so badly, I could taste it."

"Why didn't you?"

"No privacy. If I could have gotten you alone for two minutes..."

"What are you doing now?"

"I'm lying in bed with just my pajama bottoms on. What are you wearing?"

"I'm not trying to have phone sex, you pervert. I wanted you to come over here and kiss me."

Erik sat up in bed. "Are you serious?"

"Yes. I wanted to kiss you, too."

"I'll be there in seven minutes."

"Seven minutes? How do you know it only takes seven minutes to get here?"

"I've been known to drive by your house a time or two." Make that ten times in the past two weeks.

"Am I inviting a stalker over to kiss me?" Frannie said, laughing softly.

"Technically, it isn't stalking unless the behavior of the stalker isn't desired by the stalk-ee."

Frannie laughed. "I don't even think that's a word. See you in seven. Just lightly tap on the front door."

When he got there, Frannie opened the door at the first sign of his knock, and pulled him inside. After quietly closing the door, she pressed his back against it, went up on her toes, and kissed him.

Erik was prepared for her assault this time. He held her in his capable arms and met her passion with his own. He loved her. He knew it as well as he knew that his heart was most certainly going to be broken by her.

How could he wish that someone so fragile, so beautiful, so strong could ever belong to him?

Chapter 15

November arrived, wet and stormy.

Sara's mood matched the weather. She had sent Eunice her letter of resignation via e-mail more than a week ago, and had not heard a word back. Admittedly the secretary of state was a busy woman. Sara attributed her impatience to wanting to sever ties with the organization as quickly as possible so that her marriage to Jason could go forward.

Was that unreasonable?

She didn't believe so. She'd given Aminatu's Daughters six faithful years of her life. In fact, she and Frannie had almost given it their lives. They should give them medals.

Over breakfast this morning, Frannie helped her pinpoint why she was in such a funky mood. In Frannie's opinion it had nothing to do with Eunice's tardiness.

Sara had been complaining about not hearing from Eunice, and Frannie peered into her eyes, and said, "I'm not trying to trivialize your concerns. But Eunice's lack of communication is not what's got you in a horrible mood. Do you remember what was happening around this time last year?"

Sara, in the middle of putting butter on her toast, froze. "Mama died, Daddy moved to Florida, and I was depressed as hell. But not everything going on in my life was negative. Jason and I got closer at that time, too." She smiled, remembering. "We became lovers."

"You're smiling," Frannie said, rising. "I've done my good deed for the day. I'll open up the store this morning. I've got to leave before five this afternoon."

"All right," Sara said. "Only the truly loyal will come out in this rain, anyway."

Upon settling the matter, Frannie grabbed her umbrella and left through the kitchen door. Sara leisurely finished her breakfast as her mind wandered back to a year ago.

They had buried her mother, Janie, in late December. The days had been overcast with flash downpours. One minute it would be clear and the next a deluge would commence.

The day of the funeral was like that. Thunder rumbled and lightning flashed while the minister gave the eulogy. However, as the pallbearers left the church, the sun came out and the rain ceased.

She rode to the cemetery with her father, Jim, in a limousine directly behind the hearse. She'd had to be the strong one that day because her father had been inconsolable. He silently wept during the service. He wept on the way to the cemetery. He couldn't watch as they lowered the casket into the grave. Sara held his hand throughout, at intervals squeezing it for reassurance.

He had seemed paralyzed with grief that day, so it was a complete surprise when he announced, as soon as they got home from the cemetery and had a few moments alone together, that he was moving to Florida to live with his brother, Edward, a confirmed bachelor in Coral Gables. Uncle Ed lived in a condo and was reputed to be quite the ladies' man. Sara had stared at her father. She knew that he and her mother had not been intimate in a long time due to her mother's illness, but did he have to go sow his wild oats so soon after her death? "Why?" Sara had almost shouted.

"I had to let the workers go months ago," her dad began. "This hasn't been a working farm since then. Your mother was the one who loved the farming life. Her enthusiasm fueled me, but now that she's gone, I really see no point. I'm sixty, still healthy, and I don't want to spend the rest of my life here without Janie. The house was going to you after my death anyway. I'm signing it over to you now. Sell it if you want to. But I hope you'll hang on to it and, maybe, raise your children here. If not, please sell it to someone who'll love it. Janie and I made some good memories here."

He was a tall, hefty man with copper-colored skin and golden-hued eyes. His black hair was silver at the temples and he was still handsome. A fine figure of a man. Sara, in pain from her mother's death, felt somehow slighted that her father was preparing to move on so soon. It felt as though he was not adequately honoring her mother's memory.

She bit her tongue, though, and didn't voice her misgivings. There had been enough pain. For two years she had taken care of her mother. Her father had done it longer than that. It had taken a lot out of him to have to phone her in New York and ask her for her help. She was not going to burden him with empty recriminations. Her mother, and his wife, was gone. The last thing Janie Johnson would have wanted was for her husband and daughter to be at odds.

"I just want you to be happy, Daddy," she said.

Her father had hugged her tightly and started crying again.

A few days later, she was waving goodbye to him at the airport.

A day or so after that, she awakened out of a dream and clearly remembered how solicitous Jason Bryant had been to her ever since her mother had passed. She'd been in a grief-induced daze the whole time but now it all came back to her. Upon hearing of her mother's death, he'd come to the house bearing flowers. He'd sent a formal sympathy card. He'd gone with her to pick out the casket, a chore her father firmly refused to be a part of. All of this after she had told him she couldn't go out with him because she was still grieving Billy.

On the day of the funeral he had attended with his parents. He'd stood in the rain in the back row at the gravesite, holding an umbrella over his mother. And later, when friends and family had gathered at the house, he and his mother and Frannie had helped her organize things in the kitchen so that everybody got fed in a timely manner. She'd been on automatic pilot that day, doing everything that was expected of her. Everything a good daughter would do.

It was on a Sunday morning that she'd had her

epiphany. At that time, Frannie hadn't moved in with her yet, so she was alone in the big house. Rain pounded the roof and spattered the windows. She got out of bed, showered, dressed, had a bite to eat, went and brushed her teeth, grabbed her raincoat and umbrella, and ran to the unattached garage a few feet beside the house.

She owned a Toyota Camry back then. Dependable as always, it started right away and she backed it out and pointed it toward the Hacienda. The last time she'd been there was to attend Erica's wedding. It was during the reception that Jason had spirited her away to the wine cellar and had kissed her for the first, and last time. She'd avoided all intimate situations with him since then. He had not voiced his disappointment with her attitude. He'd simply been there for her at every turn.

Today, she was simply going to the Hacienda to thank him for his support. That's all. Really. She worked herself into quite a state of nervousness as she drove.

By the time she was standing on the portico of the Hacienda, her palms were sweating, and when Jason opened the door, she was rubbing them on her jeans' legs and silently berating herself for being such a ninny.

She hadn't been watching the clock. Didn't care what time it was. However, when she saw that Jason was still in his pajama bottoms, she wondered what time it was and was immediately apologetic. "Oh, no. Did I wake you?" she asked. "I'm so sorry!"

Jason laughed and stepped back so that she could enter. "Don't be. I was up. I was brushing when I heard the doorbell. Excuse my apparel." He touched his bare chest. "Or the lack thereof. Come in, come in."

Sara stepped inside and he closed the door after her then stood smiling down at her with amusement apparent in his eyes. "You still look startled," he said. "I'll go put on some clothes. Maybe you'll be more comfortable then."

Sara was looking everywhere except at his beautiful bare chest, arms, and that slit in his pajama bottoms. She tried not to notice that every time he bent his arms, muscles flexed. Or that even his feet were beautiful.

"Don't rush on my account," she hurriedly told him. "I just came over to thank you for being there for me following Mama's death. You went out of your way to be kind to me and it occurred to me, this morning, that I hadn't thanked you."

Their eyes met and held. "You're welcome," Jason said.

He moved a little closer to her, and Sara stiffened in panic. Why, she wasn't sure. She only knew that the closer he got to her, the more she felt like bolting out of there.

Looking away, she said, "I should be going so that you can get back to what you were doing."

Jason must have sensed how nervous he made her. He didn't attempt to get closer to her again as he walked over to the door and held it open for her.

"All right, Sara. Thank you for coming."

At the door, she once more felt confident enough to look him in the eyes. "You're welcome. Have a good day."

Jason had looked out at the rain. He watched as she put back on the raincoat she'd left in a chair on the portico. She didn't know what he found attractive about her that day because with her damp hair and clothes she must have resembled a drowned rat, but he said, "God, you're beautiful."

Sara smiled at the compliment. "I don't feel very beautiful."

"I'm not surprised. You've been through hell lately."
He slowly took a step toward her. "Let me know if you
ever need anything. Anything at all. I'll come to you."

He looked at her with such sincerity, such longing, that
she felt her cheeks grow hot with embarrassment. How
could he want her when she felt like the least desirable
woman on the planet at that moment? It was then that she
realized why he made her nervous. It was because he *did*
find her desirable and she hadn't been pursued by a man
in a long time. She'd been living like a widow for four
years. Attempts at dating had failed miserably. The last
date she'd gone on, the guy tried to kiss her and she'd
been so awkward she'd moved when he'd gone in for the
kill, his nose had collided with her forehead and he'd
gotten a nosebleed for his efforts. He hadn't called again.

Now, Jason Bryant was looking at her as if he wanted
to kiss her, too. Jason Bryant, the boy who had stood
aside while bullies called her terrible names. The boy
she'd had a crush on until that day.

Which long-ago memory would determine how she
would behave?

He came closer and bent his head. She didn't move
but her heart hammered in her chest and she felt a little
weak in the knees.

"Sara," he whispered with longing as his mouth descended on hers.

She kissed him. Opened her mouth and surrendered
totally to the male strength of him. His hand firmly held
the back of her head and he bent her over backward and
thoroughly made love to her with his mouth and tongue.
She didn't think, she only responded to his stimuli. It was
elevating. She had forgotten what a sexual experience a
kiss could be. Her body came alive. What had been dead

to emotions breathed again and came back from the dead eager to experience everything life had to offer.

Jason raised his head and, holding her in his arms, gazed into her eyes. "There's no denying it, Sara, I've fallen in love with you. I tried to just be your friend. My brother Franklyn's advice was to do that. Not to pressure you. And I've tried. But knowing how emotionally raw you are at this moment, only makes me want to comfort you. To hold you."

"To make love to me?" Sara asked, her voice soft and hopeful.

"It's too soon for that," Jason told her, smoothing her brow with the pad of his thumb. "I would feel as though I were taking advantage of you. Grief can make you do things you may regret the next day."

"You're right," Sara said. She placed the palms of her hands against his chest. His nipples were erect, and she could feel the quickened beat of his heart. She gazed at him with sensual intent. "But it's been years since I've made love, and I'd like you to be the one I give up a life of celibacy for."

Jason picked her up and carried her inside. He kicked the door closed. "You talked me into it!"

They stayed in bed all day that Sunday.

So, now it really irked Sara that she had had to put Jason off for over a year when he had confessed his love so long ago. She was weary of having to lie to him and wished to put the organization behind her once and for all. Elizabeth, her final charge, was safe in the arms of the Northern California branch of Aminatu's Daughters. She had completed her mission.

Her meal eaten, she got up from the table and washed the dishes.

She was drying the last of the dishes when the phone rang.

Picking up the receiver, Sara said, "Hello?"

"Sara, it's Jody Easterbrook. I'm not supposed to be phoning you but I couldn't live with myself if my hunch is right, and I didn't warn you. All this time that we thought we had Sean Gamble in custody, I believe we've had his brother. Everything about Jon Gamble checks out. His wife arrived from Ontario and showed us family photo albums of the two of them. They have two children. Airport surveillance cameras show a man who looks exactly like him getting off a flight from Canada on the same day he came into the morgue to see his brother's body. The authorities still think he's lying and his wife is lying for him. But I have a theory."

"Yes?" Sara asked. She was standing next to the nook in the kitchen, barefoot, naked beneath her bathrobe, still in need of a shower. Jody's call had brought back that horrible day when she'd been in a killer's sights. She felt sick to her stomach.

"I think they were triplets. I interrogated Jon, and whenever I asked him if he was close to his brother, singular, his eyes would shift to the left, then down, before focusing on me again. I think he's hiding something. I think he's telling the truth about being a dentist from Ontario who has never been in trouble with the law. But I think he knows how John and Sean made their living. He knows and he's not talking. And I can't prove any of it. Nobody's listening to me!"

Sara could hear the frustration in Jody's voice.

"Sean, John, and Jon?" she said. "Yeah, their names

could be the result of unimaginative parents of triplets. So, you think Sean is still out there somewhere?"

"Yes," Jody said. "I do. That's why I want you and Frannie to be extra careful."

"It's been days since the incident. Don't you think he would have struck by now if he were planning to?"

"Why? His brother is in custody and the authorities believe they've got *him*. He has time to plan. Time to get revenge for the murder, as he sees it, of his brother."

"But how can he possibly track you all down?" Sara asked, puzzled.

"That's why I phoned you, Sara. He can't track us down. But he knows where you are. You and Frannie were in the red Mustang that he was trailing the day his brother got shot. He undoubtedly believed the gunfire came from the Mustang. He had to move fast after John was shot. He didn't have time to check the trajectory of the bullet. No, he will focus on you. I would have told you that the day you were at the mansion, but we truly believed he would be apprehended swiftly. And when Jon was arrested, we thought we had him."

"But now you don't," Sara concluded.

"Now I don't," Jody said.

"So, what are you going to do about it?" Sara asked.

"I'm going to take some time off from my job and come watch over you and Frannie for a while."

"Come on," said Sara. "We've got two spare bedrooms."

"I can't live with you. I'll use one of the surveillance vans. If I stayed with you, and he's watching, he'll know something's up."

"Okay, when can we expect you?"

"I'm already here," Jody said. "I'm phoning you from the van. I'm parked down the street."

"By yourself?"

"No one else is available."

Sara sighed. "Well, thank you, Jody."

"Thank me after I apprehend his behind," Jody said. "Goodbye, Sara."

She hung up before Sara could respond.

Paranoid now, Sara hurried upstairs to shower. She locked the bathroom door and left the shower curtain open. The floor got a little wet while she hastily bathed, but she felt better being able to see the door's handle.

She was also cautious opening the bathroom door when she finished showering.

She was beginning to feel a little foolish when she'd dressed and was going out the front door. Jody could be way off base. If Sean Gamble had any sense he would be in a country that didn't have any extradition laws by now.

Grief made you behave recklessly, though. His brother was dead. He might not be thinking like a cold-blooded assassin at this point, but like a loyal brother.

On the drive to the bookstore, she continued turning over in her mind the possibility that Sean Gamble was still out there. If he were being honest with himself, he would admit that he was the one at fault for his brother's death. John could have survived a clean shot to the shoulder. However, going headfirst through a wind-shield at over sixty miles per hour probably was not something a lot of people walked away from.

Psychopaths were not known for taking respon-sibility for their actions, though. Sean was most assuredly a psychopath. He would blame the people he was targeting for murder. He would want revenge because in his mind they had defended themselves. While being in the bull's eye, they had chosen not to go down without a fight like calves to the slaughter. He would think it his obligation to retaliate.

When she got to the store, she immediately went to Frannie and asked to see her in her office. After she'd told Frannie about the call from Jody, Frannie, sat, ashen, her eyes wide. "I'm sorry, Sara, but that makes sense to me. Their being triplets, I mean. Two of them were paid assassins while the third led a life above reproach. The killer brother phones him and tells him their brother is dead, to get to San Francisco, but when questioned not to mention he has another brother. John was his sole sibling. It's the stuff that writers turn into suspense novels or action films."

Pacing the floor, Sara said, "Well, I don't want to be in anyone's novel or film. This is my life and I want to live it without fear! Do you still have that gun you used to carry?"

Frannie nodded. "Yeah, and still know how to use it. Believe me, I'm going to have it on me from now on."

"Where is it?"

"In a lock-box in my closet."

"That's the first place a killer would look for his victim's weapon," was Sara's opinion.

"Excuse me," Frannie said. "But seeing as how we've never been targeted by a killer before, I had no idea I had to hide it!"

Sara plopped down in her chair behind the desk. Looking at Frannie, she laughed suddenly. "You know, you just have to laugh at life. I'm all ready to stop behaving like Harriet Tubman, leading the downtrodden to safety, and get married. And you're in love. Finally. Then, this guy comes along and throws a wrench in our plans."

"Who said I was in love with Erik?" Frannie asked, frowning.

"You didn't have to say it, it's written all over your face," Sara told her. "Now, stop denying it."

"Okay, I love him, but if he thinks I'm going to marry him, he's mistaken."

"Has he asked you?"

"Not in so many words, but I can tell he's building up his nerve to ask. He just doesn't want me to shoot him down. Plus, since he's such good friends with Jason, he knows what he's been through with you. He may think you've rubbed off on me."

"I'm a bad influence, huh?"

Frannie laughed. "Jason has never accused me of being a bad influence on you?"

"No, he just thinks you're a lesbian and you're in love with me."

Frannie laughed harder. "Why? Because I followed you from New York?"

Sara nodded in the affirmative.

"I love you like a sister," Frannie told her. "But only like a sister. I just wanted us to work together as partners in the organization. It's been a good relationship. I'll miss working with you when you marry Jason."

"I'll miss working with you, too," Sara said. "But I won't miss the weird hours or having to lie to Jason."

"That's why the organization puts you out once you get married," Frannie explained. "Women, as opposed to men, know how to keep a secret. But we don't believe you should have to keep secrets from your husband. It's not conducive to a happy marriage."

"How about a happy relationship?" Sara asked. "My relationship was strained because of all the secrets I had to keep. It's not conducive to a good relationship!"

"I had no trouble keeping it from every guy I ever dated," Frannie said.

"Because you haven't been in love with any of them. Watch. The longer you're with Erik, the more lying to him will bother you. And he will become suspicious. It didn't take long for Jason to start asking me questions about my whereabouts, the people I hired to work here. And he's been very curious about the tattoo. Just a few days ago, he mentioned that Erik had told him he saw your and Willow's tattoos, and Jason told Erik that I had one, too. Now he knows I lied when I told him I'd gotten it in college."

"I always thought tattooing members was a bad idea," Frannie said. "You've got thousands of women worldwide with crossed spears tattooed somewhere on their bodies. If the organization is exposed, we can all be easily identified."

"But who thinks that way?" Sara asked. "Lots of people have similar tattoos. How many times have you seen a woman with a tattoo of a rose on her upper arm? Is she a member of The Secret Order of the Rose? No. Jason is suspicious now because he knows you, Willow and I belong to the same service organization. That's all."

"Maybe you're right," Frannie said. "And at any rate, the organization doesn't have sinister goals. If we're found out, and Eunice is booted out of the president's cabinet, they wouldn't be able to convict us of anything. What have we done except save peoples' lives? Eunice would be seen as a hero. Women all over the United States would want her to run for president."

"She would make a great president," Sara said sincerely.

"She would," Frannie agreed. "Now, though, we have a killer to catch. How do you suppose we should do it? Because I'm gonna tell you right now, I'm not going to be anybody's sitting duck. If he's coming, we're gonna be ready for him."

"Amen," said Sara. "You've got a gun. I need a weapon, too."

"What do you know how to use?"

"I was on the softball team in high school and college. I can swing a mean bat."

Frannie laughed. "You and Willow."

Sara laughed, too. "I didn't tell you. I got an e-mail from her yesterday. She said Elvin tried to press charges for assault. Then, when he got her alone, he told her he'd drop the charges if she would take him back. Willow promptly tracked down his lover, and the woman told the police exactly what had happened the day Willow had discovered them naked in her closet. Elvin had lied to her, too, and told her he was a widower and all the women's clothes in the closet belonged to his dead wife. He was just too broken up to get rid of them."

"What a creep," Frannie said. "I'm so glad she met a sweet guy like Joe. Did she mention anything about him? Whether they're going to try a long-distance relationship or not?"

"No," said Sara. "Not a word about Joe." Sara looked at her friend soberly. "Do you think the Wal-Mart in Santa Rosa carries wooden baseball bats?"

"They should," said Frannie.

* * *

At the winery, Jason was having troubles of his own. With the torrential rains had come flooding. He was having to put sandbags around the perimeter of the entire vineyard. He'd hired six temporary workers to help him, Claude and Erik who seemed to be around for the long haul.

They were out in the rain, now, stacking sandbags two deep, hoping to hold the deluge at bay for as long as possible. Being heard over the rain was nearly impossible so they worked in silence, muscles straining, putting their backs into it.

His father was in the midst of it all, doing his part, but after two hours, Jason had insisted he go home. Eric hadn't wanted to, but Jason wouldn't take no for an answer. After he'd reminded him that his wife would be livid if he came down with pneumonia, Eric gave in and went to the house.

They worked on until night fell, then Jason paid the temporary workers and he and Erik went to the Hacienda to dry off and drink a couple of beers.

"Can you believe this rain?" Jason asked as he handed Erik a cold domestic brew. He sat down across from Erik at the kitchen table. They'd come through the mudroom, removed their raincoats, knocked the mud off their boots and grabbed towels to dry off with. Erik still had a towel on his head. His raincoat's hood had blown off as they were walking to the house.

"Sara told me a few weeks back that some of the ladies who come in her store had mentioned that we were going to have a bad rainy season, but I didn't pay much attention to her. Now, I don't know. Maybe they were right."

"It's a hell of a way to make a living," Erik said. "Being at the mercy of Mother Nature. I don't envy you. It's hard work. And you can lose everything at the drop of a hat, or an act of God."

"I respect my parents more and more every day," Jason told him. "I used to take what they did for granted. But now, I know what they went through, and I'm really proud to say I come from that kind of strength."

"I know what you mean," Erik said. He tossed back a long swallow. "When I was in high school, I would have been thrilled to have an old man like yours. My dad was a pillar of the community, but at home he was a tyrant. I once overheard your mother say that my parents were wonderful people. She had it half right. My mother was. My dad controlled us all with an iron fist. My mom was afraid of him. All of us were afraid of him. I was so happy to go away to college. Going to college on a football scholarship was my first act of rebellion."

"Damn, man, I had no idea you were catching hell."

"Nobody did," Erik said. "At home he would stomp me underfoot and I would behave the same way with my peers. It took me years before it occurred to me that I was acting just like him. I was in college by that time. Heather told me she was pregnant. I was foolish enough to call home for advice and he told me to make her get an abortion. Can you imagine? He said the baby was probably not mine. If she would have sex with me, she'd have sex with any number of other guys. He was disgusting. That's the last time I ever went to him for advice. I couldn't stand to be around him."

"Is that why you waited until he'd died before moving back home?" Jason asked.

Erik's brows came together in a frown. "You know, I never even thought about that. But probably. When I moved back with Melissa after the divorce, all I was thinking was that this would be a good place for her to grow up. And I definitely wouldn't have thought that if my dad were somewhere around to influence her. After all, he hadn't even wanted her to be born."

"You're a good father," Jason complimented him.

"I try to be." Erik grinned. "Now, if I can convince Frannie to marry me, she'll have a good mother, too."

Jason laughed. "Good luck with that."

Chapter 16

Sean had been staying at the inn on Arnold Drive for two days now. It had a lovely, homey atmosphere and somewhat soothed the rage simmering underneath the surface.

He'd dyed his blond hair brown, and gone were the togs that reminded him fondly of his favorite Schwarzenegger movie. He'd prepped-out, a long-sleeve cotton shirt in pale blue, dark blue cotton duck dress slacks, and black loafers. When he looked in the mirror he thought he looked disgusting.

However, the woman behind the desk apparently thought he was attractive. He was masquerading as a magazine writer doing a story on the area wineries. Each day, after he returned from spying on Sara Minton's house, he would stop by the desk and ask if he had any messages.

He was approaching the desk now. The woman, a blonde in her early twenties, looked up and smiled expectantly at him. Sean thought of walking past her without saying a word just to see a deflated expression on her face. That would be out of character, though, so he stopped, smiled, and said, "Hello. Did I get any messages while I was out?"

Her brown eyes took on a sympathetic aspect. "I'm afraid not, Mr. Baldwin. Maybe tomorrow." She knew he'd paid a week in advance.

What she didn't know was that Sean was leaving tomorrow. He was done watching Sara Minton. Tomorrow night he was going to end this one way or another. Either she would be dead, or he would. He'd had to be cautious because even though she appeared harmless, somehow she had known that she was being followed, and before John could squeeze off a shot she, or someone in the red Mustang with her, had fired.

Sean smiled graciously at the clerk. "Yes, maybe tomorrow. Thank you."

"Have a nice evening, sir," the clerk called as he turned away.

"Same to you," Sean said and climbed the stairs to his second-floor room. The inn was small. The first day he'd gotten there he'd learned everything he would ever want to know about it. They mostly catered to wine lovers. Their rooms were booked months in advance because those wine lovers who liked this part of Sonoma Valley knew there was a lack of hotel accommodations. Indeed, the inn was the only place a visitor who wasn't staying with friends or relatives could find a bed.

Once in his room, Sean closed the door, made sure

it was securely locked, and went to lie down on the bed fully clothed. Hands behind his head, he stared at the ceiling, thinking about Sara Minton. He couldn't figure out her connection with Elizabeth Mbeki. Old man Oswald had been no help when he'd phoned to tell him John was dead and that they had missed the target.

His eyes narrowed with hatred when he thought about their tense conversation.

"Dead, how?" asked Oswald.

"Shot by the people who're helping Elizabeth Mbeki. You obviously left out pertinent facts when you hired us. We didn't know we'd be going up against trained operatives."

"Don't be ridiculous. She got out of the country on her own. You read the e-mail she sent her lover. She said she was staying with friends. Friends, not a group of trained agents. Maybe you're mistaken. Maybe someone else killed your brother." The cold-blooded bastard had not even offered his sympathy. "At any rate," he went on, "you can still collect the payment once the job is done."

"I don't care about Elizabeth Mbeki anymore," Sean ground out. "My brother's dead and I'm going to get the person who killed him."

"Then, you're a fool," Oswald told him. "You should go with the plan. Find her, watch her and strike when she's alone. You're going to wind up getting killed, or worse, getting caught. Just don't let my name be on your tongue when they catch you."

Sean had laughed. "If I go down, you go down, you old fart!" He'd hung up then.

Sean knew he couldn't afford to wait any longer. He was worried that his brother, Jon, was soon going to crack under the pressure and tell the authorities everything. In fact, he expected the spineless worm to spill his guts sooner rather than later.

He'd gone to visit him in jail shortly after he'd donned his disguise. Jailhouse personnel, burnt-out, and entirely uninterested in visitors to their facility, had not paid close attention to him. If they had, he would be wallowing in jail now himself. The man who checked IDs had given his a cursory glance, handed it back to him, and said, "Walk through the metal detector." Sean had gladly done so. He wasn't carrying anything more lethal than a wooden toothpick, which he had stuck between his surly lips. He was doing his Elvis. Not that anyone would notice. So many people affected the confident swagger of the king of rock and roll nowadays.

Soon, he was sitting across from his brother, separated by glass. Jon had looked shocked to see him. He looked so much like John, that Sean felt like crying again, but he held himself together. "I just wanted to make sure you understood me when I called," he told Jon. "If you talk, I will make sure I pay a visit to you the next time I'm in your neck of the woods and you and your lovely wife and two ugly kids won't be happy to see me. Got me?"

Jon had frantically nodded, looked comically like a bobble-head doll.

"I don't expect you to stay in jail forever," Sean said. "You can tell them about me after November fourth. I'll be out of the country by then." He rose. "Goodbye, little brother. I hope we never lay eyes on each other again."

"I second that," Jon had the temerity to say.

Sean leapt toward him in a rage and Jon fell off his chair on the other side of the protective glass. Sean roared with laughter. "You coward. How am I going to hit you through inch-thick Plexiglas?"

He turned and left.

On the bed in the Glen Ellen Inn, he smiled. Tomorrow, he was going to get satisfaction.

That night, Sara made dinner for Jason at her house. Frannie was out, having gone to have dinner with Erik and Melissa. Nobody was venturing very far in this weather. Since morning, there had been a steady downpour. Driving any great distance was difficult, if not hazardous.

Sara even tried to talk Jason out of coming out in it. She phoned him at seven. He was supposed to be there at eight. When he answered, she said, "Sweetie, why don't we postpone dinner for a better night?"

He immediately knew to what she was referring. Lately, it was the most-talked-about topic in Glen Ellen. "I'll swim if I have to," he told her. "Don't worry, I'll take it slowly. Besides, if the road washes away while I'm with you, I'll have to spend the night."

"Don't say that!" Sara cried. "This weather scares me."

"All right, all right, chill, baby," he said, laughter evident in his tone. "Look, I'm going to come over early. You sound like you could use the company."

She really could use the company. Since she and Frannie had heard Jody's theory that Sean Gamble might want to do them harm, she'd been one step away from a nervous breakdown. But she and Frannie had agreed that they needed to carry on with their normal routines, except their weapon of choice should always be within reach at a moment's notice. Her baseball bat stayed close by.

She was looking at it leaning against the pantry door while she told Jason, "Yeah, I could use the company, but I'd really feel better if you wouldn't risk life and limb to be that company."

"Sorry to have to disappoint you, darlin', but I'm on the way. See you soon," Jason said, and hung up before she could protest further.

Sighing, Sara hung up the phone. She could hear the rain on the roof. Thunder shook the foundations of the house. She was fairly safe inside, but she wondered how Jody was faring in the surveillance van parked somewhere nearby.

Jody was wide awake after sleeping away the afternoon. She'd decided that her best bet was to sleep during the day, and stay awake all night. More than likely, if Sean Gamble was going to try anything, he would do it under the cover of darkness. Unless he were exceptionally bold, which didn't seem to be his normal way of doing things.

She'd read his file. He liked thinking things out. Being cautious. His brother had been the hotheaded one. Although, who knew how John's death had affected him? He might very well get impatient.

The cameras Jody had set up in a couple of trees were aimed at Sara's house. Front and back. Monitors inside the van displayed exactly what was going on in the targeted areas.

She was sitting in front of them now, drinking coffee and eating a stale ham sandwich. She had to remember to restock the minifridge tomorrow. She hoped she wouldn't be here tomorrow. But, in case she was, a girl had to eat.

Her bladder screamed as if reminding her of something else a girl had to do on occasion. She looked at the coffee cup in her hand. What was she thinking drinking two cups in quick succession?

There was nowhere in the van to relieve herself. And unlike a man, she couldn't pull an empty milk carton from under the seat and do her business. So, she reluctantly got up and went outside.

Two minutes later, she was peeing in bushes at the back of the van. It was a good thing Sara lived in a wooded area. There wasn't another house around for several blocks. Farm country. She hated it. She preferred the city where there were bathrooms on every corner.

Fortunately, the rain had somewhat let up, and she only got slightly soaked. Finished, she wiped with the wet cloth, balled it in her fist to dispose of later, and zipped her jeans.

She hurried around to the side door of the van and collided with someone in a black, hooded poncho. "What the hell!" she said, just as the blade of a knife sliced into her abdomen. She stared up at her assailant, a look of utter confusion on her face.

Sean smiled at her. "I guess you didn't see that one coming, bitch."

He savagely pulled the blade out.

Jody sank to the cold, wet ground and he stepped across her, and into the van.

Certain that she would be dead in a matter of minutes, he sat down and observed the monitors. He was patient. Well, not that patient. He hadn't been able to wait until tomorrow night to get on with it.

He'd lucked out this afternoon when he'd spotted this van and recognized it for what it was. Someone was looking over Sara Minton. His first move would be to get rid of her guardian angel. If his instincts were right, her guardian angel would be a *real* angel any minute now.

He laughed softly. This was fun.

"Uh-oh." He saw an SUV pulling into Sara Minton's driveway. A tall guy got out and ran onto the porch. Sara opened the door and kissed him. Whore. Yeah, he was going to enjoy offing her. He had every confidence that his luck would hold.

He'd certainly been lucky when he'd learned her identity. He was buying gas at a convenience store when he'd struck up a conversation with a chubby kid in a black Camaro. She was cute with red hair and an innocent aura about her, and she was drinking a bottle of apple juice while she filled her gas tank. Sean liked it when kids opted for nutritious drinks instead of drinking all those empty calories sodas provided.

"Nice car," he'd said.

"Thanks," she said, her green eyes sparkling. Poor kid probably didn't get many compliments.

Sara Minton just happened to drive by in her red Mustang at that moment, and he'd said, car lover that he was, "Man, what a beauty. And the babe behind the wheel ain't bad either."

The girl had giggled. "That's Sara. She owns the bookstore on Arnold Drive. And don't get your hopes up, she's taken."

Sean had thrilled to his good luck. He never got the kid's name, but he had Sara Minton's. After that, it was no trouble at all chatting up the clerk in the convenience store who conveniently supplied Sara's last name. It seemed she was known and liked by quite a few people around there. He was sure she would be missed after he killed her.

He sat watching the monitors, trying to formulate his next move. If he attacked suddenly, shooting off the front door's lock and kicking his way in, he would have the element of surprise and terror on his side. All that violence and noise often frightened the victim so much that it rendered her helpless due to panic. On the other hand, Sara Minton had not panicked when she saw John's gun trained on her. She'd calmly, and maliciously, put a bullet in him. He would wait awhile.

His wait lasted a full two minutes, then he got up and left the van.

Stepping across the body of the guardian angel once more, he didn't notice that she hadn't expired as he'd expected. This particular angel had had the foresight to wear a bulletproof vest. It wasn't designed for knife wounds, but it had adequately prevented the blade from penetrating any vital organs. She was bleeding. It hurt like hell, but she was determined to live.

She lay in the mud with her face turned to the side, breathing shallowly. She saw him leave. When he had been gone for what she judged to be a full minute she pulled herself up and went into the van.

Sean crossed the street. It had begun to rain a bit harder now. His new shoes squished. A man who wore only the best, most expensive clothing, he cursed this lousy weather.

It was ruining his shoes, his clothing and his gleeful

consideration of how satisfying it was going to be to watch Sara Minton die in the arms of her lover.

Surely, by now, they were naked and doing the nasty. That kiss had been more than adequate foreplay.

As he walked up onto the porch he screwed on the silencer. Not that he thought he necessarily needed it. She didn't have close neighbors. No one to run to her rescue. But better safe than sorry.

He stepped back a few paces and pumped four rounds into the place where the door and the lock met. Wood splinters and minute pieces of metal flew in the air. The sound was minimal compared to the report of a gun without a silencer. But he knew it had to have been heard by Sara Minton and her lover. He kicked the door open and prepared for a fight.

Sara and Jason were in the kitchen when they heard the shots. There was no mistaking that sound, however muted. Sara immediately grabbed the bat leaning against the pantry door. Jason hadn't even noticed the bat until she did that.

"Sara, what's going on?"

Sara didn't have time to explain because at that moment, the invader was kicking the front door in. Thinking quickly, she said, "The basement. We've got to get to the basement!"

She pushed him toward the basement door. "Now, Jason, damn it!"

Jason moved quickly, pushing her in front of him toward the basement door in case whomever had broken into the house so violently came into the kitchen and started shooting. He would get him in the back, not Sara.

Once they were through the door, Sara locked it, and

they ran down the steps to the large basement. Sara went directly to the breaker box and turned off the electricity to the entire house.

"We know this house better than he does, it'll give us the advantage," she explained in a whisper.

Upstairs, Sean paused in his tracks when all the lights in the house went out. He was in the hallway. Even if there had been a full moon, no rays would have penetrated into the hallway. No windows. Momentarily disoriented, he cursed under his breath and stood still, listening. Closing his eyes, he waited a couple of minutes before opening them again. Slowly, his eyes became acclimated to the dark. If he didn't panic, he would be able to find his way around. He would find them, too, eventually.

In the van, Jody pulled off the vest and looked at the wound in her abdomen. It was still bleeding, but not gushing, which she was grateful for. As a soldier and later as a police officer, she'd received worse injuries in the line of duty.

She grabbed several paper towels from the console beside the steering wheel where she kept little necessities, and pressed them against the wound. Then, she sat down and placed a phone call to Frannie Anise. When she was finished with that call, she rang the mansion in San Francisco and requested backup.

Once she got off the phone, she sat down and breathed deeply. Someone had to go in there and rescue Sara, and she was the only "someone" available.

Okay, Sean thought, *my plan for a quick in and out isn't working.* She'd slowed him down by shutting off the electricity. She definitely was not the sort to panic.

He could really use John's help about now. John would welcome the chance to go bananas and trash the house in a bid to terrify her. No one was better at acting crazy. *Let's face it, John was crazy!*

He would be needling him right now for being so cautious. You only live once, he'd say, get in there and get the little tramp. Show her who's boss!

Sean laughed nervously. To hell with John. He needed to exorcise his ghost so that he could think clearly, figure out what Sara Minton was up to. Where would she hide? Then, he remembered a salient point from his childhood. The breaker box was in the basement. He strained his eyesight in the darkness, trying to find the kitchen. Once he was in the kitchen, he felt along the wall until he located the basement door.

"Give me the bat, Sara, and find a hiding place," Jason said, his hand firmly around the base of the bat.

"No," Sara said in a vicious whisper. "He's here because of me, and I'm not letting you get yourself killed."

"Woman, I'm your man. I'm not going to stand by and let you fight for me!"

She gave him the bat. "Okay, you can have it, but you've got to listen to my plan before you go off half-cocked."

Jason hefted the bat in his hands. "I'm listening."

"You're going to wait down here, hidden near the foot of the stairs. I'm going to trip him when he comes down, and then you're going to whale on him with the bat."

"And if he doesn't lose his balance and fall?"

"Oh, he's going to lose his balance all right," Sara said. "I'm going to pull his feet right out from under him."

Several gunshots were heard at the top of the stairs. "He's coming!" Sara said, and, her eyes accustomed to the dark by now, she ran to get under the stairs. Jason moved back into an alcove at the bottom of the stairs so that his silhouette wouldn't be the first thing the home invader would see when he started down the steps.

Sean, being careful, shot a couple rounds into the room before he started down. He wanted them cowering below. He wanted them worrying about their bowels turning to water, instead of ways to defend themselves.

One round lodged into the wall not two inches above Jason's head. The other went into the concrete floor of the basement.

Because Sara had grown up in this house, she knew all of its creaks and all of its nooks and crannies. She knew that the third step creaked louder than the rest of them.

When Sean Gamble's full weight was on the third step, she ran forward, grasped him around both ankles and jerked backward.

She heard the pings of the gun's report as he got off two more rounds before letting go with a volley of filthy expletives on his way down.

Jason stepped forward and began swinging with the bat. Every time he connected Sean Gamble cried out in pain. Sara scrambled from under the stairs and spotted the gun lying on the floor about a foot out of Gamble's reach. She went and picked it up then ran over to the breaker box and switched the electricity back on.

By that time, Jody, who had heard the gunshots when she came into the house was at the top of the stairs with her gun drawn. "Sara!" she called.

Sara almost felt sorry for the pitiful heap of human trash that was Sean Gamble. He was curled into the fetal position on the basement floor, whimpering from pain. He had tiny cuts on his face, obviously from the splinters he'd produced by shooting through the doors, a split lip, and a gash across his left eyebrow. Sara imagined he'd be black and blue all over tomorrow from the hits he'd taken from Jason's bat.

"It's okay," she told Jody. "We're okay."

Jody descended the stairs slowly. She leaned against the wall halfway down. "Then maybe somebody can come up here and help me. The bastard stabbed me."

Sara handed Jason the gun, he tossed the bat onto the old couch down there, and held the gun on Sean. "Shoot him if he moves," Sara said before hurrying to give assistance to Jody.

Sara helped Jody down the steps and led her to the couch. Peering into Jody's eyes, she asked, "How bad is it?"

"I'll live," Jody said. She gave Sara a weak smile. "You and your guy did all right."

Sara looked up at Jason. "Yeah, he kept his head about him. What about you? Should I call the paramedics?"

"No, a medic is coming from headquarters," Jody told her, keeping her voice low because of Jason's presence. "I'll be okay until then. Hospitals report gunshot wounds and knife wounds to the authorities. I'm fine sitting here. What I want you to do is find something to tie Gamble up with. He's a sneaky bastard and I want him hog-tied."

Rising, Sara knew just the thing. The laundry room was in the basement. Her mother had kept a length of thick twine in the cabinet next to the washing machine in case she had to replace her clothesline. She loved hanging laundry to dry in the bright sunlight of a Northern California day.

Sara enjoyed tying his hands behind his back at the wrists, then tightly tying his ankles together. He didn't give her a fight, but he did have questions for her. "Who are you people?"

"I'll tell you who we *aren't*," Jody told him. "We aren't killers. Otherwise your behind would be toast."

"Why did you hide Elizabeth Mbeki?" he asked.

Jason wondered who Elizabeth Mbeki was, but didn't say anything. He was also curious as to the identity of the tall, practically bald, muscular babe with the gun.

His questions would have to wait though, because there was more commotion above them and soon, Frannie was running down the stairs screaming, "Sara!"

When she appeared he saw that she was armed and was holding the weapon as if she knew exactly how to use it. More disturbing was the vision of Erik, behind her, brandishing a shotgun about the size of a cannon.

"Lower your weapons!" Sara shouted, smiling. "Gamble's trussed up like a turkey and ready to be carted off."

The relief on Erik's face was priceless. "Damn. What are you women involved in?"

"That's a very good question," Jason said, looking at Sara.

"I'll explain it all later," Sara promised, her eyes pleading.

"I've heard that before," Jason said tiredly. He walked over to her and handed her Gamble's gun. "I'm outta here." He looked at Erik. "And if you had any sense, you would be, too."

Chapter 17

"Jason!" Sara cried.

She put the gun down on the couch next to Jody and appealed to Frannie. "Look after her, she's been stabbed in the stomach."

"Oh, my God," said Frannie, rushing to Jody's side.

Sara left them and ran up the basement steps. Jason was walking through the front door when she got to the living room. "At least hear me out!"

He didn't even turn around. "I've heard it all," he yelled to be heard over the rain. "I'm done, Sara. Go make a fool out of some other guy."

"Fool?" Sara yelled back.

He was quickly walking toward his Explorer. Sara knew that once he got to the SUV he would close and lock the door, thereby locking her out of his life. So, she did the only thing she could think to do: She tackled him.

Fueled by rage, Jason was stomping across the lush lawn in the rain when she threw herself onto his back. Her weight propelled both of them to the ground. Laughing out of shock and amazement, Jason turned onto his back. Sara sat on top of him. "You're going to listen to me, damn it!"

"I've never hit a woman, Sara, but you've pushed me just about as far as I'm willing to go. You could have been killed! Get the hell off me."

"No!"

"I'm asking you nicely."

"You're being unfair, Jason. I resigned from the organization days ago. I had no idea he had targeted me and Frannie until Jody contacted me day before yesterday and said she, against the better judgment of the authorities, thought he might come back for us. It involves Mary. Mary had to get out of South Africa because her life was threatened. We help people whose lives are endangered. What we do is hardly ever dangerous. But we're not naive, we know it's innately dangerous and we try our best to prepare for it. This case is the closest I've ever gotten to being physically harmed. The man who was after Mary hired two hit men. That guy in there is one of them. The other got killed the day I told you Frannie and I had taken Mary to the airport to catch a flight to L.A."

"That's why you were behaving so strangely that day," Jason said, remembering. "Because you'd just escaped death. They tried to get to Mary and therefore, you and Frannie's lives were threatened too."

"Yeah, Jody and her partner arrived just in time to deal with them, otherwise it could have been bad for me, Frannie, and Eli...*Mary.*"

"So, her name's not really Mary."

Sara shook her head. "No, Jason, and there are a lot of things I can never tell you. But I'm telling you the truth now, and it's up to you whether or not you're gonna believe me. I wish I could tell you everything. But look at it this way. What if *you* worked for a top secret branch of the military? Even if you and I were married, you couldn't tell me what you did on your missions. I wouldn't expect you to. A lot of innocent people's lives depend on my discretion. I will *never* be able to tell you everything I've done in the past six years. *Never!*"

She got off him and sat on the lawn, her head lowered in abject misery. "Now, if you can't accept that, then you're free to go. I can't hold you. And I wouldn't want to."

Jason sat on the lawn too, his head in his hands. "In spite of my suspicions, I never suspected you could be in this deep. Hiding foreign nationals. Bringing them into the country illegally, too?"

"Each case is different. We have lawyers who deal with that."

"I take it Gary Pruitt is one of them?"

She didn't answer.

"They really have you brainwashed."

"I'm not brainwashed. I knew what I was doing when I joined. I knew the sacrifices I would have to make. The organization saved my life, Jason."

He stared up at her. The rain had slowed down to a drizzle instead of a downpour. He could see her face clearly in the illumination from the porch light. Her braids were soaked and glistened with water droplets. She met his eyes.

"The day Frannie took me to meet her sisters in the organization, I was sitting at the kitchen table in my apartment, playing with a knife, trying to get up the nerve to slash my wrists. It was a few weeks after Billy got killed. I wanted to die too."

"Oh, Sara!" He sounded appalled that she had gone through such suffering, but he didn't move to pull her into his arms. He waited for her to continue.

"Frannie showed up and wouldn't go away until I let her in. She made me get up and shower, get dressed, and then she took me to a building on the West Side. That day, Jason, I found a new purpose. Suicide never entered my mind again. Don't worry, I'm not unstable. I spent the next six years helping other women who found themselves at the ends of their ropes. I don't regret it for a minute. I'm not going to lie to you and say that."

"I love you, Sara. And I'm glad you found the strength to go on after losing Billy. But this organization took advantage of you when you were in a fragile state."

"No, they didn't. They offered me an alternative. They gave me a way to make a difference in the world. How many of us talk about doing something good for somebody else but never get around to doing it? How many of us see starving children on TV, or hear about terrorists attacking a school bus or a crowd of women and children, and say 'Oh, God, that's awful!'. But that's all we do? The organization didn't take advantage of me, I took advantage of them! And, now, I've met a man I want to marry. I'm prepared to give them up. You can't remain a member if you get married."

"Then you're telling me you're willing to give up all that for me?" Jason asked, sarcasm evident in his tone.

"All the secret trips, crazed hit men, and a group of Amazons to play spy with?"

Sara laughed. She was emotionally wrung out. What else could she say? Getting to her feet, she said, "That's all I have to say on the subject. I'm going inside out of the rain. Good night, Jason."

Sara went inside.

Jason slowly got to his feet. He felt like a heel. The woman he'd proclaimed his love for had just told him that she had once contemplated suicide and he hadn't offered her any comfort whatsoever.

The fact was, he was mentally and physically exhausted. First the vines were attacked by root rot, then flooding threatened the vineyard. Now, his woman turns out to be some kind of spy with a secret organization of female do-gooders. He was dizzy. Dizzy, and wet.

He walked to the Explorer. He had to go home and think. Think about everything Sara had said tonight. Think about what life would have been like from now on if that guy had killed her. Think about how close that bullet had come to his head a few minutes ago. Think about whether his faith in Sara was strong enough to get them through this crisis. Or if it was truly over between them.

Four operatives and a medic arrived from headquarters about an hour and a half after Jody had phoned them for backup. The inclement weather had slowed them down.

Sara, Frannie and Erik walked outside with two of them as Jody was carried out on a stretcher and put into the huge unmarked van. Sara went and kissed Jody on the cheek. She didn't care any longer that Jody's demeanor was above sentimentality. "You saved us," she told her. "If not for you, we might have been helpless."

Jody smiled. "Just looking out for my sisters."

Sara jumped down out of the back of the van, and soon they were watching it drive away.

Sean Gamble was led away, limping, by two more operatives who'd replaced the twine Sara had used on him with handcuffs. They put him in the back of a specially built sedan that had iron mesh separating the back seat from the front, and no handles on the back doors.

When they drove off, Sara breathed a sigh of relief. She looked at Frannie and Erik. "Did Jody interrupt your dinner? Where's Melissa? You'd better get back to her."

"Melissa's fine," Erik said. "The house is more secure than the White House. You need us more right now."

Sara smiled at him. Life was funny. When she'd been that insecure chubby kid, she would never have imagined she would one day actually like her tormentor. But she did. "That's sweet of you, Erik. I'm okay, though. I would really prefer to be alone."

Frannie went and pulled her into her arms. "You wouldn't lie to us, would you?"

Sara peered into her best friend's eyes. Her expression was determined. Definitely not despondent. "I'm not the same woman I was six years ago. I can handle losing Jason behind this. I made my choices. I have to live with them."

"I'd like to knock some sense into his head," Frannie said with vehemence.

Sara laughed softly and playfully pushed Frannie toward Erik. "Erik, take her with you before she hurts somebody."

"Okay, I'm not going to argue with you," Erik said, satisfied she was all right. "I'd better go get my shotgun. This is the first time it's been out of its display case."

"It *was* loaded?" asked Sara.

"Oh, yeah," he said. "Frannie showed me how to load it."

Smiling, Sara watched him jog back to the house. She and Frannie followed more slowly. It had miraculously stopped raining for the moment, but thunder could be heard in the distance. Sara suspected the storm front hadn't yet passed.

"Jason freaked out, huh?" Frannie said resignedly.

"Uh-huh. I think my almost getting killed tonight was the last straw for him," Sara said. She sincerely understood Jason's point of view. She would be outraged too. However, she didn't believe she would let it come between them. "I love him, but if he doesn't have it in his heart to understand that I did what I had to do under the circumstances then maybe it would be better if we didn't marry."

"Give him time," Frannie said comfortingly. "He'll come around."

"I'm not holding my breath," Sara said.

By the time they stepped onto the porch, Erik was returning with the brand-new shotgun in his right hand. "Frannie, maybe you should teach me how to use this thing if our life together is going to involve nights like this."

Frannie kissed Sara's cheek. "Good night, sweetie. Let me get Wyatt Earp home."

Jason didn't go home; he kept driving. The rain had let up, and he pointed the car south, toward San Francisco. He needed to talk to someone, and his parents would not do. They would take Sara's side. He'd learned that when they had told him not to expect to know everywhere she went and to "suck it up" concerning his gripes about her secretiveness. They seemed to think that love was all that mattered.

It was Saturday night, and he knew where Franklyn would be until midnight—the Vineyard, his restaurant near Chinatown. His stomach growled. He was hungry. He and Sara hadn't had the chance to get to dinner what with having to cope with the house invasion.

He laughed, sounding insane to himself. What did she expect of him? He was only a man. He didn't want to have to deal with his woman getting shot at. He didn't want to worry every time she was out of his eyesight. Or having his heart plummet to the pit of his stomach every time the phone rang in the middle of the night.

Franklyn was glad to see him and gave him a warm bear hug, then promptly went back to work juggling several individualized orders for his hungry patrons. Jason talked throughout the chaos, wait staff rushing in and out of the swinging doors to the kitchen, chefs, two of them, filling orders of their own, and support staff like the chefs-in-training who did all the grunt work like cleaning up after the chefs, keeping the work stations clear of vegetable peelings and so forth.

Franklyn never stopped moving, but he insisted on Jason telling him his troubles while Jason ate from a plate Franklyn had piled high with delicious food. Jason told him everything, leaving nothing out. Franklyn listened patiently as he chopped vegetables, made exquisite sauces, braised lamb, roasted chicken, grilled salmon. Jason didn't know how his brother did it. He'd go crazy inside of a week.

He finished the food on his plate. It had been just what he needed. And by the time he'd completed his tale of woe, he realized that Franklyn had provided him with physical sustenance and spiritual sustenance in the form of a brother's love.

"Don't call it quits with Sara," Franklyn said as he whipped potatoes. He looked Jason in the eyes. "It's obvious she was trying her best to be as honest with you as she possibly could. Her quitting the organization for you was a big step in that direction. What happened tonight was out of her control. Entirely. You're afraid, aren't you?"

"Damn straight, I'm scared," Jason said. "I'm scared that next time she won't be so lucky!"

Franklyn smiled at him. "Have you noticed that life is dangerous in and of itself? Sara's husband, Billy, died when a man fell asleep at the wheel. We have no control over anything except whom we choose to let into our lives. Choose wisely, brother. From all indications, Sara is a loyal woman. She would give her life to save others. I don't see how you could ask for a better woman than that. Don't let your fear of losing her keep you from sharing your life with her. You both deserve to be happy but for different reasons. You've never known love before Sara. Sara has known a great love and lost it. She invested her heart in you. Don't let her down and make her regret it."

Jason's heart broke when Franklyn said that. It *had* been fear that had made him react the way that he had. He was a twenty-first-century male, for God's sake. The closest he got to combat was playing video games.

And those didn't involve live ammunition. Yeah, a guy shooting doors down would scare the crap out of anyone. Sara had been terrified too, he'd seen it in her eyes, but she had reacted calmly in the heat of battle. For that matter, he hadn't been a craven coward himself. He had been prepared to take a bullet for her. He had been prepared to beat the gunman to death with a baseball bat. Franklyn amazed him with his next words. "Just ask yourself this," he said. "If the situation were reversed, would you want Sara to believe in *you?* If so, then your only choice is to forget about the organization and go get Sara and take her in your arms and love her forever. That's my advice." He laughed. "But then, I'm a man who's totally in love with his wife."

After Frannie and Erik left, Sara went to the garage, got a large piece of plywood, a hammer and nails, and covered the front entrance to the house. Gamble had destroyed her front door. She cleaned up pieces of it as best she could, but the carpenter would have to remove the damaged door whenever she could get him out here. For now, nailing a piece of plywood over it was the best she could do. It would keep wild animals and, hopefully, other home invaders out until the door was replaced.

Following the carpentry work, she went to the kitchen to see if dinner could be salvaged. She'd prepared spaghetti and meatballs. The meatballs in red sauce were still simmering on low, and she hadn't yet cooked the pasta, so at least she wasn't going hungry tonight.

She boiled the pasta until it was al dente, then sat down to eat. She forced herself to finish her meal. She refused to make herself sick over Jason Bryant. She

refused to waste precious time on self-recrimination,
either. She'd done the best with what she had to work
with. She was thirty-one. Life was short. Look at how
short it had been for poor Billy. Craving a man the way
she did Jason was a habit, just like any other habit. She
could unlearn it. She could cleanse her system of him
inside of a week if she worked diligently enough at it.
Which meant, she couldn't let herself mope around.
She had to stay busy.

At the conclusion of her meal, she washed the dishes,
dried them, put them away, scrubbed the kitchen floor
and took the trash out. Then she went upstairs and took
a bath. She felt dirty after her encounter with Gamble.
Plus, her hair could use a good wash and a condition
after getting soaked in the rain more than once.

She was soaking in the tub when her cell phone rang.
It was lying on the bath table right next to her. She
quickly dried her hands on a towel, and picked it up to
see who was calling. She saw Jason's name and number
and set the damn thing back down without answering
it. She wasn't going to talk to him tonight. Maybe
tomorrow. Or the next day. For tonight, she didn't want
any more drama.

What could he have to say, anyway? I'm sorry? Yet,
again? He was always apologizing but never with real
sincerity. The last time he'd apologized he'd told her
that he would always have her back, no matter what.
Let a little thing like a home invasion happen, and he
was out of there!

She laughed, her voice resounding off the large
bathroom's walls.

She didn't need someone as wishy-washy as Jason
Bryant. That spoiled ex-playboy. Why, he hadn't even

sold his house in Bakersfield yet. Obviously because he wanted a backup plan when his dalliance with the winery—and her—didn't pan out. Yeah, she saw it all clearly now. He was not the type of man for the long haul. She was lucky she'd turned down his marriage proposal. They would've been headed for divorce court inside of two years, three, tops.

She tried to soothe herself with these thoughts. But she wound up crying anyway. Who was she fooling? Not herself. Jason was the best thing that had ever happened to her. And she'd lost him because of her loyalty to Aminatu's Daughters. She was a big girl. She couldn't regret loving him. And she couldn't regret loving her sisters, either. It was too bad she was the loser in all of this. But, that's life.

She got out of the tub, dried off, flossed and brushed her teeth and went to the adjacent bedroom to get a nightgown from the lingerie drawer. She sighed tiredly as she climbed underneath the covers.

She dimmed the lamp on the nightstand. She didn't feel like sleeping in complete darkness tonight. Images of Gamble kept floating through her mind. She glanced at the clock. It was nearly half past midnight. My, how time flies when you're under assault. Closing her eyes, hoping that she would be able to sleep, she wondered where Jason was and why he'd phoned her. She should have answered the phone.

She sat bolt upright in bed. Maybe he'd been in some kind of trouble. A woman whose husband had been killed in a car accident never stopped having thoughts like that. She would return his call.

Picking up the cell phone from the nightstand, she dialed his number and waited as it rang several times without his answering. She didn't want to leave a message so she hung up when the message function kicked in. Where was he?

She stared at the clock again. It was too late to phone his relatives to ask if they knew where he was. Certainly not his parents. Franklyn would still be up though. After all, he didn't close the Vineyard until midnight. He would probably get home about an hour after that. She would wait a few more minutes and then phone him at home.

She didn't have to wait that long, however, because Jason phoned her again ten minutes later. This time she quickly answered. "Hello?"

"I'm glad you answered because I refused to leave a message," he said. "Are you all right?"

"I'm physically all right," she told him.

"Good. Who nailed the plywood over your front door?"

Her heart leapt. How would he know there was plywood over the front door unless he was outside her house or had been outside her house since she'd done it? "I did."

"When I got to San Francisco, I thought about that. But I figured Erik would do it before he left."

"I think Erik was preoccupied with Frannie, but he was very nice to me. I had to make them leave. Told them I wanted to be alone."

"Do you really?"

"What?"

"Want to be alone?"

"That depends, Jason. Are you asking because you want to come to me or are you asking out of some warped sense of obligation?"

"I'm asking because I want to come to you."

"Then, no, I don't want to be alone."

"I'm standing on your back porch."

"I'm on my way," she said, and hung up.

Swiftly throwing her legs over the side of the bed, she hit the floor running.

"You went to see Franklyn?" she asked the moment he stepped into the house.

Jason picked her up and squeezed her tightly. She smelled wonderful. A lot better than he probably did after getting soaked in the rain and driving to San Francisco, standing in a kitchen redolent with all kinds of food smells. The scent had probably permeated his skin, his hair, his clothing. "Yeah, I went to see my big brother," he told her. "I had to have someone unbiased to talk to. My parents are always on your side."

"I love your parents," Sara said, smiling.

"They love you, too. A little too much. You can't do any wrong in their books. They want grandbabies by you, and the sooner the better. Franklyn is more logical. He can see both sides of the situation and he cares for my happiness."

Sara was helping him out of his jacket. It was still damp. She hung it on the nearby coat rack. "What did Franklyn say?"

"He said he didn't think I'd ever be able to find a better woman than you."

Sara, a bundle of nerves, burst into tears. "I love your brother!"

Jason picked her up again and held her close. "I was terrified, Sara. When I left here tonight, all I was thinking was that having your house invaded wasn't something that happened to people living right. It wasn't a part of normal everyday life. You could have been killed!"

"I know!"

"We could all have been killed by that lunatic!"

"I know! I'm sorry."

"Stop apologizing," Jason said as he set her feet back on the floor. "I realized that I'd rather go through the agony of the possibility of losing you one day rather than not have you in my life at all. Life's tough. As my grandma Monique says, often while sipping whiskey, it ain't for sissies."

Sara laughed as she wiped her tears away. "That's true." She thought of Frannie and Willow and their personal histories. She thought of so many others who had gone through pure hell but had pulled themselves up and kept on living. She looked into Jason's eyes. "Then where do we go from here?"

"Vegas," Jason answered. He sniffed himself. "But first, I need to use your shower."

They walked upstairs with their arms about each other's waists. Sara gave him fresh towels and a new toothbrush and watched him while he stripped down. "Just put them on that chair next to the door," she told him.

Naked, Jason stood before her. "Sara, will you marry me?"

"Yes," Sara said quietly.

Then he kissed her for the first time since she'd let him in the back door. After which he got in the shower and she picked up his smelly clothes and went to put them in the wash.

She came back into the bedroom a few minutes later and put his wallet, car keys and the two condoms she'd found in his pocket on the bureau top. He was still in the shower. She'd smiled when she'd seen the condoms. She supposed he'd thought he was going to get lucky after dinner. What he'd gotten was shot at.

It would take her a long time to forgive herself for endangering his life. She figured around fifty years would be sufficient time to make it up to him.

Thinking better of it, she went and got the condoms from the bureau and put them on the nightstand. Then, she got into bed and picked up a paperback novel by one of her favorite writers. She couldn't concentrate on it, though.

Less than ten feet away, the man she loved was naked in her shower for the first time. Whenever they'd been together in the past, they'd always been at his house.

With his parents at home again, they'd had to be creative. Once they were married, though, she wouldn't feel any qualms about making love to him while his parents were somewhere in the house. Or would she? She'd have to wait and see. If she found it still made her uneasy, she would have to learn to live with it. They were going to have children someday, and they would certainly be in the house when they made love. She would have to get in the habit of locking doors then.

Jason strolled into the bedroom buck to the bone. He had a good excuse. Her bathrobe was way too small for him, and he had nothing else to put on.

He went to Sara, pulled her to her feet and bent his head to kiss her, but stopped when he was within two inches of her mouth. He'd noticed the condoms on the nightstand.

"You washed my clothes?"

"You can't put back on dirty clothes."

"You see, men don't think that way. We think that as long as our bodies are clean, the state of the clothes we put on them doesn't matter."

"That's why a man will wear his clothing until they can practically walk around on their own?" Sara asked sweetly.

"Exactly," Jason said. "We'll only wash them when they smell so badly they almost make you puke. Then, they're dirty."

"It's a good thing God created the woman," Sara told him, bringing him down to kiss him. "Otherwise you men would be living in your filth." She knew he was joking. Jason was almost as fastidious as she was. It was fun being this free with him again, though.

Their mouths came together in a slow, wet kiss. The taste on their tongues was sweet and satisfying after a terrifying night. To be back in each other's arms was such bliss that they both felt like weeping. Instead, they fell onto the bed. Jason reached down and raised the hem of her nightgown above her waist, pressed his hardened penis against her warm vagina. Sara opened her legs farther. It felt so good she could think of nothing except having him inside of her. A few minutes ago, she had been in this bed alone wondering where he was. Now he was holding her, soothing her fears, making her moan with anticipatory delight.

She raised her hips, encouraging him to take his pleasure. Jason, so grateful to be about to make love to her again, simply followed her lead. Nothing would ever make him ignore her needs again. Tonight, he had become a man. Tonight, he had made the choice to love her completely.

No more fears. No more second-guessing. He thrust all of himself into her. Their bellies were rubbing together, he was so far into her as she writhed beneath him, calling his name in a voice rife with passion. What a fool he'd been to doubt her love. To ever doubt her capacity for truth. This was the truth: They loved each other.

He bent and kissed her deeply. She clung to him,

giving as good as she got. He licked her breasts, suckled her nipples, and all the while his thrusts were long, deep and oh so fulfilling. Sara's body was so soft, yet strong. She didn't lie passively but met his thrusts, her vaginal muscles quivering with sexual stimulation.

She gave a loud sigh, bucked wildly underneath him, then fell back on the pillow, momentarily spent. Jason smiled at the seductive image she made, her eyes dreamy as they gazed into his, her mouth soft, her hair splayed across the pillow. He felt his own impending orgasm and it was at that moment that he remembered he didn't have on a condom.

He stopped, but he knew if only a little sperm had been released, Sara could already have been impregnated. He reached over and grabbed a condom anyway. He showed it to Sara. She smiled. "It's too late now."

He dropped the condom and continued thrusting. He seemed to grow harder inside of her. Sara felt it too. Her expression was at once surprised and delighted. She gasped as she came again, and he rolled with her and had a powerful orgasm. He threw his head back as he filled her with his seed. It was wonderful. Sara raised her hips off the bed, meeting him thrust for thrust.

When he lay beside her on the bed, face to face with her, he said, "Is it agreed? We'll fly to Las Vegas, get married, and not tell anyone until we get back?"

"When do you want to leave?"

"Tomorrow morning. Pack light."

Chapter 18

Frannie was so happy when Sara told her she and Jason were going away together for a few days that she didn't ask any questions. She waved goodbye to them as Jason's Explorer pulled out of the driveway, then she went to phone Erik with the good news. Sara and Jason were back together!

She spent Sunday with Erik and Melissa. On Monday morning, she opened the bookstore, accepted several boxes of books from Baker & Taylor, their distributor, and did pretty brisk business for a soggy day.

She envied Sara and Jason being in sunny Las Vegas.

In Vegas, on Monday morning, Sara awakened in Jason's arms. She took a moment to admire her engagement ring and wedding band. Jason slept on, with her panties at a cocky angle on his head. She laughed softly. She couldn't attribute his craziness to too much champagne because neither of them had drunk more than two glasses. He was just nuts that way.

She tried to pry his arm from around her waist and slip out of bed, but the moment she touched his arm, his grip on her tightened, and he came awake. He opened his eyes. "Where do you think you're going?"

"To the bathroom," she told him, looking at him with narrowed eyes.

He let go of her. "Hurry, I don't want to lie in a wet bed."

She thumped him on the forehead and got out of bed.

Watching her hurrying toward the bathroom, her behind very enticing, Jason said, "Oops, I thought I saw some leaking out."

"Shut up!" Sara cried, laughing. "You're horrible." She closed the bathroom door so she wouldn't have to hear his comments.

Jason came into the bathroom while she was sitting on the toilet. This was the first time he'd ever come into the bathroom when she was on the toilet and Sara was embarrassed. "Is this what I have to look forward to?" she asked. "Your coming into the bathroom while I'm using it?"

"We've showered together, babe. I've seen you naked."

"Yeah, but you've never seen me on the toilet. What if I was doing something other than peeing?"

"You mean having a bowel movement?" Jason smiled at her. "I would close my nose and come on in."

Sara watched him with her mouth open in disgust. "No, you won't! You are not to come in the bathroom when I'm on the toilet, Jason Bryant! Get out!"

"But baby, we're married. We share everything now."

"Not bowel movements! Out!"

Laughing, Jason left, closing the door behind him.

He quickly ducked back in. "Um, how about when you're peeing. Am I permitted to come in then?"

"No," Sara cried. "Always knock before you come in."

He looked crestfallen, but Sara knew that was a ruse. He was having fun at her expense and she was incensed. For a while, anyway.

To punish him, she went ahead and showered while she was in the bathroom. When she returned to the outer room, he'd already had breakfast delivered and it was set up on the table near the window. A fresh rose in a vase sat in the center of the table.

He was sitting at the table in his bathrobe, reading the morning paper.

He looked up and smiled. "Your breakfast is served, Mrs. Bryant."

Her irritation with him fled.

Breakfast done, Sara sat at the desk with her laptop in front of her. She needed to check her mail to see if Eunice had finally answered her e-mail. She didn't hold out any hope of that, though, because that morning she'd heard on the news that the United States was in talks with North Korea about missile tests. More than likely, Eunice would be in the thick of it.

Jason was in the bathroom taking a shower.

She logged onto the organization's Web site and clicked on her messages. She scanned the sixteen addresses and was surprised to see a message from Eunice:

Writing fast, so bear with me. I heard about the attack on you and your fiancé. I'm so relieved you were not injured in any way. We really screwed up this one. Thank God that Jody followed her instincts and went to watch over you. She'll get a commendation. As for you: Congratulations. I wish you all kinds of happiness. Marriage is a wonderful institution if you don't mind being committed. So, join the rest of the nuts, and enjoy yourself! You know where to send my invitation. On a serious tip, you have been a wonderful operative and I hate to lose you. Remember, you are still my sister. Don't be a stranger. Love, Eunice.

Smiling, Sara fired off a reply:

We eloped. However, we will have another ceremony and a reception at the Hacienda sometime soon. Hope you can be there, but I will understand if you can't make it. After all, you *are* saving the world. And I won't forget that you're my sister. Much love, Sara.

She then shut down the laptop.

Jason came out of the bathroom, drying his hair on a towel. "Sweetheart, what do you want to do today?"

Sara got up, walked over to him and pushed him onto the bed. "Let's start by getting you all funky again."

She straddled him. On his back, Jason grinned his approval as he pulled her down for a long kiss. He hadn't had the chance to go buy any condoms. He'd neglected to pack any and, the fact was, he liked having sex with her without using them.

Two days later, they returned to Glen Ellen and went straight to the Hacienda to tell his parents they had gotten married. They were disappointed, though, because his parents were not there. The mystery of their disappearance was solved when they went into the kitchen and found a note from his mother on the bulletin board next to the pantry door.

Turn on your cell phone sometime! it read. Erica gave birth to a little girl last night. Baby and mother are both fine. We're in Healdsburg. Call as soon as you get this message. I'll answer *my* phone.

Sara noticed that the date on the note was two days ago. Erica could be home from the hospital by now. "Call them!" she urged Jason.

Jason picked up the phone in the kitchen. His cell phone needed recharging.

His mother, as promised, answered right away. She also started in on him right away. "Where have you and Sara been? We've been trying to get both of you!"

Jason was pleased to be able to shut her up with, "Sara and I eloped, Mom."

Simone screamed in his ear. He could hear when she held the phone away from her mouth to tell everybody else in the room with her about his and Sara's nuptials. She got back on the line with him. "Is Sara pregnant?"

Jason laughed. "You've just received one grandchild. Don't be greedy, woman. No, Sara isn't pregnant. We just didn't want to wait, so we flew to Las Vegas and got married."

Simone was laughing and crying simultaneously. She obviously was too emotional to continue talking because the next voice was Erica's. "Congratulations, brother dear. Give Sara my love. I'm so happy for you both."

"Congratulations to you, little momma," Jason said, laughing softly. "We'll get there as soon as we can to meet our niece. What's her name?"

"Noelle Simone," Erica said.

"That's beautiful."

"*She's* beautiful, Jason," Erica said, understandably biased. "She looks just like her daddy. He's holding her now. Can't keep his eyes off her. He keeps sniffing her as if she's something good to eat. Get one soon. You'll see what I mean."

Jason laughed. Looking at Sara with his love for her shining in his eyes, he said, "Stop telling me what to do. Because of your interference, I'm no longer a confirmed bachelor. Now you want to rush me into fatherhood."

Erica laughed too. "Oh, please, Jason. You can't fool me. You and Sara are gonna fill the Hacienda with rug rats. Mark my words."

"There you go again, pontificating and prognosticating."

"I'm not sure what those words mean," Erica said. "But if they mean I'm predicting you'll be a father within two years then, okay, I'm guilty."

"Get some rest," Jason said. "We'll see you soon. Bye."

"Bye," Erica said happily, and hung up.

Jason turned to Sara. "She sounds strong," he reported on Erica's condition. "The baby's name is Noelle Simone." He pulled her into his arms. "You're an aunt."

"And you're an uncle."

Jason grinned. "I hadn't given it much thought until now, but I like the sound of that. Uncle Jason. If Noelle Simone is anything like her mother, she'll be ruling the roost by the time she's three months old."

"I can see you haven't been around babies a lot," Sara said. "They pretty much rule the roost as soon as they get home from the hospital."

* * *

Thanksgiving arrived, and all of the Bryants, Sara included now, were expected to go to Franklyn and Elise's Victorian in San Francisco. The house had five bedrooms so there was room enough for everyone to spend the night. They arrived the night before the holiday, and sat up well into the night cooking, talking, laughing and catching up on each other's lives. Sara had never felt uncomfortable around Jason's family because of Erica. When she'd returned from New York to take care of her mother, Erica had come out to the farm to welcome her back. And when Sara, with Frannie's help, opened the bookstore, Erica had been one of their most loyal customers. What's more, she'd made sure that everyone she knew in the area heard about what a great place Aminatu's Daughters was to visit. Sara joked that she needed to hire Erica as her publicity person.

It was through Erica that she became reacquainted with Simone. Simone was an old friend of Janie Johnson's but since Sara no longer lived in Glen Ellen she hadn't seen her in a long time. Simone had been so warm and loving to her upon their coming face-to-face again that Sara had instantly liked her.

Sara knew from experience, though, that when a woman married another woman's son, sometimes the mother became curiously resentful of the new wife. Her former mother-in-law, Teresa Minton, had enjoyed her company until she'd married Billy, but then she had openly vied with Sara for Billy's attention. It was as if Teresa was worried that now that Billy was married, he wouldn't have any time for her. Sara had tried everything to convince Teresa that she would never keep Billy from her, but the woman had resented her anyway.

Therefore, Sara was a bit apprehensive about how Simone would see her. As a daughter or as an interloper who would now command most of her youngest son's time and devotion?

Sara had not been able to spend much time in Simone's presence when she and Jason had gone to Healdsburg to see Erica and baby, Noelle Simone.

They would all be under the same roof together for two days for Thanksgiving, though. There would be plenty of time for her to interact with Simone and the rest of the family.

In Franklyn and Elise's home a grand staircase led to the five bedrooms upstairs and, farther up, there was a second staircase that led to the widow's walk on the roof. Sara loved it up there, and that's where Simone found her on Wednesday night.

"Hi, sweetie," Simone said as she joined Sara on the narrow lookout. "Isn't this a beautiful city? I've always loved San Francisco."

"So have I," Sara said softly. "When I was growing up in Glen Ellen, I dreamed of living here."

"Do you still dream of living here?"

Sara smiled at her new mother-in-law. Simone's short, brown, wavy hair had soft blond streaks in it. She wore a minimum of makeup. Sara had often heard her say that the older a woman got the less makeup she should wear. To age gracefully was her goal. "No, like many of my childhood dreams I forgot all about it once I went away to college."

"There were new horizons to explore," Simone said knowingly.

Sara nodded. "Yes."

"When I was a little girl, I wanted to live in Paris.

Eric and I have visited many times, but after a few days, I always long to be home again. Some places are nice to visit but I wouldn't want to live in them."

"That's how I feel about New York," Sara said. "I lived there for about four years but now, whenever I visit, I can't wait to get back to Glen Ellen."

"Maybe home," Simone said, "really is where the heart is."

Sara laughed softly. "It is, it truly is. I couldn't wait to get out of Glen Ellen when I was in high school. I never imagined I'd end up living there one day. And then I came back home to take care of Momma. I met Erica, you and then Jason. Now, I wouldn't want to live anywhere else!"

"I'm glad," Simone said, gazing wistfully out at the San Francisco night. The neighboring houses were all lit up and farther away tall buildings lent their glamorous glitter to the landscape. Night blooming jasmine wafted in their nostrils. "I want you to know that I've come to love you like a daughter and my fondest wish is that one day you'll regard me as a second mother."

Sara had tears in her eyes when she met Simone's.

Simone reached up and gently patted her cheek. "None of that, now. Being my daughter is not all it's cracked up to be. I can be bossy and critical and way too honest. I'm not the kind of parent who gives any slack. I'm not the kind of parent who loves with half her heart, either. So, you and Jason—be good to each other. Eric and I had planned on being out of the house by the time you and Jason got married. We're building a house somewhere on the property. But you guys sprang it on us, so we're going to have to coexist for a little while. I know how uninhibited honeymooners like to be and I hope being on the other end of the house will give you the privacy you need. I promise not to enter a room without knocking."

"Please," Sara said. "That won't be a problem because that door will be locked whenever Jason and I, well, you know!"

Laughing delightedly, Simone said, "Yes, indeed, I know. And if he's anything like his father that door will be locked quite often."

Sara couldn't believe she felt so at ease talking to Jason's mother about sex. However, Simone was so down-to-earth, she believed she could talk to her about anything. She felt foolish now for thinking Simone might begin to treat her the way Teresa Minton had. "I'm glad we had this talk," she told her.

"The beginning of a long mother-daughter relationship," Simone said.

After which they simply enjoyed the breathtaking view.

The next day at dinner, Franklyn rose to offer a toast. "Elise and I welcome you to what we hope will become a Thanksgiving tradition." He smiled at his parents who were sitting side by side at the long table. Everyone had dressed semiformally for dinner. The women were in nice dresses, the men in ties and jackets. "For years we've celebrated Christmas morning and Thanksgiving at the Hacienda. Elise and I want to at least take Thanksgiving off your hands."

"We'd like to keep Christmas morning at the Hacienda," Jason spoke up. He smiled at Sara.

She smiled back. She liked the idea. In recent years she'd missed celebrating the holidays in a family atmosphere. "Sounds good to me," she said.

"Well, then, we want Easter," Erica said. "Y'all can come to Healdsburg and we'll have dinner and hide Easter eggs for Noelle Simone to find."

"Then, that's settled," Franklyn said, raising his glass. "To family, may be always be as one."

"As one," Eric said, smiling at Simone.

Everyone drank to it and expected Franklyn to sit down so they could say the prayer and start eating the delicious food he and Elise had prepared.

But Franklyn had more to say. Elise was sitting next to him looking beautiful in a simple black dress and with her long hair in an elegant chignon. Franklyn knelt beside her, grasped both her hands in his, turned them palm up and kissed them. Raising his head, he said, "My wife has made me the happiest I've been since our wedding day."

At that point, Simone got happy and pinched Eric on the arm. Eric yowled in pain.

Looking deeply into Elise's eyes, Franklyn ignored the antics of his parents and continued. "A few months from now, she's going to make me a father."

Simone pinched Eric again and he slapped her hand away. "Woman, can't you express your happiness in some other way?"

Simone got out of her chair and went to hug first Elise, then Franklyn. "My cup truly runneth over! A new granddaughter, and one on the way."

She was jumping up and down so much, that Franklyn worried for his toes.

"I'm happy for you two," Jason said.

"Yes, that's wonderful news," added Sara. "Congratulations!"

Erica had tears in her eyes. "Hormones," she said.

She looked heavenward. "Thank you, God. I finally get to be an auntie." She turned her gaze on Sara. "Y'all get busy, now. I wouldn't mind two nieces or nephews. I'm not choosy."

"Give us time," Sara said, smiling. "We just got married."

"Yeah, but Jason has always been an overachiever," Franklyn put in. He bent and kissed his mother's cheek, scooted her back to her seat, then bent and kissed Elise's forehead and whispered, "I love you!"

"Love you more," she whispered back, lovingly looking up at him.

Franklyn sat down and said the blessing. Following the prayer, he asked his father to carve the turkey.

Ten minutes into dinner, Noelle Simone could be heard wailing in the room her parents shared with her. Erica went to get up, but Joshua told her to remain seated, he would see to their daughter.

In Joshua's absence, Simone asked, "Is he always that good with her?"

Erica smiled. "I've got it like that, Mom."

Simone laughed. "Bless his heart!"

In December the rains finally trickled down to a once-a-day sprinkle. As in years past, the vineyard flourished, the vines lush and healthy. Jason couldn't have been more relieved. His second year had really been stressful, but they'd emerged relatively unscathed.

He and Sara decided to have their second wedding ceremony there at the Hacienda in early March. In the meantime, his parents hired a building contractor and in late December ground was broken for their cottage on a hill overlooking the Hacienda. Now there would be three residences dotting the property: the Hacienda, the house in which Claude and his family lived and Eric and Simone's house.

Sara moved into the Hacienda and their routine ran fairly smoothly. She went to work every morning. Simone had insisted on taking care of the cleaning along with the housekeeper they had employed for many years. Sara would not think of their doing everything and took care of the wing in which she and Jason lived. She was used to cleaning a big house, and didn't want to get out of practice. After all, Simone would not be living there forever. She didn't want to get spoiled.

Frannie continued living in Sara's house, although she spent a lot of time with Erik at his place. Sara was thrilled with the change in her best friend. She was still her old acerbic self, but she'd also mellowed. Formerly, she'd said she would never get married; now she was actually helping Sara plan her wedding, and making comments like, "I'll have to remember to use that when I get married."

Sara found herself simply staring at her in amazement.

In early January they got an update on Sean Gamble's fate when Jody phoned Sara at the bookstore and said, "They think he and his brother were responsible for nearly forty murders in the United States and abroad. He's not talking, but he doesn't have to. CSI has physical evidence that match his and his brother's DNA. He's going to spend the rest of his life in prison."

"What about his brother?" Sara asked. "Jon?"

"The authorities let him go. He did what he did because Sean threatened his family. He has said that he will testify in court if it helps the case. But that isn't needed. You did good, Sara."

"I didn't do anything except survive," Sara said, laughing. "Any woman scared out of her wits would have done the same."

"No, you and Jason beat the crap out of him. You outsmarted him."

"How are you healing?" Sara asked, changing the subject.

"Oh, I'm doing great according to my doctor. I was lucky I was wearing that vest. Otherwise it could have been the bone yard for me. Hey, I received your wedding invitation. I'll be there."

"Wonderful, I'm looking forward to seeing you again."

"Me, too," said Jody fondly. "Well, I'd better go. Goodbye!"

"Bye!"

Sara hung up the phone and continued working on the accounts on the computer in her office. Frannie was taking care of the bookstore side of the store. Linda Ramirez was working on the coffeehouse side. Since the Sean Gamble incident, Aminatu's Daughters had not given Frannie another assignment. Sara would soon have to hire someone else to do the duties her charges used to. She would put it off as long as possible, though. Frannie could get a charge at a moment's notice.

Over lunch in the office that day, Sara happened to mention how long it had been between assignments. They usually brought lunch and kept it in the mini-fridge in the office. It saved them time and money. Frannie was sitting in the chair in front of the desk, dressed in jeans and a frilly lavender shirt. Her hair was behaving today, hanging soft and wavy down her back. Sara wore a bronze-colored blouse over dark brown dress slacks and brown leather ankle boots. She sat behind the desk, nibbling a thick turkey sandwich on brown bread. Frannie, a fast eater, had already devoured her ham and Swiss sandwich.

Sara looked up at her and said, "Don't you have any qualms about eating ham all the time?"

A puzzled expression crossed Frannie's features; then she smiled when she deduced to what Sara was referring. "Oh, you mean because I'm half-Jewish."

"Ham isn't kosher, is it?"

"I'll tell you a secret, Sara. Some Jews don't keep kosher. If I thought that due to my genetic makeup pork was bad for me, I wouldn't eat it. But I don't eat it every day and I've had no adverse effects from eating it, so I keep eating it. Do you think I'm going to hell?"

Sara laughed. "You don't believe in hell, do you?"

"No. I believe hell is on earth. At least that's how it seems sometimes."

"Shall we change the subject, it's too depressing. I was wondering why you haven't gotten a new charge yet? It's been several weeks since Elizabeth had to leave."

Frannie's cheeks colored. Her skin was so fair in spite of the melanin in it that Sara was always able to detect when she blushed.

Sara smiled. "Something's up. What are you hiding?"

Frannie didn't answer. She simply sat and sipped her soy milk. Sara's eyes were on the carton in Frannie's hand. Something was strange here. Why was Frannie drinking fortified soy milk, the kind with a double boost of calcium and antioxidants? Frannie loved food. She wouldn't drink soy milk unless…Sara leaped from her chair and went and hugged her. "Jason and I have been having sex without a condom for weeks and you're the one who turns up pregnant! Congratulations, sis!"

Frannie laughed. "My God, you figured it out just like that, and that lummox, Erik, hasn't noticed anything. I can't marry him. I won't do it, Sara. No matter how much he begs. I'm going to have this baby by myself."

Sara held her at arm's length. "That's just your hormones talking. Of course you'll marry him. You want your baby to have a father. Plus, there's Melissa to think about. You can't raise her little brother or sister separate from her."

In her excitement, Sara had forgotten the initial question she'd put to Frannie. Why hadn't she been assigned another charge? "Did you resign from the organization when you found you were pregnant?"

Frannie nodded in the affirmative. "I'm not risking something happening to this child."

Sara hugged her again. "Way to go. So now, we're a couple of ex-Amazons."

"Eunice wasn't too happy about it," Frannie said. "But she wished me well."

"Same here," Sara said.

They sat back down, basking in the warmth of their friendship, and Frannie's wonderful news. "I take it you haven't told Erik yet."

"No, I'm working my way up to it. How do you think he'll take it?"

"He's going to be ecstatic. Now, you'll *have* to marry him."

Sara wished she could be a fly on the wall when Frannie told him.

"We'll see," said Frannie. She finished her soy milk.

Frannie wasn't the only Amazon coping with a surprise pregnancy. A few hundred miles away in

Seattle, Willow was sitting on an exam table in her doctor's office waiting to hear the results of her blood tests. Lately, she had been feeling excessively sleepy and milk products suddenly were making her sick to her stomach, when formerly she had devoured them with abandon. The words *lactose intolerant* were not in her vocabulary.

Dr. Gail Latson quietly entered the room, a clipboard in her right hand. "Willow! Long time, no see. How was your trip to the jungle? Meet anybody interesting? Maybe an attractive field guide?"

Willow was not amused. She'd known Gail Latson, a tall, thin brunette with brown eyes and an ever-present smile, more than ten years. They were friends as well as patient and doctor.

That's why Gail knew from the grim expression on Willow's face that she needed to get on with it. "You're pregnant."

Willow fainted.

After Gail brought her around, Willow lay on the examination table a while, getting her equilibrium. Gail was standing over her looking concerned. She held Willow's wrist between her fingers and thumb, checking her pulse.

"You don't just blurt out to a forty-seven-year-old woman that she's pregnant!" were Willow's first words to her friend and doctor.

"I'm sorry. I thought you'd take the news better. What's wrong? The father really is a South American field guide you never expect to see again?"

"No," said Willow. "He's a half-Greek, half-Italian olive grower from Northern California and he wants to see me again but I haven't been returning his calls."

"Why? Don't you like him?"

Willow sighed and sat up. "I do like him. I like him a lot. But it would never work out between us."

"Why?" Gail asked.

For the life of her, Willow could not come up with one reason.

She looked at Gail. "Are you done with me?"

"Yeah, as long as you feel all right."

"I feel fine. That's the first time I ever fainted in my life."

"Well, watch it," Gail warned her. "You're not as young as you used to be. Don't go sky-diving or anything."

"I wasn't planning to," Willow told her, getting to her feet. "Thanks, Gail."

Gail smiled. "My pleasure. Stop by the desk and one of the office personnel will give you the name of a good ob-gyn."

Gail left the room. Willow got dressed. Pregnant. Joe was going to die! She certainly hoped he'd been joking when he'd mentioned taking his heart pills on the night they went out to dinner. She didn't want to give the poor guy a heart attack.

She didn't want to tell him over the phone either.

This called for another visit to Glen Ellen. It would be nice to see Sara and Frannie again. She missed them. Did she miss Joe? She told herself she didn't. But that wasn't the first time she'd lied to herself.

Willow went to the ob-gyn on a cold day in February. It had rained and she looked like a native Alaskan, she was so bundled up against the cold in an anorak, scarf and boots. A six-foot-tall bundle of nerves, that's what she was. It seemed lately she was always in some doctor's examination room, waiting to hear dire news.

Because of her advanced age, she'd had to have certain tests to determine the genetic health of the fetus. She tried to think in terms the doctor had used to distance herself from the very real human being growing inside of her. She would be devastated if something was wrong with her, or him.

Dr. Adam Gordon was smiling when he entered the room. He was young. Willow was older than he was, and taller too. He was in his midthirties but he looked all of seventeen. Dark hair and eyes, slightly built and an easygoing manner. She'd liked him when she'd first met him. That's why she had chosen him to be her obstetrician.

"Willow, the baby's fine!" he said. "All the tests came back exactly the way we would wish them to. It's time to celebrate."

Smiling broadly, Willow thanked him profusely and left his office with all speed.

It was time to tell Joe he was a father.

Sara and Jason were having their reception in about three weeks. She could wait until then. Somewhere in the back of her mind, she knew why she was hesitant about telling Joe. She didn't want to face it just yet, though. Maybe soon.

In the meantime, her child was healthy!

She went home and ate some ice cream.

Sara woke up in the middle of the night feeling as though her dinner were threatening to come back up. She hurried out of bed and ran to the bathroom just in time to throw up in the toilet bowl.

Jason awakened when he felt her getting out of bed, and

upon hearing the violence with which she was vomiting, he was instantly at her side. The sight froze the blood in his veins. He'd never known Sara to be sick once!

He had visions of her mother lying sick in bed. Poor Mrs. Johnson. Gone of cancer at fifty-seven. He panicked. "Sara, what can I do? Just tell me what to do!"

Sara couldn't answer for throwing up.

He ran to get his mother.

Sara looked after him, fear in her eyes. She didn't know what was wrong with her. Could it be food poisoning? She knew it could make you vomit explosively. She tried not to think about the many times she'd watched her mother regurgitate her food.

More came up. This time, she felt as if that might be it. Maybe her stomach was empty. But, no, more followed. She was mortified when Simone came into the bathroom and immediately took charge. Taking a clean wash cloth from the linen shelf, she wet it with cool water at the sink and pressed it to the back of Sara's neck.

"Relax, sweetheart," she said soothingly. "Just let it all come out. It won't take very long."

To Sara, it felt like an eternity until she finally stopped vomiting. Sara removed the wet cloth from her neck and handed it to her. She helped Sara to her feet. "Come to the sink now and wash your face in cool water, then go lie down with this on your forehead."

"But I need to clean up first," Sara said, referring to the vomit in the toilet that still needed flushing, and the vomit on the toilet seat that hadn't made it into the toilet.

"Honey, I'll do that," Simone told her. "Do as I say."

Sara washed her face and rinsed out her mouth at the sink.

Simone looked at Jason who was hanging back with a concerned look on his face. "Jason, make her lie down like I said."

Jason clasped Sara by the arm and led her to the bed. Simone stayed in the bathroom.

"After she lies down, go get her a glass of water," she instructed him.

Weak and puzzled by her body's sudden need to get rid of everything in her stomach, Sara lay on the bed. She was glad she'd worn a nightgown to bed tonight. Other nights she hadn't had a stitch on. She knew Jason wouldn't have given her nakedness a second thought when he'd gone to get his mother. He'd been just that panicked.

She glanced down at the front of her nightgown. She hadn't gotten anything on it.

Jason sat beside her. "Did you eat something that didn't agree with you?"

"I don't think so. I ate what you all ate today."

"How about at the bookstore?"

"I had a sandwich I brought from home. I've had the same thing dozens of times."

"Baby, if something happened to you I'd lose my mind!"

She touched his dear face. "Nothing's going to happen to me. It's probably a twenty-four-hour virus, or something."

In the bathroom, Simone quickly flushed, got the Lysol from under the sink and cleaned the toilet seat and the floor around the toilet. She was done in about five minutes.

She washed her hands at the sink and went out to the bedroom where she found Jason sitting on the bed next to Sara. "Where's the water I asked you to get the child?"

Jason immediately got up and went to get it.

Smiling, Simone took his place beside Sara. "Darlin', when was the last time you had your period?"

From the mystified expression on Sara's face Simone could tell she couldn't recall.

"It's understandable that it wouldn't be on your mind. You got married, moved in here. Things have been moving too fast, too chaotic. But try to remember."

Sara shook her head in the negative. "I would always write it down on a calendar in the kitchen at the house. The date it started and the date it went off. I haven't done that since before Jason and I eloped. But, I don't think I've had a period in about two months. I don't remember having to tell Jason we couldn't have relations."

"You can call it sex, honey," Simone said. "I've heard the word a time or two." She smiled at her daughter-in-law. "I think you might be pregnant. Make an appointment with your doctor as soon as possible. But one of those home pregnancy tests would give you the answer quicker. Tell Jason to run over to Santa Rosa and pick one up at a twenty-four-hour drugstore. You can go with him, it might do you good to get some fresh air."

"You mean right now?"

"Why not? You're young. What do you need with sleep?" Simone said. She bent and kissed Sara on the forehead. "I'm going to bed. See you in the morning. Get some saltines from the pantry on your way out and take them with you. At the first sign of nausea, eat some of them. And be careful you don't get dehydrated after all that throwing up."

Sara smiled at her. "Thank you. Thank you for everything."

"That's what mothers are for," Simone said, then she left.

When Jason got back, Sara was pulling on a pair of jeans.

"What are you doing?"

Sara was worked up into a frenzy by now. She had to know if she was pregnant. She would drive to Santa Rosa tonight by herself if she had to. "Your mom thinks I might be pregnant and I can't sit around wondering about it. We're going to buy a home pregnancy test."

"In the middle of the night?" Jason asked incredulously.

Sara cocked her eyes at him. Darned if she wasn't beginning to master the looks his mother always gave him when she wouldn't brook any disobedience. That construction company needed to hurry up with his parents' house before Sara turned into another Simone Bryant.

"Okay, okay," he said walking into the closet to find some clothes and shoes.

Five minutes later, they were in his Explorer pulling onto the highway adjacent to the winery. Sara sat munching on saltine crackers. When he reached over to grab a couple, she slapped his hand away. "Mine," she said. "I may need them all between here and Santa Rosa."

Chapter 19

Sara was pregnant.

Simone and Eric floated on air. Jason wavered between panic and elation. Sara was so sick for the next few weeks, she contemplated calling off the wedding. However, Simone assured her that her sickness would pass soon. She had to bear with it.

She was thankful that Simone was nearby. They got closer every day.

As for Jason, she loved him dearly but for some reason he irritated her, especially when he got amorous. For Jason's part, approaching Sara for sex was tantamount to stepping into a pit of vipers. You got bitten, no matter how softly you treaded.

His mother assured him that "this too shall pass."

* * *

A week before the wedding, Willow phoned Sara at the bookstore. Sara was helping a customer at the time, and told Willow she'd call her right back. A few minutes later, she did, and Willow told her she was coming to Glen Ellen tomorrow. Sara didn't even think to ask why she was coming early. The wedding was a week away. She was simply too happy to hear from Willow. But Willow told her anyway. "I've got some unfinished business to settle before I'll be in the right frame of mind to party with you guys," she said.

"Joe?" Sara guessed.

"Yes," Willow replied, her tone a little sad.

"What's wrong, Willow?"

"I'm over three months pregnant and I haven't told him yet," Willow said. It was the truth. It had been staring her in the face for months. It was about time she owned up to it.

Sara was glad she was sitting down. She was in a booth in the coffeehouse section of the store, the cordless phone at her ear. Three Amazons down for the count! "You're not going to believe this Willow, but Frannie and I are pregnant, too!"

"Oh, I believe it all right," Willow said. "There's something in the water in that town! I've been wanting another child for years, and I finally get pregnant when I come there. And by a fifty-nine year-old. This ain't funny."

"You're obviously happy about it," Sara said, laughing.

"I am," Willow said, laughing too. "This is my last chance. That's why I didn't tell Joe about it. I was afraid that he wouldn't want the child. Maybe he never wanted children and that's why he and his wife didn't have any."

"I wouldn't know," Sara said. "You're going to have to ask him."

Frannie came and sat down across from Sara in the booth. "That's Willow?"

"Uh huh."

Frannie reached for the phone. "Hey, girl. What's shakin'?"

"I try not to do much shakin' anymore," Willow said. "I might shake something lose. We're all pregnant at the same time. Our children are going to be contemporaries."

"Lay off that professor-speak," Frannie joked. "If you mean our children are going to grow up together, then you're going to have to move to Glen Ellen."

"I've tendered my resignation," Willow told her. "I'd like this child to know his father. I'm willing to move there if Joe will have me."

"Joe says he hasn't heard from you since you got back home. He's not happy about it," Frannie informed her.

"I know that. So showing up with a bun in the oven might not go over well."

"That's tough, but you're not the type of woman to turn down the hard assignments."

"Speaking of assignments, I quit the organization," Willow said regrettably.

"Ditto," Frannie replied. "Sara, too."

"Eunice wasn't happy about it," Willow said, laughing softly.

"Ditto," Frannie said again.

"I'll be in Glen Ellen tomorrow afternoon. I'll rent a car at the airport."

"No, you won't. I'd be glad to pick you up," Frannie offered. She looked at Sara. Sara nodded. It would be like old times. Picking someone up at San Francisco International Airport. "Sara's coming too. What time?"

Willow told her the time, then they chatted a while longer, and rang off.

Frannie handed the phone back to Sara. "You started all this."

"All of what?"

"Our downfall. You had to go and fall in love with Jason. Willow caught the bug, and now I've come down with it. We're fallen warriors. Felled by Cupid's arrows."

"Are you on something?" Sara asked.

"Just prenatal vitamins," Frannie cracked.

"Well, give me some. Because you are definitely feeling good if you think I'm to blame for your falling in love with Erik and getting pregnant."

Frannie felt herself up. "My breasts are sore as hell. Are yours?"

Sara winced. "Yeah. I nearly cold-cocked Jason when he touched me last night."

Frannie got up to leave. She laughed all the way to the stock room.

Willow waited a day after her arrival in Glen Ellen before phoning Joe and asking him if she could come over. He was heartrendingly happy to hear from her. She could tell by the sound of his voice that he'd been dreaming about her for months.

She hoped he would keep that in mind when he saw her.

She borrowed Frannie's Mustang and drove out to his place on the outskirts of town. He was waiting for her in the yard when she got there. He had been so excited to see her again, he couldn't wait in the house.

Willow unfolded her long limbs from the sporty car. She was wearing an attractive caramel-colored tunic that was almost the color of her skin, over a black pair of slacks, black leather flats and her trusty leather jacket.

Joe couldn't tell from simply looking at her that she was more than three months pregnant. He would have to feel her bump underneath the tunic. Willow didn't hug him, she stuck out her hand. Joe looked strangely at her, but shook it.

She looked as lovely as he'd remembered. Her hair a bit longer, perhaps, but the same. Willow smiled at him. Why did he have to be so striking? He wasn't classically handsome in spite of his Greek ancestors. But he had a powerful masculinity. Healthy, and swarthy from working outdoors.

It startled her when she realized she genuinely wanted to be with this man. The next few minutes would determine the outcome. She leaned against Frannie's Mustang.

He went and leaned against it too. He regarded her with knowing eyes. "What is this, Willow? You've come to tell me why you haven't returned any of my calls. You've come to tell me you never intend to?"

"No, what I've come to say to you is much more important than that."

Joe narrowed his eyes at her. He was irritated with her seemingly nonchalant attitude concerning their relationship. When she'd told him she had the tendency to run from good men, he had hoped that their last night together would convince her to change for him. Take a leap. But, no, she had run and kept on running for three months.

Now that he had her here he intended to give her a piece of his mind. "I don't know what kind of woman you are, Willow Quigley, to love me and leave me so heartlessly. I had feelings for you. I would have come to Seattle whenever you wanted me there. That's how good I felt about us. About what we could have had together."

The day was bright and cool. Willow loved these California days. She wished she could wake up to a day like this the rest of her life. "I didn't want to believe in a happily ever after with you, Joe. You were too good to believe. You wanted to court me, for goodness sake. I've lost a lot in life and it's going to take me a while to start believing that my life can be what I make of it. I've been kicked around by fate too much."

"We all have," he said quietly, looking at her with such sincerity it almost made her cry. Damn her hormones! "But that doesn't mean we should stop trying to be happy. Sometimes we win, and sometimes we lose. But you stay in the game."

"Well, honey," said Willow, smiling at him. "When we made love we rolled the dice and hit the jackpot." She took his hand and placed it on her abdomen.

Joe didn't snatch his hand back as she suspected he would after detecting her bump. He went to stand in front of her and put both hands on her stomach. Their eyes met and held. "It's healthy and everything?" he asked.

"Yes, it's fine. I've had all the tests."

He fell to his knees and clasped her around the waist, his ear to her belly. Then he kissed her there. Rising, he pulled her into his arms and held her tightly. "I never thought I'd have a child. Lydia and I tried for years. But she couldn't conceive and for some reason was adamant that our child would have our genes, no one else's. I wanted to adopt so badly. Then when she was killed, I figured no one would allow a man my age to adopt. Don't even get me started on ever hoping I'd find the right woman, get married and have a child with her. Women my age are finished with child-bearing and I wasn't attracted to someone half my age. I wanted to have deep conversations with the woman I would share the rest of my life with and I didn't think someone in her thirties would be capable of that. Then, I met you and I wanted you the moment I saw you. At forty-seven, I never thought you'd still be…"

"Fertile as all get-out?" Willow provided.

"Something like that." He grinned at her. "Are you going to marry me, Willow?"

"I was hoping you'd ask," she said, her eyes moist with tears.

Joe kissed her sweet mouth, and kept on kissing her.

Willow moved into his house that night.

By the day of the wedding, Sara was pleased to note that Simone had been right. The morning, noon and night sickness she'd been experiencing had subsided. She was feeling healthy again. Jason, a direct beneficiary of her improved health, was relieved.

She didn't smack him in the middle of the night anymore when he touched her. And her lovely breasts were no longer off-limits. He was a happy boy.

The guests began arriving at 11:00 a.m. for the noon nuptials. It wasn't a very big list. Sara had invited some of her old friends from New York. And a few of her sisters in the organization, most of whom she didn't believe would actually show up even though they had each sent a RSVP saying they would. The rest was family. Her father was going to give her away. Her cousins from Florida were coming. She hadn't seen them in ages.

She and Jason had chosen not to have bridesmaids or grooms. Frannie would be her maid of honor and Franklyn would be his best man. Jason had family coming from all over the United States. His grandmother, Monique, had arrived two days early and had him fetching her bourbon which his mother made him water down. He knew his grandmother was pouring the defiled whiskey in the plants. She knew where the bourbon was kept and he'd caught her stealing some late one night.

The weather was lovely that day, hardly a breeze and the temperature in the low sixties. Workers set up the elegant white gazebo in the garden. Chairs were lined on either side of the aisle. The bride would walk down a red carpet to reach her groom.

Sara wore a simple sleeveless cream-colored dress with an empire waist. The hem fell two inches above her knees. It had a sheer train that trailed behind her. On her feet were exquisite cream-colored leather sandals. She did not wear anything on her head. Her braids were done up on top of her head in an intricate style that had taken her stylist six hours to complete. Diamond stud earrings were in her lobes. She wore her mother's pearls and her engagement ring.

Jason had on a black tuxedo with a white bow tie, highly polished black dress shoes, and the only jewelry he wore was his watch. He owned the tuxedo but he hadn't had an occasion to wear it in over two years.

The ceremony started promptly at noon. Jim walked proudly down the aisle with his daughter on his arm. He was silently weeping. Sara had given him her linen handkerchief before they'd begun the stroll down the aisle but he wasn't using it.

She fought to keep her own tears at bay.

Jason sighed when he saw her. He was standing beside Franklyn in the gazebo. The minister was standing behind a podium, his book of vows open before him. Jason looked around him and then he looked at Sara again. Somehow this ceremony affected him emotionally more than the one in Las Vegas had. Then, their sentiments had been sincere, but it had seemed almost like a lark. Now, they were standing in front of everybody who meant anything at all to them, taking vows that were supposed to last a lifetime. It was a little nerve-wracking. However, when Sara smiled at him after her father placed her hand in his, he forgot he was nervous. He got lost in her eyes.

He bent his head and kissed her before he could control himself. Everyone present laughed good-naturedly.

In the back there was a commotion following the kiss. Two big, burly men in dark suits came down the aisle. Behind them was an attractive African-American woman wearing an expensive navy-blue skirt suit and a white silk blouse. On her small feet were conservative black pumps. She was followed by two more huge men in dark suits. She sat down in an empty chair in the back. The men stood.

Jason could have sworn that the woman was the Honorable Secretary of State, Eunice Strathmore. He blinked and turned his attention back to his bride. His eyes must be playing tricks on him.

The minister read the vows and had them repeat them after him. They exchanged rings, then he said, "By the power invested in me by the state of California and our loving Father above, I pronounce you husband and wife. *Now,* you may kiss the bride."

More delighted laughter as Jason and Sara kissed for two whole minutes. The guests pretended to be restless. Somebody called out, "Hey, save some for the honeymoon!"

Jason and Sara finally came up for air. He picked her up and carried her down the aisle to thunderous applause, then the party moved to the back patio, where tables had been set up to accommodate the seventy-five guests.

A live band began to play as soon as the bride and groom came through the French doors. The song was "The First Time Ever I Saw Your Face." They would play throughout the afternoon. Jason and Sara immediately began dancing. Other couples held off until their song ended. Then the dance floor was filled with dancers.

As Sara and Jason left the dance floor after their dance, two of the latecomers blocked their way. "Excuse me," said one of the fellows, his voice deep and well-modulated. "But someone is here to see you, Mrs. Bryant."

They parted and Eunice stepped forward, her arms open wide to Sara. "Hello, darling girl. My, don't you make a beautiful bride!"

Sara hugged her tightly. Smiling, she said, "I thought you'd be in North Korea."

"I'm on the way," Eunice said. "But I thought a detour was in order." She eyed Jason speculatively. Sara introduced them.

"It's a pleasure, Madam Secretary," Jason said, smiling warmly.

"Call me Eunice, honey," the secretary said. "All of my friends do."

The band began playing "Skylark." Eunice looked

expectantly at Jason. "That's one of my favorites." She smiled at Sara. "Mind if I steal your groom for a few minutes?"

"Go right ahead," Sara said.

She stood watching as her husband and the secretary of state cut a rug. She wasn't standing for long, however, because her father came to claim a dance with her and while they were dancing, she revealed that she was going to have a baby. He started crying again. As for Sara, she couldn't stop smiling.

A couple of months later, Sara, Frannie and Willow were taking their usual morning walk when Melissa pulled up next to them in her black Camaro. "Good morning, ladies," she greeted Sara and Willow.

Sara and Willow returned her greeting.

"I'm off to school," Melissa called. "Have a good day, ladies. Love you, Mom!"

"Love you, too, sweetie!" Frannie yelled back.

After Melissa had sped off, Sara and Willow smiled at Frannie with dumbfounded expressions on their faces.

"When did she start calling you Mom?" Sara asked.

Frannie screwed up her face, thinking. "It must have been after she found out I was pregnant and I was going to marry her dad."

"You haven't married him yet," Willow said. She and Joe had gotten married about a week after Sara and Jason's ceremony. They'd done it at his olive ranch. Lord, why the man called an olive grove that didn't even have one horse or one cow on it a ranch, she'd never know. But she loved him anyway.

"I know," Frannie said. "But I'm going to marry him before I give birth."

"How soon before you give birth?" Sara asked.

"When they're rolling me into the delivery room," Frannie quipped. "I'm hanging on to my Amazon status for as long as I can."

Laughing, the three ex-Amazons waddled on down the road.

Dear Reader,

This book is for all of you who loved *Waiting for You* and *Constant Craving*. Thanks for your letters. They meant so much to me. You told me you had a wonderful time reading the books and that they took you to another world. A writer couldn't ask for more. And if you're just discovering the books, Enjoy!

One Fine Day is my farewell to the Bryants. I was not happy having to leave them behind after a more than two-year relationship. I probably know more about wine now than your average sommelier. :0)

If you'd like to drop me a line, you can do so at Post Office Box 811, Mascotte, Florida 34753-0811. Or if you prefer online communication you can leave a message in the guest book on my Web site on the World Wide Web at JaniceSims.com. Either way, I'll write you back.

With warmth,

Janice Sims

National bestselling author

ROCHELLE ALERS

No Compromise

In charge of a program for victimized women,
Jolene Walker has no time or energy for a personal
life...until she meets army captain Michael Kirkland.
This sexy, compelling man is tempting her to trade
her long eighteen-hour workdays for sultry nights
of sizzling passion. But their bliss is shattered when
Jolene takes on a mysterious new client, plunging
her into a world of terrifying danger.

"Alers paints such vivid descriptions that when Jolene
becomes the target of a murderer, you almost feel as
though someone you know is in great danger."
—*Library Journal*

Available the first week of October
wherever books are sold.

ARABESQUE®

www.kimanipress.com

KPRA0181007

Trouble was her middle name...his was danger!

Elaine
OVERTON

His Holiday Bride

Fleeing from a dangerous pursuer, Amber Lockhart
takes refuge in the home—and arms—of
Paul Gutierrez. But the threat posed by the man
who's after her doesn't compare with the peril to
Amber's heart from her sexy Latin protector.

THE LOCKHARTS
THREE WEDDINGS AND A REUNION
FOR FOUR SASSY SISTERS, ROMANCE CHANGES EVERYTHING!

*Available the first week of October
wherever books are sold.*

KIMANI™
ROMANCE

www.kimanipress.com

KPE00361007

Never Without *You*... *Again*

National bestselling author
FRANCINE CRAFT

When Hunter Davis returns to town, high school principal Theda Coles is torn between the need to uphold her reputation and the burning passion she still feels for her onetime love. But her resistance melts in the face of their all-consuming desire and she can't stop seeing him—even though their relationship means risking her career...

"Ms. Craft is a master at storytelling."
—*Romantic Times BOOKreviews*

**Available the first week of October
wherever books are sold.**

KIMANI™
ROMANCE

www.kimanipress.com

KPFC0371007

He looked good enough to eat...and she was hungry!

The Trouble *with* Luv'

PAMELA YAYE

When feisty, aggressive, sensuous Ebony Garrett
propositions him, Xavier Reed turns her down cold.
He's more interested in demure, classy, marriage-
minded women. But when a church function reveals
Ebony's softer side, Xavier melts like butter.
Only, is he really ready to risk the heat?

"Yaye has written a beautiful romance
with a lot of sensual heat."
—*Imani Book Club Review* on *Other People's Business*

*Available the first week of October
wherever books are sold.*

KIMANI™
ROMANCE

KPPY0391007

It happened in an instant.
One stormy December night, two cars collided,
shattering four peoples' lives forever....

Essence Bestselling Author

MONICA McKAYHAN

The
EVENING
After

In the aftermath of the accident that took her husband,
Lainey Williams struggles with loss, guilt and regret over her
far-from-perfect union. Nathan Sullivan, on the other hand, is
dealing with a comatose wife, forcing him to reassess his life.

It begins as two grieving people offering comfort and
friendship to one another. But as trust...and passion...
grow, a secret is revealed, risking the newly rebuilt
lives of these two people.

The Evening After is "another wonderful novel
that will leave you satisfied and uplifted."
—Margaret Johnson-Hudge, author of *True Lies*

*Available the first week of October
wherever books are sold.*

sepia™

www.kimanipress.com   KPMM0371007